I0638267

Reach the Shining River

KEVIN STEVENS

First published in the English language worldwide in 2014
by Betimes Books
www.betimesbooks.com

Copyright © Kevin Stevens 2014
Kevin Stevens has asserted his right under the Universal Copyright
Convention to be identified as the author of this work

All rights reserved. No part of this publication may be reproduced,
copied, stored in a retrieval system, sold, or transmitted, in any form or
by any means, electronic, mechanical, print, photocopying, recording,
or otherwise, without the prior permission of the publisher and the
copyright owner.

ISBN-13: 978-0-9926552-5-9

Reach the Shining River is a work of fiction. Names, characters, places, and
incidents are either the product of the author's imagination or are used
fictitiously. Any resemblance to actual persons, living or dead, events, or
locales is entirely coincidental.

Cover design by JT Lindroos

For Janice

Also by Kevin Stevens

Fiction
Song for Katya
The Rizzoli Contract

Nonfiction
The Cops Are Robbers
The Bird Era

For Younger Readers
This Ain't No Video Game, Kid!
The Powers

1

It was Wardell found the body.

He was walking along a cutbank north of town, snapping heads off cattails with his cane pole and checking the river for sunfish. The corpse lay face down in the mud between the railroad tracks and the river path. A man, hard to say what age. His jacket was pulled over his head and his shirt was ripped. The skin on his back was a mess of ugly.

A colored man, like him.

He ran along the railroad tracks towards the city. Couldn't get the tore-up body out of his mind. Ahead, the packing houses and railway yards wiggled in the hot air. He crossed the bridge and ran past the factories, breathing like a plow horse. Tarred road burning his bare feet. He followed Grand all the way to the Negro district. By the time he reached Jesse's house he was hog-sweaty and shaking like a jitterbug.

They sent for Mr. Watkins.

"Go on, Wardell. Tell the man. Go on, now."

He wore a pin-stripe suit with a gold tie clip and a fancy watch chain hanging from a belt loop. Bald-headed and dark around the eyes, but kindly.

Wardell told him.

Mr. Watkins listened and nodded and said to Jesse's dad, "You did right to send for me, Les." He asked Wardell if he would like some lemonade.

"Yes sir."

Jesse's mother fetched him the drink. Her dress rustled like old straw. Wardell's fishing pole leaned against the piano, leaf shreds wedged in the guide holes. Jesse stood near the back door.

Under his breath, Mr. Watkins said, "Not good, Lester."

Wardell peered at them over the lip of the glass. Not enough sugar in the lemonade, but cool and smooth down his dry throat.

"Where's his folks?"

"Alice knows."

"Mondays, Arlene does maid service down plaza way."

"Arlene Gray? The singer?"

"That's right."

"His daddy?"

"On the road, I believe. Some time now."

Mr. Watkins nodded.

"He can stay here," Alice said. She smiled, touched her straightened hair. "Wardell, you have supper with us this evening. Till your mama free."

"Thank you, ma'am."

Mr. Watkins checked his gold watch and looked at Jesse's dad.

"Alice," Lester said. "Take the boys out back."

The men talked for a spell and drove off in Mr. Watkins's Oldsmobile. They came back an hour later, followed by a black sedan with a ten-foot antenna. A white man in a seersucker suit climbed out, fanning himself with a straw hat. He looked around the parlor like he was in a museum. He asked Wardell some questions. Lester and Mr. Watkins watched from the doorway. Wardell had never seen a white man inside a colored folks' home.

The man led Wardell to his car. Mr. Watkins followed.

"You want me to come along, officer?" Mr. Watkins said.

"That won't be necessary."

Mr. Watkins's face was saggy and scared looking. "The boy's had a fright," he said.

The man put his hat on. "I'll bet he has."

He led the man to the body. Afterwards, the man spoke into the car radio for a while. He didn't say a word to Wardell until they pulled up in front of Jesse's house.

He grabbed Wardell's arm. Tight. His teeth were dirty and his breath was bad. But his eyes were the worst. Wolf eyes. "You listen to me, boy. You forget where you took me today, you got that?"

Wardell nodded.

"Those people inside ask where we went, you tell 'em you can't remember. I don't care how many times they ask you."

"Yessir."

His grip was so hard Wardell wanted to cry.

"I will find out if you say anything. I will find out, you hear me? And I'll come looking for you."

Wardell nodded. His throat was too tight to make words.

He and Jesse played in the back yard while Alice fixed supper. Jesse was a blabbermouth, but he wasn't saying squat. They threw the baseball back and forth, pitches first then grounders and fly balls. Next door, old Mrs. Aldridge was singing in her kitchen.

Steal away, steal away
Steal away to Jesus
Steal away, steal away home.

Alice called them in and they ate. Everyone acted like nothing happened. Wardell kept glancing over his shoulder. Like someone was at the kitchen door. All the windows were open and the sound of the crickets was way too loud. The air smelled like trash.

He ate all his biscuits and gravy, said his thank yous and yes ma'ams, waited for his mama on the porch with the cane pole between his knees, all quiet and polite like he was supposed to. But he was running scared. Something was out there.

That night he dreamt of a hoodooman chasing him with a Randall knife. When he woke his throat was on fire and his mother was stroking his forehead.

"There now, Wardell. You safe with your mama. You safe with your mama, child."

2

"Emmett, will you help me with this?"

Fay sat at her vanity, head bent so that her hair draped over her shoulders. The delicate lines of her neck caught the bedroom light. Between her fingers she held the ends of her pearl necklace. He secured the clasp and, on impulse, kissed the white skin. Slightly, but obviously, she flinched.

He stepped back.

"Thank you, darling," she said. With fierce strokes she brushed her hair. Its copper tones glowed against her clear skin and silk dress. In the mirror her green eyes were stony and glinting.

Since the miscarriage there had been this distance. Nearly a year now. As if it was his fault.

He buttoned his suit coat. "You'll need to get a move on, we don't want to be late."

"Don't worry about that. Isabel will be a half an hour late. *At least* half an hour."

The wedding was at Trinity Episcopal; the reception, for two hundred and fifty guests, at the Muehlebach Hotel. Highlight of the Kansas City summer calendar. Fay's Uncle Robert was not shy about showing off his wealth, and Isabel was her father's daughter. Maine lobster on the August menu, Dom Perignon to wash it down. Her dress by Philippe Marchand in Chicago and a cream-colored 1935 Rolls Royce to ferry her from the Perkins mansion to the church.

"Your dad," Emmett said, "wouldn't appreciate us ducking in just ahead of the bride."

Fay stood, checked her earrings. "Father gets difficult I'll deal with him."

"I didn't say difficult."

"God forbid."

Today, anything he said or did would annoy her. She was miffed that she hadn't been asked to be her cousin's bridesmaid. *It's because of you*, her manner said, though she would deny it. Assistant county prosecutor, sure, but still on a shitheel salary that forced her to go to Daddy for handouts. And way down the social scale. Whereas Isabel's catch, Dickie Brewster, was heir to one of Kansas City's biggest fortunes and, at twenty-seven, already on the board of the National Union Bank.

"Bring the car around," Fay said. "I have to give instructions to Hattie."

Driving down Prospect Street, the sun's rays fierce and fragmented on the windshield, he thought back to their own wedding two years ago. His mother wearing a frumpy frock when Fay's mother had offered to have a gown made for her at Goodman's. His father in his cups before the first course, his arm around Pat O'Malley as they forgot the lyrics to "Shamrock Shore."

"If Peter Lawson is invited," Fay said as he drove, "I will *die*."

"Who is Peter Lawson?"

"Darling, I must have told you a hundred times. He proposed to Isabel at Nancy Chatham's debut."

"There's a Lawson on the *Star*. Sportswriter."

Languidly she took in the passing streets. "Really, Emmett, you don't have a clue, do you? The Lawsons own Missouri

Asphalt, though they'd be fools to let Peter anywhere near it. Not the brightest of the clan, I'm afraid. Isabel did right to cut him."

And no-one could cut like the Perkins girls.

Fay fidgeted throughout the ceremony, picking lint from her dress and adjusting her hat with the tips of her fingers. The high-windowed church was stifling. The ceremony was long and formal. Like a Catholic mass, Emmett thought, though his mother would not have agreed.

Outside the church they paid their respects. The Brewster parents stiff and correct, smelling like old money. Big Bob Perkins with his hands behind his back, morning suit impeccable, huge head perfectly bald. Underwriter of all he surveyed. Beside him Fay's Aunt Claire, thin as a ferret, round eyes taking in the smallest social detail. And the newly married, a couple of mummies in their glad rags, phoney smiles pasted on their faces like paper moons.

Fay and Isabel hugged and wept, all differences forgotten. Emmett pumped Dickie's hand.

"Thought the minister would never get to the 'I do's'," Dickie said, running a finger under his collar. "Hot as hell in there."

Emmett could tell by the way he avoided his gaze that Dickie could not remember his name.

It took a while for a crowd that size to move from church to hotel, and what with the high sun and river air, Emmett's courtroom suit was dark at the armpits by the time he plucked a soft drink from a waiter's tray in the tea foyer of the Muehlebach. He took a long pull from the soda and wiped his face with his handkerchief. Fay was across the room, hat in hand, perched on the edge of a wicker chair opposite the society columnist Henrietta Kincaid and busting a gut trying to impress.

A dance band played Guy Lombardo tunes. Faces well-fed and familiar floated past. The guest list was long but not diverse. It was south-side and deep-lawned. Made up of Mission Hills and other Ward 16 residents who voted a straight Republican ticket, shopped at the Plaza, and lunched at the Terrace Grill. The kind of people his mother would call "quality" and his dad "country-clubbers". The kind of people who wouldn't let him forget where he came from.

"Hey, Emmo."

No country-club stiff ever called him that. He turned and saw Mickey McDermott behind the bar, hair unruly, eyes morose.

"What the hell are you doing here?" Emmett said.

"That's funny. I was about to ask you the same thing."

"What does it look like? I'm a guest."

"Then I'm your man. Name your poison."

Emmett raised his glass. "OK for the moment, Mick."

"Go on. Bird never flew on one wing."

"Soda water, so."

"*Soda* water?"

"Off the drink two years now. You not know that?"

Mickey topped up his glass and poured a shot for himself. They clinked. Like being back in the old neighborhood.

"How's Mrs. Mac?" Emmett asked.

Mickey grimaced. "Touch of the arthritis. Had to give up work."

"And the Da? Still pouring cement for the boss?"

"When he's not losing his shirt at the track."

"Here's to their health."

Again they touched glasses, drank, went silent. Behind the bar the long mirrors reflected the foyer's floral-chintz lounge chairs and silk-shaded lamps. Mickey ran a cloth along the gleaming counter, a solid slab of mahogany lying between them like the run of life itself.

"How long you been moonlighting, Mick?"

His face darkened. "You didn't hear?"

"Hear what?"

"Laid off."

"You're joking."

"I am not."

Emmett put his glass on the bar. "Since when?"

"Eddie Plunkett's the manager here. Gave me a start two months ago. No WPA make-work for me, Emmo."

Emmett and Mickey had grown up a mile from each other, graduated high school together, and played ball for the same American Legion team. Mickey had been the best shortstop in Jackson County and spent two seasons with the Kansas City Blues. After busting up his knee he quit the club and applied for the force. Turned down twice because of the injury, he finally took his old man's advice and climbed the stairs to the second floor of the Jackson Democratic Club on Main Street. Boss Pendergast asked him where his dad worked then nodded at Jim Aylward. Like that, Mickey was in. So why was he out now?

"I don't get it, Mick. What's the deal?"

He shrugged, swirled dregs in his shot glass. "It's tough out there. Not like when I was coming up. They're going for a higher class of recruit. College boys."

A glance at Emmett's serge.

"But you're a veteran. They don't – "

"Hey. The breaks."

From the get-go Mickey had been a good cop. When Emmett was still in law school, he was on a detective track, shrewd and ambitious, always popping up in the right place at the right time. Beneath the cowlick and surly manner was a mind keen and analytical. Emmett would often have a drink with Mickey at Billy Christie's, pick his brains on who was on the take, who was muscling who, how far a watch commander or cranky captain could be pushed outside the lines. A Pendergast boy but straight as a rail and straight with an old friend.

But he was holding back now.

"You gonna tell me?"

"What's to tell?"

"If I know, maybe I can help."

Mick rapped his knuckles on the bar and shook his head. "What's the point? You of all people should know. Used to be you kept your mouth shut and they'd leave you alone. The Union Station massacre changed everything. The Feds are breathing down everybody's neck, Milligan is out for blood, the ministers are pushing for reform."

"All good things."

"Sure, Emmett, good. But what do you think happens on the inside? With the bagmen and juicers and fixers? The grease that keeps the wheels turning?"

Emmett raised a palm. "Whoa, Mickey. Lower your voice."

"You think they're the exception? *I* was the fucking exception. The way it's turned, those boys feel the heat they come down on the good guys. You join the club or they cut your balls off. And I wasn't joining."

He turned his back in disgust, rearranged the pewter measures beside the whiskey bottles. His shoulders were high and his head was forward, reminding Emmett of the view from left field as a pitch was thrown and Mickey readied himself for a ground ball.

"Mick, listen to me."

He waved dismissively. Near the entrance to the ballroom, Fay talked to a man in a drape cut suit with big shoulder pads. Something he said made her laugh, and she let her hand rest on his arm.

"Come to my office on Monday," Emmett said. "Any time during the afternoon. Come on in and we'll talk."

"Talk, talk."

"Mick. Promise me you'll come in."

"We'll see."

He wouldn't turn around.

Emmett rejoined Fay and they filed into the ballroom. The band played "We're in the Money". Oriental carpet beneath their feet, potted palms in the corners. The vast room a dazzle of white linen and fuchsia.

"Who was that you were laughing with?" Emmett said.

"That awful bore Peter Lawson."

"You didn't look bored to me."

"Why on earth were you talking to staff for so long?"

Staff. It was amazing the shape ordinary words could take as they fell from Fay's lips.

"That was Mickey McDermott."

"Who?"

"An old friend. Fallen on hard times."

She made a face as if she'd eaten something rotten.

During dinner his father-in-law came to their table and put a hand on Emmett's shoulder.

"Mr. Perkins."

"Don't get up, Emmett. You youngsters enjoying yourselves?"

"*Youngsters,* Daddy?"

"Oh yes. Very young from this old man's vantage."

Lloyd Perkins didn't look like an old man. Sixty years old, he was lean and leathered, still the wiry Rough Rider he had been nearly forty years ago, when he won a Purple Heart helping Teddy Roosevelt take San Juan Hill. Unlike his brother, he owned a full head of iron gray hair. His face was thin and crowded: eyes set close together, front teeth overlapping. A hunter's face. His law practice was one of the most successful in Kansas City, thirty years in business and the firm of choice for corporations nationwide needing counsel in western Missouri. Early in the century he had bartered his war-hero rep and friendship with Teddy R to land several large anti-trust cases. Successful young and hadn't looked back.

"How's my girl?" Lloyd asked. "Not used to being out of the spotlight, are you?"

"I can handle it, Daddy."

He barked a laugh, gazed at the head table. "Isabel looks fine today," he said. "Though not in your league, sweetheart."

"Daddy!"

He looked down at Emmett.

"No argument from me, Mr. Perkins."

Lloyd nodded curtly, cleared his throat. Scanning the room, he said to Emmett, "You busy tomorrow?"

"Sunday?"

Lloyd waited.

"No, not busy," Emmett said, glancing at Fay. "I'm free."

"Meet me at Mission Hills. Two o'clock. Some men I'd like you to meet."

He touched his daughter's shoulder and moved off. Short strides, parade-ground swing of the arms.

Fay raised her eyebrows. "Mission Hills Country Club," she said. "*That's* an invitation you don't get every day."

A gust of warm air stirred the curtains, a whiff of moisture and a change of pressure. White-coated men hustled to the windows and extended long, brass-hooked poles to close the fanlights. Bad weather on the way.

"He didn't invite me to play."

"One step at a time, Emmett."

3

On Saturday night, Eddie hadn't shown for work. Arlene was in the Sunset Club dressing room, if you could call it that, putting on her make-up. Piney Brown came in without knocking.

"Where is he?"

"What's a lady got to do to get some privacy around here, Piney?"

She sat on a beer barrel peering into a shard of broken mirror. Her hand shook, making it tough to get her lipstick straight. Behind Piney was the buzz of a full house.

"I can't wait no longer."

"Then get Otis to play," she said. "He knows the tunes."

"Otis all gowed-up."

"So what? The man plays better when he's high."

She drew in her lips to seal the color and carefully wiped the corners of her mouth. She did not want to think about Eddie right now. It was all she could do to get ready for the show. Busiest night of the week. He wanted to get all personal about this, well, that was his problem. Otis might lose the rhythm once or twice, but nobody would notice.

Piney fretted. "I don't know, Arlene."

She stood up, smoothed the sequins of her gown, adjusted the camellia in her hair. "Get Otis to warm 'em up," she said.

"What you opening with?"
"'Lady Be Good'. In G."

A full house was tough on the nerves but easier to gather and please. If you knew what you were doing, and Arlene did. Had known from the beginning when, eleven years old, she sang "Go Tell It on the Mountain" in the Mount Zion church choir. Hitting the notes, yes. But plenty of singers could carry a tune. You had to get the audience involved. Start a conversation with them. You had to have soul.

Otis was at the piano, warming the crowd with a little boogie-woogie. Piney gave him the high sign and he segued into the first song.

The audience stirred, and faces turned stage left. Draymen, day laborers, housecleaners, cooks, domestics: these folks worked with their hands but knew their chord progressions. "Lady Be Good" was Arlene's calling card – not the white-bread Fred Astaire arrangement but Bill Basie's Kansas City version, up-tempo, swinging, with Lester Young soloing on tenor like he was making love to the long-legged gal serving drinks.

Arlene stepped into the light, singing just a shade behind the beat, her hands moving down along the sequins of her dress, from breasts to hips to thighs. It wasn't the words that carried the soul but the ghost of Young's saxophone, its sexy lines floating in her mind. Voices called out from the semi-darkness, filled with lust and admiration and surprise. Glasses clinked. The air was blue with cigarette smoke. Ecstasy and longing and gospel shouts. But this wasn't church.

> *Listen to my tale of woe*
> *It's terribly sad but true*
> *All dressed up, no place to go*
> *Each evening I'm awfully blue.*

The audience went with her from the start. Otis was just good enough. She followed with "All of Me", "If You Were Mine" and "It's Too Hot for Words". Then another of her torch songs, "Body and Soul".

My heart is sad and lonely
For you I sigh, for you dear only
Why haven't you seen it
I'm all for you, body and soul.

Out of the lyrics he appeared. Unexpected. Looming in her mind, cool and easy, pork-pie hat pulled low over his brow and cigarette glowing between his lips. From between the lines of a song, like Young's tenor sax.

Her heart lurched. She struggled to continue.

Eddie. My man is gone. Her piano player for three years, her loverman for two. To her bed he had come, once, twice a week. To comfort her with long-fingered hands and marijuana-scented breath. To hum the blues as he stroked her hair.

It was too much. Onstage, she faltered. Dropped a line, missed a beat. Otis glanced at her. The audience allowed the lapse, willed her to get back in the groove. But they knew she was lost.

Something bad had happened, she knew that as clearly as if the police had shown up at her door. The song told her. Eddie would never have abandoned her to someone like Otis. Especially not over a silly argument.

She moved to the side of the stage, out of the lights, overcome with tears. Otis let the ballad die out and shifted to a brisk blues. But her throat was frozen. Piney paced the floorboards in a panic as the audience grew restless.

Big Joe Turner rescued her. Standing behind the bar, a glass in each hand, he belted out:

Goin' to Chicago, sorry that I can't take you
Goin' to Chicago, sorry that I can't take you
There ain't nothin' in Chicago
For a monkey woman like you to do.

The audience revived. Arlene slinked off to the dressing room, slowly closing the door behind her.

4

Fay's ambitions were simple but expensive: a house on Ward Parkway, a wardrobe from Bancroft's, a European tour, and a social life that snagged regular mention in Henrietta Kincaid's *Tattler* column. Emmett's role was even simpler: serve his time with the county and move to Perkins & Graves. Lloyd Perkins had no sons. Emmett would have to be as thick as Dickie Brewster not to slide in as partner when Lloyd retired. And Emmett was not thick. He had finished second in his law school class. And though he'd dreamed since graduation of becoming district attorney and some day (some day!) running for Congress, time with the city's best law firm would do no harm, whatever his aim.

Mission Hills was part of the package. Membership meant you were among the elect; more business got done on its greens than in all the boardrooms in Kansas City put together. Mind you, you could count the number of Catholic members on one hand, but a word from Lloyd, and the stain of Emmett's original sin would fade away. The man had that kind of pull.

Emmett made sure he was on time. He left his car with the valet and passed though the porticoed entrance into the grand vestibule. It was plush and subdued. Staff glided silently beneath slowly rotating ceiling fans. The trophy cases gleamed and the walls were full of photographs of bright young Protestants lifting golf and tennis trophies. From distant rooms came the low rumble of male laughter and the clink of silver on good china.

"Emmett."

Lloyd tripped across the vestibule flags, ruddy and relaxed after eighteen holes and a solid lunch.

"Let's go to the cigar room."

Lloyd's pals were in the far corner, grouped around a cold fireplace. Bob Perkins sat heavy in a leather armchair, his egghead sparkling with sweat. Perched at his ear was a small man with inflamed cheeks and shifty eyes and a notebook at the ready. Beside the fireplace, two men in dark suits stood smoking stogies and holding snifters of brandy at their belts. They looked sated and content but alert to possibility. Lloyd's friends never slept.

"You know Robert, of course."

"Wonderful wedding yesterday, Mr. Perkins."

The big man nodded, did not rise.

"Will Hutchins and Charles Hayes. My son-in-law, Emmett Whelan."

They all shook hands. Bob's assistant clearly didn't merit an introduction.

"You the county prosecutor?" Hutchins said. He had a Mark Twain mustache, crinkly eyes, and a mouth that grimaced as it asked a question.

"Assistant," Emmett said.

"You know... what's his name, Charlie? The Hudson kid?"

"Roddy."

"Hell of a name."

"I do know Roddy Hudson," Emmett said. He was a year ahead of me at law school. Heads the Criminal Division now."

"Frank's boy," Lloyd said.

"Francis Jeremiah Hudson. Commanded the American First at Verdun."

"On the board at National Commerce."

The older men went silent, contemplating a time when the glories of war added luster to a man's standing and stock values rose like the summer sun.

"I wouldn't have much contact with Roddy," Emmett said. "He works out of Jefferson City."

A waiter appeared, a familiar-looking kid with ginger hair and a scrubbed face. Emmett probably knew his family.

"What are you drinking?" Lloyd said.

Emmett ordered soda water.

Charlie pointed at him with his cigar. "Your office in the new courthouse?"

"Yes sir."

"They tell me it cost four million. A million for the site alone."

"It wouldn't surprise me."

"No?" Charlie looked at Hutchins. "Middle of a depression, they come up with that kind of money. What does that tell you?"

"It tells me Harry Truman knew what card to play."

Charlie harrumphed, brushed ash from his lapels. He wore rimless glasses, and the imprint left by his hat circled his thin-haired head like a water line. "Goddamn right."

Emmett had never met Hutchins and Hayes, but he knew who they were – prominent Kansas City businessmen, insurance executives, and officers, along with Bob Perkins, of the Missouri Actuarial Committee.

There was a lot of money in insurance, and no-one knew that better than Lloyd. For several years Perkins & Graves had been representing the committee in pursuit of fire insurance premiums impounded by the federal government. The insurance industry was charging its customers big increases. The Democrats in the Missouri legislature wanted to keep the rates down. So while the industry and the politicians argued, the Feds were taking the increases and putting the money into escrow. The case had been dragging on for four years, and the impounded money was huge – nine million bucks at last reckoning. Guys like Hutchins and Hayes were counting on Lloyd getting that money back. And if his firm could swing a settlement in favor of the committee, he stood to make a lot of dough himself.

But others wanted that money too. And the big question was: who in the legislature did Boss Pendergast have in his pocket?

And more to the point: what did these guys think *Emmett* could do about it?

Hayes flicked cigar ash into the grate. "Pendergast got his thumb on the scales down in county?"

"We keep our distance from the city boys," Emmett said.

"And just how do you manage that?" Bob said, coming to life in the chair with sudden heat. The man with the acned cheeks jotted in his notebook.

Emmett took measure of the big man: the set of his shoulders, the stomach mounded beneath the expensive suitcoat, the broad hands splayed on the scuffed leather of the chair arms. "Well, the Attorney General's office has a record of going after – "

Bob cut him short with a nasty laugh. "Tom Pendergast has the governor on a short leash, and you're trying to tell me those shitheads on Oak Street are free of influence?"

"I'm one of those shitheads."

Bob shrugged. Emmett saw a smile pass between Hutchins and Hayes.

"Emmett's his own man," Lloyd said. "I can vouch for that."

Bob took a handkerchief from his breast pocket and patted the huge curve of his brow, as round and smooth as a honeydew. He had been battling the Pendergast family and the Democratic political machine since the turn of the century. Getting rid of Tom Pendergast had become a personal obsession.

"I'm sure there are some fine men in Jackson County government," Bob said without conviction. "But how much can one man do inside a political structure that's rotten to the core?"

"Boss Pendergast manages to do a hell of a lot," Hutchins cackled, nearly spilling brandy on his suitcoat.

Lloyd hitched his shoulders. "His day of reckoning is coming, mark my words. You don't consort with thugs and gangsters and get away with it. Look what happened to Johnny Lazia."

Flushed and agitated, Bob struggled up from the chair.

"Goddamn it, Lloyd, he doesn't consort with gangsters. He *is* a gangster. He let Lazia steal and pimp and murder at will, and now he's letting Carrollo do the same. Under our noses. And this is the man who's *running our city!*" He gestured impatiently at his assistant. "Newt, get me a drink."

Newt was the right name. He slithered to the bar.

Standing up had loosened Bob's tongue. "The bastard's even got the Feds duped. Everybody said the New Deal would be the end of the patronage system. Take the handouts out of local hands. Well, *now* look: Pendergast controls that racket too. CWA. WPA. The whole goddamn federal relief program under his direction. Now he can hand out jobs and he doesn't even have to pay for them."

A grandfather clock chimed and they all looked at it, as if the tones were visible. Bob's assistant handed him a drink.

"We can all do something to bring about change," Hutchins announced. "We can all do our part."

He looked at Bob, but the big man continued staring at the clock.

"Business, state government, law enforcement." Hutchins lifted his glass in Emmett's direction. "We can all help clean up."

"You don't have to go far to find the rot," Hayes said. "Look at the North End. Filled with guineas with no money in the bank and a bundle in their wallets. Diamond cufflinks and bad skin."

"That right, son?" Hutchins asked.

Emmett sipped his soda. "It's an Italian neighborhood, isn't it?"

Bob was watching him closely, his mouth twisted, eyes bulbous.

Offhandedly, Hutchins said, "Another murder this week."

"You don't say?" Charlie said. "Didn't catch that."

"Colored fellow."

"Well."

Bob set his drink on the mantelpiece. Newt wrote in his notebook.

"Not what you think," Hutchins said. "Respectable man. Professional musician. Played organ at church. I'm sure our young prosecutor here could tell us more about it."

The smoky air caught at Emmett's throat, and he coughed. "Not much more than what you just told us, Mr. Hutchins. It's a city case."

"I believe there's some vagueness about the crime scene. Some say by the river, some say in the hills."

"I wouldn't know."

"Shot is what I heard. Gangland style."

Emmett squared his shoulders.

"Come now, Mr. Whelan," Hayes said. "You're among gentlemen."

"A neighborhood spat, I suppose.

"Since when are niggers using hit men to settle disputes?"

"I really couldn't say."

Hutchins threw his cigar butt in the fireplace. "Doesn't take a whole lot of brains to figure out the score here, it seems to me. When the North End boys stray from their neighborhood, they're on a mission. And we all know who they serve. Smart young man like you should be able to make the connections. There are no coincidences in this town."

These men knew what they wanted. And if Emmett played it smart, he'd reap the benefits. That's how it worked in this city.

But were they asking him to do what he thought they were?

"I'm not sure I get your meaning."

Bob gestured impatiently. "Look, Whelan, everyone knows Carrollo's gang killed this man. And everyone knows that Pendergast and Carrollo are hand in glove."

"Like I said, this is a city case, and when the police are finished with their investigation – "

"Pendergast *owns* the police!" Bob said fiercely.

"What about the FBI?"

"They're after Pretty Boy Floyd, not Tom Pendergast."

"Pretty Boy Floyd is dead."

"You know what I mean."

Emmett spoke carefully. "A connection between the city's Democratic organization and the murder of some poor Negro is a great deal to assume."

"Nobody's asking you to assume anything."

"Then what are you asking?"

Bob cleared his throat, licked his lips. "That poor Negro was a citizen of this state and this county. And if you county boys keep your distance from the city boys like you say... well, the guy that can prove what we all know is true – and *make it stick* – he'd be doing the whole state a big, big favor." He pointed at Emmett's chest. "And himself an even bigger one."

The longest silence so far.

"Talk to Roddy Hudson," Hutchins said at last. "He'll help you out."

Emmett nodded. What was there to say? All the loose chat of the last half hour fell into place like tic-tac-toe.

Lloyd gestured towards the door.

While they waited for Emmett's car, Lloyd said, "These men come on strong. That's their style, especially when they're looking for justice." He leaned close and spoke softly. "You must act as you see fit, of course. Investigate. Assess. Proceed with prudence." He set his jaw and narrowed his gaze, looking as if he were about to storm San Juan Hill all over again. "But remember one thing: the gentlemen guiding you are the backbone of this town. Of this country. Impress them and you will do no wrong."

The valet pulled up in Emmett's worn Packard.

Lloyd frowned. "We're going to have to get you a new vehicle, son."

5

Word in the neighborhood was that Satchel Paige was coming to the funeral. Wardell heard it from Jesse, who heard it from his Uncle Josh.

"He seen him. In Chicago."

"He seen Satchel?"

"That's right. Struck out nine batters in the East-West Game. Smoked 'em with his pea ball."

The boys played catch in Jesse's back yard. They weren't allowed to leave the house. Their mothers were in the kitchen, cooking for the funeral. Wardell's mama stuck her head out every couple of minutes, her eyes all sad and spooky. She wore a red apron with flour all over it.

"So how he know the man's comin' here?" Wardell asked.

"Porter in Grant's Hotel said so. Told Uncle Josh what he heard with his own ears: Satch say Kansas City has the bestest barbecue and music in the whole country. Always goin' to the Sunset Club when his team in town. That's how he knowed Eddie Sloan."

The locusts were screaming. Wardell wished Jesse wouldn't say the dead man's name. He couldn't get it out of his head that it was Eddie lying dead by the river. It was Eddie he found.

Jesse said, "And if he knowed Eddie, he musta knowed your mama. Did you ask her?"

"No."

"Ask her! This Satchel Paige we talkin' 'bout."

Wardell shook his head. His mama had done changed on him. Had her times when she stared through him like he was a ghost. Then went all weepy and squeezed him till he was fixed to burst.

"Uncle Josh he said he's comin' to the Monarchs," Jesse said. "Next year. Gonna sign a contrac'."

At the back of Jesse's house was a plank fence with pieces missing, like an old man's teeth. Wardell could not look at the gaps. When he did, the locust buzz got louder, and it was like he was smothering, and he knew, just *knew*, that something was going to bust through those holes and savage him. So he worked on his pitches, stretching out his leg like Satch. Snapping his wrist through the ball. They said the man pitched so quick you couldn't see a thing. Not even a blur. Like watching shadow ball.

If Satchel showed, maybe his daddy would. Wasn't he a diamond rat too? Played in North Dakota, Minnesota, Pittsburgh one time. Shortstop and second base. "Playing ball somewhere," his mama said when Wardell asked where his daddy was. His hands were hard and leathery, Wardell remembered that. Couldn't remember his face.

Jesse kept jawing. The ball whizzed back and forth. Mama stood behind the screen door. Her cheeks were shiny where the tears had dried.

No Paige and no papa at the funeral, but a bunch of ballplayers, looking funny in their Sunday best: Newt Allen, Bullet Rogan, Sam Crawford. A beanpole named Leroy who played right field, in front of the cheap seats. At the burial the minister's glasses kept slipping to the end of his nose. His voice was like a tenor saxophone. He lifted his hand and the people sang "Just a Closer Walk with Thee".

The women fanned themselves. At the edge of the cemetery a mule peered over a wire fence, twitching its tail. Wardell stood beside the gravediggers, and when they lowered Eddie, he peered into the hole. He could smell the cool earth and the bouquet of flowers. When the first clump of dirt hit the coffin lid, his mama cried out, and a shiver went through his body.

Eddie's kin did not live local, so the mourners went to Jesse's house. On the back porch was a trestle table crammed with food: sugar-cured ham, jambalaya, ribs, sweet-potato pie, and hot biscuits with red-eye gravy. Alice and Arlene served, shooing away the flies. They told the boys to wait until the guests had their plates before helping themselves.

The Monarch ballplayers came to the house, and other grown-ups Wardell knew: the preacher, neighborhood folks, Mr. and Mrs. Watkins, people from the newspaper. And musicians, of course. Bill Basie and Jimmy Rushing, five foot wide. Herschel Evans and Hot Lips Page. Mary Lou Williams. And some Wardell didn't know. They were friends of Eddie, and of Wardell's mama. The guests took their food to the front porch and back yard. Ate with plates on their laps and white napkins tucked in their shirtfronts. At the back of the yard, near the fence, someone opened a jug of corn whisky.

Wardell sat beside Jesse on the porch edge and ate with his eyes cast low. It was too dangerous to look up. Evil lurked in the sky, the back fence, the bushes. It was like a comic book. Through the screen door he could hear the visitors saying soft words to his mama. His heart swarmed with dark feeling, so he went into the parlor and sat behind the piano.

"A gentleman. You ask anybody. You ask Piney Brown."

"I know."

Mr. Watkins and Sam Crawford were talking. Wardell could see the cuffs of their suit pants jigging above their two-toned shoes.

"There is an element down there," Mr. Watkins said.

"Large element."

"Well, we're all aware of it. But Eddie kept his distance. That's a fact. Arlene will tell you."

"A mystery."

"What are you saying to your boys?"

Sam was the manager of the Monarchs, and still played utility.

"What can I? Some of them are scared and some are hopping mad, but what am I going to tell them – that they can't go down Eighteenth Street? Where they going to get their hair cut? Where they going to buy their clothes?"

"From me, I hope."

"My point precisely."

The feet shuffled and the voices dropped.

"The nightclubs are the problem. There's an ownership question," Mr. Watkins said. "You get my drift?"

"Surely."

"Colored folk working for colored folk – it's natural."

"I work for Mr. Wilkinson."

"That's different. Wilkie's a good man. Honest. Color blind, too. But you look at the entertainment business, it's a whole other story. We know who owns those outfits. Who they're associated with. A body can get mixed up in trouble, not even know it. What happened to Eddie, it would appear."

A short silence. Laughter from the yard, the murmur of women's voices from the kitchen.

"Some of my boys have taken it hard," Sam said.

"That right?"

"My third baseman, George Barlow" – Sam's voice dropped – "he knew Eddie, worked with him. He's gone missing."

"A number of folks missing."

"Especially with the rumors."

"What are they saying? You tell me."

"Death consistent with certain methods, shall we put it."

The cloth in Mr. Watkins's pants shimmied, change jangled in his pocket. Wardell felt the floor shake beneath him. A silence stopped his ears and a chill came over him. He sneezed.

Mr. Watkins peered behind the piano. "Wardell? What are you doing? Come on out of there."

He was trembling. Mr. Watkins bent over him. "What's the matter, son? You all right?"

"Yes sir."

"How long have you been sitting back there?"

"Don't reckon I know, sir."

Mr. Watkins put a hand on the boy's shoulder and stared at him. He smiled and said, "You heard about this young man's curve ball, Mr. Crawford?"

"Don't believe I have."

"How old are you, Wardell?"

"Eleven years old."

"Eleven years old. With a bona fide breaking ball and a wind-up like Satchel Paige hisself. Am I right, Wardell?"

"Yes sir."

"Always use another pitcher on the Monarchs," Sam said. "Can't have enough good pitching."

Mr. Watkins winked at Sam and gently steered Wardell towards the kitchen. "This is a tough day for your mama, son. You know that, don't you?"

"Yes sir."

"You do the family thing, you hear? You look after your mama."

In the kitchen Arlene sat with Alice and several other women drinking coffee. His mama's face was puffy and covered with tiny dots of sweat. She wore a dress she had made herself, black wool with matching velvet collar and pockets.

And a brooch Wardell loved. It was the shape of a treble clef and shiny with small bright stones.

"Come here, honey."

Her voice was like falling water. She held him close, so that he smelled her perfume mixed with the aromas of food and something musty in the folds of the dress. The other women patted his head and stroked his mama's arms.

"That's a hard week."

"Nobody knows what y'all been through."

"Your mama loves you, baby."

His mama cried as she held him and the women fluttered around them. And though his heart was breaking for his mama, he felt safe at last within her arms and within the bigger circle of women, with their warm bodies and voices like honey.

Evening fell. Most of the guests left. The ballplayers and musicians stayed on, the night people, and the atmosphere went back door and down home. More whisky. The house grew smoky. The piano came to life and Mary Lou Williams stuck her head in the kitchen door.

"Pete Johnson's playing," she said. "Y'all come in and listen."

Like Eddie, Pete played at the Sunset. A boogie-woogie man. He was playing "Honky Tonk Train Blues" and the room was rocking.

"Roll for me, Pete. Come on, roll 'em."

"Make 'em jump."

"Yeah. I say yeah."

After several choruses Arlene joined in, singing with her eyes closed. They followed with "Shuffle Boogie" and "You Don't Know My Mind". A harp appeared. Hot Lips found a trumpet. The jam session had begun.

A little later Sam Crawford told Wardell to come out back. The stars hung above the cottonwoods like Christmas lights.

At the dark end of the yard were low voices and the glow of cigarette coals. The sweet smell of reefer. But Wardell felt safe with Mr. Crawford.

"Can't see much," Wardell said.

"That's all right." He took up Jesse's mitt and tossed Wardell the ball. "Stay close to the porch light. Show me your stuff."

He threw. Curve ball. Fast ball, such as it was. Little blooper thing he liked to try.

"Not bad, kid. Keep it coming."

The night pressed in. The air hummed and the ball smacked leather. The house beside him was like a big ship, all lit up. He threw, Jesse's mitt a tiny bull's eye in the gloom. The darkness out there so big. Nothing for it but to stay close to the light, eyes on the right now. He looked hard at his target and threw. The music and the rhythms flowed around him, the rolling boogie-woogie and his mother's sorrowful voice.

Roll 'em. Make 'em jump. Throw hard and don't look back, something might be gaining on you. Satch knew that. Satch knew how to stay ahead of the hoodoo man.

6

Mickey showed. He stuck his head through the office door on Monday afternoon. Emmett was reviewing arrest reports.

"Must be in the wrong place. Looking for Emmo Whelan."

On the tenth floor of the new county courthouse, the office looked north and west over the business district. Emmett laughed and Mickey shuffled in, sizing up the burnished oak, the soft leather, the plate-glass view.

"Not bad for a kid from the north side," Mickey said.

"It'll do."

"Guess you're pretty high in the pecking order."

"Not so high."

Side by side, they surveyed the panorama, a boomtown density of redbrick businesses and granite public buildings: the Federal Reserve and US Courthouse, Police Headquarters and the Kansas City Club. Directly opposite, work was proceeding on the new City Hall, and on the streets below they could see the law school campus, where Emmett had sweated for five years, and the offices of the *Kansas City Star*. A depression going on? What depression?

But Mickey's gaze was beyond downtown.

"Look at it."

"What?"

"West Bottoms."

The old neighborhood. Beyond the boom. The packing houses and factories. The pinched streets.

"Awful small from this high," Emmett said.

"Not much when you're down there, either."

"Be fair, Mick. You couldn't find a truer place."

Mickey turned from the window with a sneer. "Depends on your vantage, I guess."

"It's home, isn't it?"

Mickey squinted, his dark blond hair sticking out above his ears like ripe wheat. "Last I heard you were living in Oakwood."

"Just making my way in the world, Mick."

Mickey patted his pockets. "No law against smoking in here, is there?"

"Ashtray on the coffee table."

He lit up and circled the room, waving his cigarette at the paneled walls, the brass spittoon, the custom-built furniture.

"I figured it was something in here, but little did I know."

"You get used to it quick enough."

"Is that right? I hear you got a hanging tree."

"Upstairs. Thirteenth and fourteenth floor are the county jail. The execution chamber's up there."

"Trap door, I heard. Hit a button and, boom, the poor lad drops. Wouldn't know what hit him."

"I haven't seen it. Those floors have separate elevators."

"I'll bet they do."

The light up here was sharp at this time of day, the room warm in spite of the building's cooling system. Mickey had a manic edge. His skin was rough and mealy, his clothes unfresh. He favored his bum knee as he paced and had the look of a guy with little to do and more on his mind than he could handle.

He returned full circle to the window and took a deep drag. "Trap door. Boom. See you later, pal."

Emmett sat behind his desk. He needed Mickey clear-eyed. With the chip off his shoulder. "Buddy. Sit down."

Mickey turned his head. The light behind him obscured his face. "*Buddy*? You gonna give me a pep talk? Show me how to win friends and influence people?"

"No pep talks. I need a favor."

Slowly he backed away from the window and eased into a chair, pressing the padded arms with his palms and avoiding Emmett's eyes. "Shoot," he said.

"You heard about this murder last week?"

"There were two murders last week. In Kansas City there were two murders. Vagrant kicked to death outside the Roberts Building and a musician executed and dumped by the river."

"You keep in touch."

Mouth downturned, Mickey shook his head. "I read the papers like everybody else."

"I didn't see anything in the papers about an execution. Or a river dump."

Mickey reached back and tapped his cigarette over the ashtray.

Emmett lifted a Connemara marble paperweight from his desk and passed it from hand to hand. "It's the musician I'm interested in," he said.

"This a county case?"

"Strictly speaking, no. The body, it's claimed, was found inside the city limits. South bank of the river. Where precisely is a mystery."

"And the boys downtown aren't sharing jackshit."

"I haven't bothered asking."

"Why alert them to your interest?"

"Exactly."

"The only people city homicide hate more than killers are county dicks."

Emmett spread his hands like a preacher.

Mickey pointed at himself. "And you'd like your old pal Mick to somehow pull the jacket for you. Discreetly, of course."

Ah, Mickey. He hadn't lost it. And now that he had a focus for his restless mind, the hostility had eased. Not quite their old rapport, OK, but common ground.

"Not that you'd find much of interest in the file," Mickey said.

"What makes you say that?"

"Manner of his death. If this is what it appears to be, the boys who pulled the trigger probably attend the annual police barbecue. No way their chums on homicide are going to do any serious digging."

"Is it as bad as all that?"

Mickey checked to see that the door was closed. "Something tells me you know this already, but here you go. Every captain in the department has to produce a list of hookers in his district and submit it to Chief Higgins's office. Update it on a regular basis. The idea being that the chief can then determine the amount of tribute due him. And who runs the trade and collects the vig? Our boys in the North End. And that's just one of many activities. Every gambling room in the city pays weekly juice to Carrollo's men. And it's not a muscle payment – it's to keep the cops away. You also got the numbers rackets, the strip clubs, the unbonded liquor. Not to mention what gets squeezed from legitimate merchants."

"I get the picture, Mick."

"It's big business. Are the cops running the show or the gangsters? Does it matter? Call it a marriage. And like every marriage you got your squabbles. That need to be dealt with."

"A man was killed."

"Because he got in the way. Or didn't make a payment. Or found out something he wasn't supposed to. If he was a club musician, that's where a lot of these activities are centered. I would guess this is not a complex case."

"It's complex for someone. A wife. A mother. Children, perhaps."

Mickey crushed his cigarette in the ashtray. "Don't go righteous on me, Emmo. Remember, I'm the one got bounced from the job because I wouldn't play ball. While you…" He blew smoke from his lungs and took in the office with a wry twirl of his hand.

Emmett ran a palm across the smooth baize of the desktop. Play games with Mickey and you better play fair.

"Well, I intend to investigate," Emmett said.

"And you still want the jacket?"

"I do."

Mickey's hands met at the fingertips and he tapped his lips with his forefingers before pointing at him. "Because of what *isn't* there, right? Because of what its gaps might tell you."

Emmett got up from his chair and looked out the window. The guy was *too* good. "Let's get the file," he said.

"I'll see what I can do. For old times' sake."

Mickey stood up. "I'm due down the hotel," he said. "Still gotta make a living."

"One other thing."

"Yeah?"

Emmett faced him. "It's not just the jacket," he said. "Maybe you can ask around. See what you scare up."

"Is this part of the favor?"

"I'll pay you."

Mickey smiled. "How much?"

"Better than whatever you're getting at the hotel, guarantee you that. And regular. I'm not going to solve case this overnight."

"I don't need any handouts, Emmo."

Emmett came round the desk. "Look, I need somebody, OK? Somebody I can trust. Somebody smart."

"Somebody from the old neighborhood."

"Whatever way you want to put it."

Mickey pulled at his ear. "Could work, I guess."

"Say we meet in Billy Christie's in a couple days. Poke around a bit. See where it takes you."

The men stood in the middle of the comfortable room, listening to the cooling system hum in the padded silence.

"What the hell," Mickey said, extending his hand. "I'll give it a go."

They shook hands and moved towards the door.

"Hey, I didn't mean to get on your case about the neighborhood."

"Forget it."

"Your old man was in Billy's last night," Mickey said, shaking another Pall Mall from the pack. "Asking for you."

"That right?"

Mickey creased his eyes against the smoke as he lit up. "Yeah. That's right."

7

The audience is white. To a man. The air is thick with cigar smoke but somehow bright, so bright it hurts her eyes. She holds the microphone in one hand and with the other clutches at her dress, which keeps slipping from her shoulders and exposing her breasts. In the front row a man in a wrinkled suit and straw hat leers at her, pop-eyed and sweating, his lips working moistly.

Where is she? How did she get here?

She is singing. The wrong song, absolutely the wrong song:

The hooded horseman and the burning cross,
Black man taken, black woman lost.

She woke. Her head ached. She rose from her bed and went to the kitchen for a glass of water. Through the open window came the drone of the locusts. Smells of baked earth and burnt grass. A whiff of garbage.

The song continued in her waking mind:

Rope and chain and poplar tree,
Weep in the moonlight, weep for me.

Oh, Eddie.

Since the funeral, grief had come in waves, foaming over her swiftly and suddenly, leaving her gasping for air. After, it left a flat, slick surface of fear. What might be done to her. To Wardell. Then the guilt. That she and Eddie had argued during their final moments. That it was Wardell, *Wardell*, who found his body.

How would it end, ain't got a friend
My only sin is in my skin.
What did I do
To be so black and blue?

Eddie liked to sing old blues tunes when he was high. He could growl like Satchmo and imitate a Hot Five trumpet solo note for note with puckered lips. Laughed and licked his fingers. And hers. He would arrive late, when Wardell was sleeping at Jesse's house, with barbecue from Henry Perry's stand and bottles of Wisconsin Club beer.

She slumped at the kitchen table and wept. Blue moonlight fell across the floorboards. The deal dresser, glass knobs of the top drawer glinting, stared at her. She dug her nails into her palms. Framed in her bedroom doorway were twisted sheets and her good shoes, her singing shoes, at attention beneath the narrow bed.

The last time they lay in that bed he'd touched her wedding ring.

"What's the idea here?"

"Keeps me honest."

"Girl, you the most honest I know."

And he the most gentle. Green eyes sleepy but searching. Sparse mustache downy above full lips. Skin light-toned and freckled, an auburn tinge to his straightened hair. My Scotch blood, he would say, if only to her. His take on the world was side-door: his language personal, his gait syncopated. A hipster, from his pork-pie hat to his crepe-soled shoes. When he played piano he closed his eyes and turned his head away from the audience, as if floating in his own universe. But the way he played – sweet, swinging, right there with her – was like his loving.

After Arlene's meltdown on Saturday night, she had let Piney Brown convince her that Eddie was all right. She had come home from the Sunset praying for a knock on her bedroom window. But he didn't show. On Sunday, after checking the club again, she went to the hotel on Wabash where he lived with Virgil Barnes. The dead-eyed morning clerk shrugged. Eddie's and Virgil's rooms were empty. Back at the Sunset she convinced Piney to go with her to the police, who took her name but refused to open a missing person's file.

On Monday night she was summoned to the morgue. The body had been stripped of wallet and jewelry, so identification depended on her witness. The morgue was a horror. Examination slabs, refrigerators, dissecting tables, bone saws, plastic sheets. Pale and ghastly under fluorescent lights and stinking of formaldehyde. A fat man in a blood-spotted smock had led her through the maze of bodies, cigarette between his thin lips. She kept her gaze on the stained floor tiles, lifting it only to see the man pull back the sheet from Eddie's face.

She had been praying that it would be Virgil Barnes.

"That him?" he said.

Dizzy, she had no choice but to grab the morgue attendant's arm. He took his cigarette from his mouth. Ash fell to the tiles.

"Edward Sloan?" he said.

She nodded.

"Lady, I'm afraid you're going to have to make a verbal ID."

Eddie's face was puffy and drained. His left eye was swollen, and a dry gash striped his cheek. His mouth gaped open; he looked confused and helpless. From her heart, waves of panic shot out to her limbs. Her stomach tumbled.

"That's him," she said. "That's Eddie." She turned away. "I have to sit down."

The attendant led her to a receiving area filled with cops and coroner's assistants who smoked manically and laughed the dark laughter of men used to death. She refused the cup of coffee he offered and sat in a metal chair while he wrote his report. Her thoughts were mangled. Her breathing was broken. She would not look up. And yet she knew that what she would remember most from this awful morning would be what she hadn't seen – his body, its shape stiff and anonymous beneath the plastic, disfigured in ways she couldn't help imagining.

Loud voices split the air. "Well, shit," a big cop said, grasping his hat to prevent it sliding from his head, "if he ain't dead, then I'm screwing Eleanor Roosevelt."

8

The paperwork lay in the buttery glare of the desk lamp. Police file. Morgue sheet. Press clippings from four papers. Stolen vehicle list from highway patrol for the week of August 12. Covering a corner of the desktop was a dusty copy of *The Missouri Revised Statutes*, thick as a bible, its pages open to the titles defining offenses against the person (unlawful killing). Across the baize were scattered Emmett's notes of the last hour, scrawled in thick pencil and stained with coffee.

He massaged his eyelids with his fingertips and squeezed the bridge of his nose. It was after eleven p.m. Apart from security and the cleaners, he was probably the only person in the building. He'd promised Mickey to return the police jacket by midnight. Not that he'd learned much from it. *Edward J. Sloan, NM, 6'2", DOB unknown, DOD 8/14/35, homicide.* This shorthand biography, stenciled on the top right-hand corner of the soiled manila folder, offered as much detail as the slim pickings inside: a vague crime-scene report and a handwritten investigation log with a single meager entry.

The investigating detective, R. J. Timmons, had not pushed himself. The report template had gaps all over it, including blanks for time of discovery and description of the victim. Place of discovery simply said "Missouri River, South Bank". There was no indication of who had found the body. The log entry, listing the contents of the deceased's room at the Park Hotel, had no distinguishing detail. No photographs or prints. No lists of possible witnesses or suspicious loiterers. No evidence of any legwork. Over a week since the murder and yet the file was so thin Emmett wondered about Timmons's motives. If the guy was covering for the Carrollo boys, you would at least expect him to *pretend* to be diligent.

The morgue report, in contrast, was thick with unsavory detail. Here Emmett had been helped by chance. The city and county morgues were housed in the same low building on Eighth Street, with a wooden screen separating the operations. Sloan's body had been delivered by mistake to the county side, ensuring a clean sheet and lowering the risk of tampering by city cops. The assistant county coroner, Joe Healy, was a pal from the old neighborhood, so Emmett got the sheet the day after the autopsy.

It wasn't pretty. Whoever killed Sloan knew what they were doing. Three gunshot wounds, one in the back of the head, two in the lower back. The .38HV slugs (since gone missing) most likely had come from a Smith & Wesson Heavy Duty. There were ligature marks on neck and wrists and cotton fibers in the mouth and throat. Brass knuckles had inflicted a lateral gash on the right cheek and crushed the zygomatic bone. The left side of the body was heavily bruised, with two broken ribs. The dead man's forehead and the knees of his black suit pants were soiled with riverside clay. His suit jacket had been pulled over his head, and his back was speckled with powder burns. Estimated time of death was two o'clock on the morning of August 14. Until picked up by the ambulance, the body had not been moved since the shooting.

Age thirty to thirty-five. Blood type O+, with .07 alcohol content and traces of THC. A marijuana user, but otherwise normal. A healthy man in every discoverable respect. But a dead man.

Emmett translated the cold detail into narrative. Some time after midnight, at least two men had driven a stolen car into the vice district and picked up Sloan, who was walking from one bar to another, perhaps, or smoking reefer in a back alley. He resisted and had his face smashed for his trouble. They bound and gagged him and levered his tall frame into the passenger seat. From the rear, one of the gang held his head in place with a rope while the driver followed a round-about route to a lonely spot somewhere on the south shore of the Missouri River, not far from where Emmett grew up. While Sloan stared straight ahead, bleeding and terrified, his murderers sat calmly in the car, smoking and waiting for the last goods train to pass. When the train was gone, they dragged him to the shore. Sloan's last earthly sight would have been the bright lights of Tom Pendergast's Kansas City, twinkling in the night sky.

Accurate? Close enough, he could be sure. Emmett had tried a few murder cases. And once a story started in his head, intuition kept it unfolding.

It got worse.

They pushed Sloan to the ground and shoved his face into the wet clay. They kicked him hard and frequently, removing the gag to hear him moan. Blood lust made them tremble. Did they call him a filthy nigger? Did they laugh at his suffering? It would not be long before they gave in to climax and shot him in the head. Breathing heavily, they stared at the twitching body. One of them yanked Sloan's jacket above his head. For good measure, the gunman fired two high-velocity rounds into the body at close range, the muzzle blast lighting the air like a flashbulb. He tucked his revolver into his holster, squared his shoulders, and allowed his accomplice to pull him towards the car. And so they roared away, leaving Edward Sloan dead in the river mud.

Emmett sipped his cold coffee and turned his attention to the newspaper accounts. The stories followed racial lines. The *Times* and the *Journal Post* blamed the murder on the atmosphere of vice in the colored part of town, neglecting to mention that most of the clubs and gambling dens on Twelfth and Eighteenth were owned by whites. The *Star* was more objective, and pointed out that Sloan had no criminal record and no apparent reason for being the target of such a vicious attack. But an editorial did say he was colored and hinted between the lines that he must have been mixed up in something dirty.

The *Call* was the Southwest's leading Negro newspaper. As expected, its report was full of controlled outrage. On successive days it ran a page-one news story, an editorial, and an obituary. Emmett read them chronologically. The obit gave him a glimpse into the dead man's character:

Sloan was known in the Negro community for his humor, his gentleness, and his talent. The son of a Tulsa minister, he moved to Kansas City as a young man and graduated with honors from Lincoln Normal School. A member of Local 627 of the AFM, he was a pianist of rare distinction, comfortable in many styles, and played regularly at Emmanuel Baptist Church. His untimely death is deeply regretted by his colleagues, friends, and family. *There Is Balm in Gilead.*

Emmett rose from his chair, kneading his lower back, and looked out the window at Police Headquarters and the US Courthouse, lit up in the darkness. Edward Sloan. A churchgoing man. A musician. Tall and sensitive and friendly. Why would Carrollo or Pendergast or anyone else in Kansas City want him dead? Emmett had the narrative. But what about motive? Was it as simple as Mickey said: the poor guy stumbling across something he wasn't supposed to see? Then why so little effort to make it look routine? Something wasn't right. It was like those news-magazine pictures of lynchings in Georgia and Florida. A black body hanging from a tree, the grinning faces of men and boys in straw hats and overalls, clubs and guns held loosely at their sides. Drawing attention to the brutality. Boasting about it.

He gathered up the police files and put them back in the folder. Before heading out to meet Mickey, he called Fay. Their maid, Hattie Renfroe, answered.

"Hattie, what are you doing there?"

"That you, Mr. Whelan?"

"Yes, it's me. Put Mrs. Whelan on."

"She ain't here."

The clock on top of the police tower said eleven-thirty.

"Where is she?"

"You axin' the wrong person, Mr. Whelan. I done finished the bakin' for tomorrow and now I'm leavin'."

"Did she say when she'd be home?"

"Didn't say nothin' to me, Mr. Whelan."

He rang off, grabbed the jacket, and left the office. In the elevator was a trace of perfume, left by some late-working secretary.

Maybe he should have stayed at home. Or taken Fay out to the Terrace Club. Tomorrow he would pay for his late night, and it wouldn't matter that he'd been working. But with Fay these days he couldn't win. He had to work flat out to break the bank *and* be on hand every minute for social calls.

As they had been getting ready for bed on Sunday, after he'd met Lloyd at Mission Hills, she had asked him, "So what did Daddy want?"

"Oh, you know. Him and his pals sounding me out. Businessmen in this town like to know what's going on. Like to hear the perspective of someone in public service."

She shed her underthings and stood naked before him. The bedroom window was open and a warm breeze blew the net curtains behind her. "Emmett, who do you think I am? One of your naïve north-side clients? I've been around Daddy long enough to know what happens at Mission Hills."

Strands of auburn hair fell across her eyes. Her parted lips were moist.

"They want me to look into a case."

"Ah, a case. An important case."

"To them, yes."

"If it's important to them, it's important to everyone. It's important to us."

"I suppose it is," he said.

His mouth was dry. His knees weak.

She slipped her nightgown over her head and sat on the edge of the bed, brushing her hair. "What did they promise you?"

"Promise me?" he said hoarsely.

She looked over her shoulder. "Are you going to make us a fortune, Emmett?"

"Could be," he said. "Come to bed."

She sighed, finished her hair, and lay beside him. He touched her shoulder.

"Not tonight," she said, and turned her back to him.

Solve the case. Make a bundle. Was that what it was going to take?

9

"The police have done nothing. Absolutely nothing."

"What did you expect?"

"I expect justice."

"Then you're in the wrong town, Reverend."

Arlene listened as the men held forth. Cal Watkins. Bill Carter, the editor. And the Reverend Lucious Jones, talking like he was in church but looking like the devil himself with his black suit and flaring eyebrows and neatly trimmed goatee.

"All this talk about reform. A change coming on. A great *change*."

"Reform is like a bus, with the Negro sitting at the back."

"*That* bus done left the station."

Laughter, but Lucious kept scowling. The scowl of anger. Of righteousness.

Leonora Watkins had talked Arlene into coming to the Watkins house for the meeting. Concerned citizens from the district, she said. Bill Carter had written Eddie's obituary and an editorial in the *Call* demanding an open police investigation of the murder. Reverend Jones had thundered from the pulpit on Sunday and on his neighborhood rounds. Time for the community to rise up. Time for the Negro people to respond to the gravity of the crisis with responsibility. *Com-mun-i-ty. Re-spon-si-bil-i-ty.* The big words rolled from the reverend's lips syllable by syllable.

The Watkins's parlor had chintz curtains on the mullioned windows, crocheted antimacassars on the armchairs, and oak shelves lined with books by Marcus Garvey and W.E.B. DuBois. Masks from Ghana and Senegal hung above the fireplace and copies of the *Call* and *The Journal of Negro Education* lay on the coffee table. Cal was president of the Colored Chamber of Commerce. He and Leonora had two sons at Howard. Good people, educated people, but careful about who they had round.

Eddie wouldn't have shown here in a month of Sundays – not that he would have been invited.

Arlene hadn't sung at the Sunset since the funeral. Piney had given her full pay for the weekend she missed. Every day, he or one of his bartenders came to the house with food and iced tea, kept her company, and looked after Wardell when she had to run errands.

"Take your time 'bout coming back, chicken," Piney had said. "No hurry."

"I have to work."

"You don't got to do nothin' but mind yourself and that sweet chil' of yours."

There was Piney's world and there was the Watkins's. Cal knew that Arlene sang in the clubs but also remembered that she was a graduate of Spelman College and a church-goer. Or used to be. Though if she'd known Reverend Jones would be here she would have made her excuses.

"An upstanding Negro citizen," Jones said dramatically, "killed in cold blood."

Leonora touched Arlene's arm. "Arlene worked with Eddie Sloan," she said.

Leonora meant well, but the weight of the room's attention shifted to Arlene. Faces severe but curious.

"He was my accompanist," she said quietly.

The reverend peered over the rims of his spectacles. "At Emmanuel?"

Arlene stared him down. "At the Sunset Club."

"And you met with the police, Arlene, didn't you?" Leonora said.

"No. With the coroner."

"Coroner?"

"I identified Eddie."

"Ah."

Piney knew about her and Eddie. No one else. It was not something the people in this room would understand. She stared at her folded hands while the others held their breath, coffee cups poised, waiting for more detail.

"Have the police spoken to you?" Reverend Jones finally said.

"No."

"What about Wardell?" Leonora said.

"Who is Wardell?"

"My son."

"Didn't he...?"

Too late, Leonora saw the pain in Arlene's face.

"What's this?" Bill Carter said, sniffing news.

Arlene drew herself up and smoothed her dress against her legs. "My son was the one who... who found the body. He led the police to the scene."

"Where?"

"He didn't say."

"He didn't tell you?"

"I didn't ask."

"What about the report?"

"I did not see any report."

Bill set his cup on the table. "How come I didn't hear about this? What's your son's name?"

Arlene couldn't speak.

"Wardell," Cal said.

Bill Carter looked at Cal. "But the boy, did he provide evidence? He must have been interviewed."

"Come on, Bill," Cal said. "You of all people asking that? Arlene was working that day, and Wardell went to the Jenkins's. Lester came and told me and I went over. Nothing for it but to call the police. Anything else would have put the boy at risk. But you know how these things go." A few throats cleared. "White detective. Senior man by the look of him. Drove the boy out there and back. By himself. I asked along but no – no discussion."

"Cal," Arlene said. "Do we have to go into this?"

The men acted as if Arlene hadn't spoken.

"No discussion and no case," the reverend said. "A cover up. A member of our congregation has been murdered, and nothing is being done."

Jones's voice was so loud his cup and saucer buzzed. Leonora said, "Let's be calm, Lucious."

"How can we be calm? An outrage. An indignity!" The reverend's hair, brushed into a wave that rose straight up from his forehead, quivered. "We must talk to the boy."

"No," Arlene said.

"*No?*"

"It's not possible."

Leonora stood up. "Who would like more coffee?"

Bill Call leaned over his coffee, peering at Arlene. "When was the last time you saw Eddie?"

Without answering him or even excusing herself, Arlene rose and went to the bathroom. She locked the door, splashed water on her face, and sat on the toilet. On the back of the door was a framed photograph of Paul Robeson. Leonora had placed little baskets along the rim of the wash basin, each filled with a different colored soap.

She covered her face with her hands and cried noiselessly. There was Eddie in her mind's eye, standing tall in her front doorway on that last evening, molding the crown of his hat with forefinger and thumb, wearing the dark suit with pencil stripes that he favored when the sun went down.

"I'm not inclined," he had said.

"Well, then, don't bother," she answered. "Don't bother on my account."

"Tomorrow night be better. Our customary evening."

This last phrase Eddie spoke with a sly tone, his way of offering to end the spat on friendly terms.

But she was angry. "You rather spend time with Virgil than me then you go right ahead. See if I care."

He frowned, put his hat on his greased head, and wandered into the night. *See if I care.* Her last words to him. Words he carried into the next world. Words she would carry through the rest of her earthly life.

And Virgil gone missing. Maybe murdered as well. What had they done? Who had they crossed?

She and Eddie had rarely argued. He was a peacemaker, even when he was unhappy with something (her wedding ring, not being able to come by the house when Wardell was home). The secrecy of their affair suited them both, and was easy to disguise because of their musical partnership. He liked to slide along the easy way, Eddie did, and keep his head low.

But lately he'd been prickly. He had to borrow a few bucks from her once or twice, which hurt his pride, and couldn't find work outside the weekend gig at the Sunset (Emmanuel Baptist didn't pay). His needs were modest, but he liked his reefer and new threads when he could get them, and bought her flowers every week. He was feeling the bite of hard times, she knew that.

Their songs would not leave her alone. Lyrics took on sharper meanings:

I don't know why but I'm feeling so sad
I long to try something I never had
Never had no kissin'
Oh, what I've been missin'
Lover man, oh where can you be?

She wiped the tears from her eyes, flushed the toilet, and washed her hands. In the hallway she could hear the righteous voices of the men and the clink of cups and saucers. Overpolished, too neat and ordered, Leonora's house was not homey. And there was no music. No piano or phonograph, in spite of all the culture. No radio.

Bill Carter's voice drifted from the parlor. "If we want the truth, we're going to have to take action."

She could not go back into that room. She crept to the front door.

"There's this man from Chicago I told you about," Bill continued. "Someone who knows the appropriate methods and procedures."

Leonora appeared. "Arlene."

"Leonora, I'm sorry. I'm not feeling the best. Please pass on my apologies."

Leonora was flushed. In spite of her sympathy for Arlene, the meeting excited her. "They want to hire a private detective."

"Do they? Well, I don't care what they want. I shouldn't have come here."

"Oh, honey, I'm sorry."

Arlene trembled. "I have to go."

"Are you all right?"

"I just need to get home."

"Of course. You go on home. Come by tomorrow. When Cal's at work."

Jones's booming voice filled the hallway. "A detective? A *white* detective?"

She hurried out the door. As she left, Bill said, "Call him what you will, Lucious. But we need someone on *our* side."

10

Friday was payday in West Bottoms, and the saloons were jammed from four o'clock. By the time Emmett got to Billy Christie's it was well after midnight, and the place was a pool of sweat and whiskey, a roaring party with a pall of smoke as thick as London fog. He elbowed his way through the din and found Mickey in a back-room booth with Jem Boyle and Fat Jack Harte. Not the boys he would choose to meet on a night like tonight, especially with a few drinks on them. At least Emmett's dad wasn't with them.

"The counselor," Fat Jack said, sticking out his lower lip. He sat squat and pear-shaped in the booth, a raw, nicked hand around his pint.

"Mr. Harte."

"Don't Mister Harte me, Sonny Boy. Man of your station needn't stand on ceremony."

He took a long slow pull of his stout and wiped his mouth with the back of his hand. Boyle smirked at Emmett's old neighborhood nickname. Sitting beside him, Mickey watched carefully.

"How's Jem?" Emmett said.

He got back the barest of nods.

"Burning the midnight oil?" Fat Jack asked.

Emmett was aware of the cut of himself: dark suit, silk tie, red-leather briefcase. Aware, too, that Jem was a street cop and reputed bagman for George Rayen, head of the car theft bureau. Word was, you wanted a deal on a second-hand Packard, you went to Jem.

"Doing what I have to," Emmett said.

"Hard work keeping the county clean."

"Hard enough."

A lot harder than drinking and bullshitting all day, Emmett wanted to say. Or shaking down gas station owners and tow truck companies at twenty bucks a pop.

"Young Mickey here has been regaling us with details of your storied success," Fat Jack said with old-country sarcasm. "Your climb up the social ladder. Your palatial workplace."

Mickey looked like he had swallowed a worm.

"A soft chair doesn't make the work any easier," Emmett said.

Boyle laughed out loud. He and Emmett had been rivals since high school, on the football field, with the girls, in the classroom. He had dropped out of law school and entered the police academy on the rebound. Out-distanced Emmett as a drinker only and carried his resentment like a shillelagh.

"Soft chair makes for a soft arse," Fat Jack said.

"All the better for taking a swift kick," Boyle added.

"Jesus, Boyle, I was beginning to think you were doing us all a favor and keeping your dirty gob shut."

"Fuck you, Whelan."

"And as for a soft arse," Emmett said to Fat Jack, "that leather you're sitting on is fucking *groaning*."

Boyle had his hands on the table and was trying to get up. Mickey, on the outside, kept him pinned. Fat Jack laughed. "Ah, don't be like that young Whelan. What would your old man think?" He cleared his throat and spat into a dirty handkerchief. "He was in earlier. As it happens."

"My dad?"

Fat Jack took another long pull of the pint. As if he knew Emmett hadn't seen his dad in nearly a month. "Always here of a Friday. You'd know that if you spent as much time with your own people as you do in niggertown."

"You lazy fat prick."

"Such language, counselor. That the way they talk in Mission Hills?"

Fat Jack stared, daring him to do something. Mickey was quickly between them, hands pressed against Emmett's shoulders.

"Emmo and I have to see a man about a dog."

"Don't let us keep you," Fat Jack sneered. "To the *spalpeens* belong the spoils."

Mickey guided him to the other side of the room.

"Goddamn it," Emmett said, "what are you gabbing with *them* for? Talking about me behind my back."

"Hey, cool down. You were supposed to be here an hour ago. O'Malley's watch ends at two, and if I don't have the jacket back by then, we're both in trouble."

"Fat bastard. Ass like a handball alley and he has the gall to say that. *Was* my old man here?"

"I didn't see him."

"Fucker."

"It wouldn't do to make an enemy of him. He knows everybody in this town."

Emmett stared across the crowded room. Boyle stared back.

"Give me the jacket," Mickey said.

"Hold your horses. What did you tell them about the case?"

"Fuck all."

"So where did the niggertown comment come from? Last thing I need is fucking Boyle catching wind of this. Company he keeps."

"The Sweeney case. The cop who killed the colored kid."

"I remember the case, Mickey. I tried it."

"Yeah. So don't be surprised when you're called a coon-lover. No one knows about the other thing. Not unless you told them."

"I didn't tell anybody."

"That makes two of us." Mickey pointed at the briefcase. "C'mon. The jacket."

"Wait. Few things we have to discuss."

The singing had started. "The Croppy Boy." Next it would be "A Nation Once Again" or "Four Green Fields". Emmett bought Mickey a whiskey and chaser, and they pressed through the swaying mass and out the back door. Billy kept a quiet courtyard for conversations more back room than the back room itself. Picnic tables. Candles stuck in beer bottles. A juniper bush. The night was warm and clear and the stars were dense. Emmett sipped his soda water to calm himself. Mickey grinned.

"What are you laughing at?" Emmett said.

"Like the old days. When you used to drink and get pissed off."

Emmett opened his briefcase, took out the manila file, and handed it across the table.

"So?" Mickey asked.

"Fuck all use."

"What did you expect?"

"More than a token report and a near-empty log. We're supposed to believe there was no ballistic evidence at the crime scene? No footprints, tire tracks, bloodstains? We don't even know where the crime scene *is*. South bank. That's ten miles of riverfront. If it *was* the south bank. This guy didn't even go through the motions."

"Why would he bother?"

"To avoid raising the suspicions of guys like me who might come across it, for one."

"You weren't supposed to come across it."

"And he wasn't supposed to forget a lifetime of police training. But he did."

Mickey drank his short in one go. "Let's say he dressed it up with phony witness statements and planted evidence. You would have bought it?"

"Doubt it. I got the autopsy straight from Joe Healy. He found three .38 slugs in the body, but they've since disappeared. *Slugs* have gone missing."

"I heard you the first time."

Emmett opened the jacket, glanced at the name. "You know this dick? Timmons?"

"Richard Timmons, a.k.a. Richie T. One of Otto Higgins's vice boys. Inner circle."

"Has the ear of the North End lads."

"He would."

"Not a guy you'd expect to be doing a river run at two in the morning. It's like he was specially chosen."

"Emmo. Can we cut to the chase here? I've got a half hour. Tops."

Richie T. The moniker rang a bell. Emmett trawled through his memory and came up empty while Mickey lit a cigarette from the candle flame.

"OK. So tell me about your week."

Mickey blew smoke at the stars. "Station-wise, even worse than the jacket. No bulletins on the case. No field reports that I could scare up. I talked to a pal in the crime lab, and the boys haven't come near him."

"Sloan have a record?"

"Clean as a nun. I checked vice sheets, Records and ID, even Motor Vehicles. Not so much as a traffic ticket. Far as downtown goes, the guy was a choir boy."

"He smoked marijuana."

"If he did, he was careful. He was never caught."

"Unless his files were wiped."

Inside the saloon the singing swelled.

"What about elsewhere?" Emmett asked.

"I visited the club where Sloan played piano. Singer there, name of Arlene Gray, she worked close with him. She was the one ID'd him at the morgue."

"You talk to her?"

Mickey shook his head. "Not back on the job yet. But she's worth a conversation, I'm sure. Had a walk around the colored section while I was down there. Not being on the inside, I don't have many sources. The snitches I do know weren't talking."

Emmett shrugged. "Would you?"

"Also snooped around the hotel," Mickey said. "Night clerk had nothing but kind words for Sloan. A gentleman, he said. Never any trouble."

"He let you see the room?"

"New occupant already. Quick turnover in those joints. Besides, Timmons cleaned it out."

Timmons. Richie T. Where had he heard that name?

"One interesting thing," Mickey continued. "This guy Virgil Barnes that's disappeared?"

"Yeah. Mentioned in the Negro papers."

"Lived in the same hotel as Sloan. Night clerk said they were best buddies."

"OK. So we scare him up."

"If he's still alive."

"Him and the singer. Not like we're going to get anything from the cops."

Mickey dropped his cigarette on the gravel, crushed it with his heel. "If this went down like I think it did, it would be in a lot of people's interest for the facts to stay fuzzy."

Emmett shook his head. "But not *this* fuzzy."

Mickey drummed the table top, thinking. Emmett took a piece of paper from the briefcase.

"There were two cars reported stolen the day before the murder. A '34 Dodge and a brand new Reo Speedwagon. Here are the details." He handed the paper to Mickey. "See where they take you."

"Jem Boyle could help."

Emmett pulled a face.

"Just kidding."

"Think you could find the crime scene? I'd like to have a look."

"Ten miles of river shore? Get me a dozen academy boys to search and *maybe*…"

"I can't believe nobody even noticed any footprints. Timmons's report had zip. And who found the body? That information is buried. There's too much missing. The slugs, the standard detail."

"I'll keep looking."

"Check out the train schedules. Goods trains do the river route on the hour. Maybe a driver noticed something across the water. And no harm to check out the vice district. The way I figure it, the perps grabbed Sloan between midnight and one a.m. The place is buzzing then, I don't care what night of the week it was. Somebody had to see something."

Mickey was grinning again.

"Now what?"

"Nothing. I was just thinking you wouldn't make a bad bureau chief. You know the drill."

Emmett snapped the buckles on his case and finished his water. "You try as many homicide cases as I have over the years, you learn something."

"County homicide."

"Murder is murder."

Mickey raised his eyebrows.

Emmett said, "And as for Richie T – "

Saying the name out loud snapped it into recognition. Richie Timmons. Implicated in the scandal following the Union Station massacre. Rumor had it that after the shootout, when Pretty Boy Floyd was being treated for his wounds, Timmons stood guard outside the doctor's office before escorting Public Enemy Number One to the city limits. Of course. Charges were dropped when the sole witness in the case, a nurse at County General, clammed up. Chief Reppert and three commanders lost their jobs, but somehow Timmons survived.

So now he was getting his hands dirty again. And feeling protected. So much so that he hadn't bothered covering his tracks. Getting cocky. And sloppy once, sloppy again. Emmett had seen it over and over. Put enough pressure on the chain of events and the weak link will break. Was Timmons the link? He felt a tingle at the back of the neck, a prickle of excitement. Here was a real lead. A way to get to Pendergast and Carrollo and tie them to a capital crime.

"Most of all, dig deep on Timmons. Everything you can find out."

"Emmo."

"He's an accessory. Isn't it obvious?"

Mickey spread his hands with exasperation. "Of course, it's obvious. Which is exactly why you *don't* dig deep."

"Just do it, Mickey. My gut is this guy didn't cover his tracks."

"Emmett. What's going on here? This a crusade? You against the world?"

"Just doing my job."

Emmett took an envelope from his inside breast pocket and slid it across the table. It was thick enough to make Mickey drop his guard.

"What's this?" he said.

"It's Friday, isn't it?"

He looked Emmett in the eye, shook his head, and slid the envelope into his own pocket. Inside the bar the rebel songs had stopped and a fight had broken out. Curses, roars, bursts of breaking glass.

"Yeah," Mickey said. "It's Friday."

11

*T*alk to *Roddy Hudson. He'll help you out.*

So Hutchins had said, almost casually, at the Mission Hills meeting. Then Lloyd reminded Emmett to call him. And reminded him again. Nothing casual about it.

Roddy was the golden boy. Son of a millionaire, college football star, valedictorian at St. Louis University. First in his graduating class at law school. Only a year older than Emmett but already headed the state's Criminal Division in Jefferson City. Six-foot-two, dark-haired and big-boned, with an aw-shucks smile and a modest air too natural to be faked.

Everyone knew Roddy. Among Fay's society friends he had been the city's most desirable catch. And the women did not stop talking about him when he married Laura Varnell, a drop-dead beauty and heir to Charles Varnell's huge ranching fortune. They were society's darling couple and featured weekly in the *Tattler*. Even after their move to the state capital, they continued to set the standard for the *beau monde* of southside Kansas City. The guy had it all.

So why hadn't Lloyd's cronies given Roddy the job? Emmett had thought hard about that before picking up the phone. For all Hudson's brilliance, he lacked a crucial advantage: proximity. He was 150 miles away, halfway across the state in a place that, for all its political importance, was still a hick town. The boys needed someone at the heart of the action, someone who could do the local dirty work, someone they could trust. So they had called on Emmett just as Emmett had called on Mickey.

After their secretaries had played telephone tag all week, Roddy and Emmett arranged to have lunch on Saturday at the Aztec Room. Roddy made it clear he expected a full report. And progress. The Perkins brothers would be busting his balls on this, that went without saying.

Needing distraction, Emmett got up early that morning and played eighteen holes on the public links. When he got back to the house, Fay's car was gone.

"The Plaza, I reckon," Hattie said when Emmett asked where she was.

"She didn't tell you where she was going?"

Hattie was rolling dough for biscuits, and her dark arms were dusted with flour. She pushed a wisp of hair from her brow with a powdered palm. "M's Whelan's whereabouts her own affair, I do believe."

"You got that right, Hattie."

He brought his clubs to the basement and cleaned his spikes. When he returned upstairs, the biscuits were in the oven and Hattie stood in the doorway, hands on her hips.

"Mr. Whelan. If I may ask."

"Yes, Hattie."

"I got me a luncheon appointment. One o'clock."

"What do you know. So do I. You're not dining at the Aztec, by any chance?"

She caught herself before answering, flashed a saucy look. The whites of her large eyes had a yellowish tinge. She had Cherokee cheekbones, straightened hair that rose high from a parting on the left, and a wide-winged nose above the fullest lips. She had removed her apron. In the heat she wore a sleeveless cotton dress and sandals. Long legs. Still in her twenties but with a shift to her hip that said she'd been around.

Emmett found himself looking elsewhere.

She said, "One o'clock on a Saturday is my usual quittin' time, but if I don't get the streetcar by noon…"

"Mrs. Whelan didn't say when she'd be back?"

"No, sir."

He walked past her into the kitchen.

"You head out when you have to, Hattie. Those biscuits ready yet? I've got an appetite."

She waited before answering, finally broke her pose and started washing cooking utensils.

"You jus' have to wait like everybody else."

He took an apple from the fruit bowl and bit into it. He needed a bath. He needed to dress for lunch. But he leaned against the counter. The radio was tuned to the Lucky Strike Hit Parade. Kay Thompson singing "Red Sails in the Sunset".

"You like that music, Hattie?"

"No, sir, I do not. M's Whelan set the station and I forget to change it."

"I think it's kind of snappy."

Another glance.

"What kind of music do you like?" he asked.

"The Lord's music be best. Songs of praise."

"I've heard you singing when you polish the floor."

"A hymn the best way to pass the time there is. Word of God be a helpin' hand."

Her voice was like good Kansas soil. She rinsed the mixing bowl, and the water flowed down her bare arms and dripped onto the linoleum. She smelled of sweat and patchouli oil.

"How about the music in the Negro district? Do you like that?"

"The clubs? You talkin' 'bout Twelfth Street?"

"Yes."

She frowned. "Not bad, considerin' it the devil's music."

"Have you been to the Sunset?"

"What you know about the Sunset, Mr. Whelan?"

His familiarity had made her bold. Her tone was coy, almost playful. Though her hands kept washing, her eyes were alert to his words.

"Not much," he said.

He waited.

"Big Joe Turner tend bar there," she said. "Liable to be shoutin' the blues at *any* time."

Suddenly she sang:

Evening
You come and you find me
Must you always remind me
That my man is gone.

She sang with her head thrown back, her eyes closed, her body swaying. Her large rump shifted rhythmically beneath the tight cotton.

"Those biscuits smell like they're done," he said.

She was looking beyond him. He turned. Fay stood in the doorway, slowly removing her white gloves. She wore a pillbox hat with beaded veil, a flannel suit, and high heels. Shopping bags bearing the names of expensive southside stores lay at her feet.

Hattie switched off the radio.

"Oh, don't stop the music on my account," Fay said.

"Hattie was just telling me that she has to leave by noon," Emmett said. "I'm having lunch with Roddy Hudson, I think I told you that."

Fay didn't respond, didn't even look at him. She folded her gloves and put them in her handbag while Hattie slid the biscuits from the oven. Her eyes on her maid, Fay clacked across the linoleum in her heels and said to Emmett, "Bring in these bags. And there are more in the car."

An hour later Fay stood in the doorway that led into the garage while he unlocked the car. She had changed into slacks and a silk blouse. Her eyes glittered and her slender throat was blotchy.

"Roddy Hudson," she said.

"What about him?"

"I suppose your business with him can't wait until the weekend is over."

"Roddy works in Jefferson City. He can't make it up during the week."

She scowled. The scene in the kitchen had filled her with fire and ice. "I know where he works," she said. "Big man in the capital, now. And yet he and his insufferable wife still act as if the whole of Kansas City hangs on their every movement."

"What does this have to do with my meeting?"

"You're out all night. Play golf all morning. I come home and find you – " She stopped mid-sentence, her hand at her throat. "Oh, go on. Have your martini lunch and leave me here alone."

As he drove away from the neighborhood, he saw Hattie waiting for the streetcar, and it was all he could do not to offer her a ride.

12

Arlene boarded the streetcar and made her way to the rear, aware of heads turning. The men smiled and swallowed. The women frowned. Some of the women, anyway. She wore a navy sequined sheath, backless, with dark stockings and ankle-strap high heels. A fabric flower at her low neckline and blue opals on her ears. She took her seat. The car rocked along uneven rails.

On her way to work. Her first night back at the club since Eddie's death.

"Fine, evenin', ma'am. Very fine." A zoot-suited young man lifted his hat and flashed a gold incisor. She cut him with a frosty glance.

She was dressed for singing, not for public transport, but had saved her cab fare for the journey home. It was too hot for a coat, and she wore a loose-knit shawl over her bare shoulders. The streetcar careened down Twelfth Street. Birds perched on the electricity wires. The street ahead was dusky and lined with the glow of Friday-night neon. Arlene peered back at Alice's house. Wardell must have gone inside; the porch was empty. The car lights dimmed. Protect him, Lord. And me so I can care for him.

Fear shaped her days. All week she had kept to the house, watching Wardell, cooking, listening to the locusts. But the world would not leave her alone. On Wednesday, a week after the meeting at the Watkins, Cal had driven her to the offices of the *Call*, where she met the detective from Chicago invited down to investigate Eddie's death. Loren Parks his name was. At first she had refused to meet him, but Cal convinced her that it was the best way to protect Wardell.

If the man was supposed to make her feel better, it didn't work. They met in a hot, cluttered room at the rear of the newspaper. He was middle-aged, with scaly skin and a high hairline. He looked like the reporter he was pretending to be, with crooked spectacles and fingers stained with black ink.

He asked her about Eddie, Virgil Barnes, the Park Hotel, the Friendship Brotherhood.

"It's a Negro men's association," she told him.

"A benevolent association?"

"If you want to call it that."

"What would you call it?"

"An excuse for men to get together on a Tuesday night when they don't want to be somewhere else."

"Ah. Eddie Sloan was a member?"

"Yes, he was. And Virgil Barnes."

"I see. Do you know where they meet?"

"You mean *met*."

"Well, yes."

"On Cleveland Street, I believe."

"Above a funeral parlor?"

"I don't know. I never attended."

He made a note. He asked her about the morgue. About Wardell's discovery. Each question was like a slap.

"I wonder if it would be possible for your son to lead me to the scene," he said.

"No."

"It would be a great help to the investigation, Mrs. Gray. A great help towards solving this awful crime and having at least a chance of seeing justice served."

"The police have no interest in justice."

"There are authorities higher than the Kansas City Police."

The small room, with its peeling walls and cracked window, closed in. Her head grew light and her breathing troubled her. "Mr. Parks, I need a glass of water."

He fetched it for her, but it did not help. She needed to be with Wardell. She asked Bill Carter to call a cab and waited in the cooler vestibule, while Parks and Carter whispered at the editor's desk.

Before she left, Parks thanked her. "You'll think about what I asked?" he said.

"I'll think about it."

"Thank you, ma'am."

It was the first time a white man had ever called her "ma'am."

At the club, Piney Brown greeted her with a bear hug and a toothless kiss.

"Ain't you lookin' good," he said.

"I've felt better."

"C'mon back here."

He led her to a rear booth, hand at her back. The club throbbed with the blues. On the bandstand was a piano trio riffing behind a huge, barrel-chested man on tenor saxophone. Arlene had never heard him before, but the guy could play. Big Texas sound. Real swing feel.

Standing in front of the stage, swaying back and forth, was a young woman who showed up most weeks, trying to make an impression on Piney. She wore a loose dress and a hair band and had her hair teased out like Bessie Smith. She closed her eyes and sang:

Then I began to fall so low
Lost my good friends, nowhere to go
I get my hands on a dollar again
Gonna hang on to it till that eagle grins.

"You going to hire that girl, Piney?"

"Why should I? She already workin' for free."

He served her shredded pork barbecue and okra. She wasn't hungry but made the effort while he sat across from her, twisting the rings on his misshapen fingers.

The band took a break. The piano player stayed onstage, vamping blues chords.

"My new partner?"

Piney nodded.

"Not Otis?" she said.

"You and me both know Otis ain't right."

"I'm not so sure, Piney."

The pork went down like a horse pill, but she did not stop eating. Piney was outright proud of his cooking.

"What you frettin' for? Think I'd pair my sweet soul sister with jus' anyone?"

"Question of familiarity."

"Question of swing, I would say." Piney pointed his chin towards the piano. "Phineas Jordan. Remember that name."

She finished eating, got ready, and took the stage. The piano man *was* good. Knew the songbook and put the singer first. Different enough from Eddie not to spook her.

But the night lay ahead of her like a hard road. Emotions had been high all day. Apt to cry at any old thing: the wail of a train, smell of honeysuckle when she hung out the wash. How would *their* tunes affect her? "Lady Be Good." "I Must Have That Man." Bedroom songs.

She turned them into requiem. Forgetting Eddie was impossible, she knew that, so she sang to him, wherever he might be. The Friday night crowd, large and local, heard the sorrow in her voice and responded with respect, more church in their calls than hoedown.

When the first set was over, she retreated to the dressing room – a storeroom behind the booths full of beer crates and broken chairs. Phineas kept his distance and sat at the bar. Piney brought her a drink and shut the door. His face was pale.

"What's wrong?" she asked.

"You seen 'em?"

"Who?"

"Ofays at the back. Pinstripe boys."

"It's a Friday, Piney. Those types like to slum it after making their dollar."

He shook his head. "These ain't your usual downtowners. They got an *interest*."

She sipped her beer. "What do you mean?"

"You know what I mean. Shit." He pressed his hand against the door, as if testing for fire behind it. "Tuesdays, same time each week, I get a visit. So much in an envelope. That be police. Thursdays a second visit, different gig. Rackets. So many percent and you be wondering how they know your take. But only a fool think he can hold back any of *that* juice."

Tight-lipped and watery-eyed, Piney rubbed the stubble on his chin and shook his head. "Them weekday boys? They flunkies. Bagmen. Gentlemen outside, they top cats. And with due respect, Arlene, they ain't here for the music."

"This have something to do with... you know?"

"Somethin' do with somethin'," he said. "That's a fact."

He stood and opened the door a crack. Peered out then left, suddenly. He was back in moments, followed by two white men in dark suits.

"When you going to get a real office, Piney?"

The room grew small. She became matronly, arranging a triangle of chairs and clearing empty bottles from a paint-stained table.

"May I get you gentlemen something to drink?"

"Take a seat, sweetheart. We don't need a drink."

There were only three usable chairs. She looked at Piney and he nodded. She sat.

The men smelled of cigar smoke and cologne. The lead man was broad and fleshy, with thick lips and oily hair. Arlene felt his attention like a rash. The other was older, with pocked cheeks, small eyes, and a lantern jaw.

"You too, Piney," the younger man said. "Sit down."

The quiet one stood with his back to the door, hat in his hand. The other sat slowly. His knee touched hers.

"Pretty singing tonight."

She nodded.

"Quite a crowd."

"Arlene, she draws," Piney said.

The man ignored the comment. He was looking at her. Close up his skin was large-pored and closely shaven. Teeth like a horse.

"You know who I am, Arlene?"

"No, sir."

"I'm your boss." He turned in his seat. "You could say that, Richie, couldn't you? I'm her boss?"

"Say whatever you want."

The seated man wiped his mouth with a large handkerchief. Gold links glinted against lightly soiled cuffs. Though well-dressed, the men were scuffed at the edges. The man beside her had a blankness around his eyes. The kind of man who could easily turn brutal.

The moments in the morgue came to her and she lowered her head. She had to concentrate not to be sick.

"You all right, sweetheart? That beer going to your head?"

"I'm all right."

He took a cigar from his pocket and let it rest unlit between his fingers.

"How's business, Piney?"

"Passable, Mr. Lococo. Passable."

Piney's pronunciation of the name was careful.

"There's a depression on. Men out of work all over the country. All of us in gainful employment should all be thankful. That right, Richie?"

Richie didn't answer.

"All be thankful."

Piney's eyes, bloodshot and alert, swiveled from one man to the other. Arlene stared at her half-empty glass of beer.

Mr. Lococo seemed to lose his train of thought. He tapped the table lightly with a signet ring.

"I'm sorry for your loss," he said.

"Wha's that?" Piney blurted.

The man gestured in a way meant to suggest generosity. "Like I said, I'm the boss around here. So to speak. I heard about Eddie Sloan. An employee of the club, after all. A tragedy."

She watched the man closely. His tone had shifted. She noticed for the first time that he had a slight lisp.

"I know the details," he said. "What the papers said, what you might have heard. I know what you could be thinking."

He extended his hand and exposed a palm, nicked and quilted. Tobacco stains on his fingers.

"And I'm here to tell you," he continued carefully, "that it is not what you might think."

He waited for a response. Piney's tongue was circling his mouth, running between gum and lip.

"You've come here to express your concern," Arlene said.

"Sympathy, I would say. Respect. And a word of caution." He shifted the cigar from one hand to the other and dug in his pocket for a lighter. "A tragedy, like I said. But over and done with. So the best thing for everybody is, say no more about it. I mean, you don't know who might come along asking questions. Trying to stir up trouble."

Piney snuffled and shifted in his seat. "You don' have to worry about us, Mr. Lococo."

"You say respect," Arlene said.

"That's right."

"How is it respectful to ignore a man's death?"

"Arlene."

She was shaking. "How is it respectful," she said, "to ignore injustice?"

Piney looked terrified. But Arlene felt only the chill of the morgue, the gashed cheek and gaping mouth.

"He was a kind, decent man," she continued. "Eddie was. Never harmed anyone. Never. Whoever killed him was evil."

Piney looked at the floor between his feet. With a click, Mr. Lococo's lighter flared, and he spent a long time lighting his cigar. Smoke billowed in the small room and caught at her throat. "Sweetheart," he said, gesturing at the bottles and empty kegs, "I own this joint. People come here to enjoy a drink and listen to the music. Eddie Sloan was a draw. Like you. I take his death personal. A tragedy, like I said." Richie had edged forward from the closed door. Mr. Lococo leaned close. "We are in agreement on this, Arlene."

She stared at him.

"Do you understand?"

"I don't know."

"Let me say this: whoever did what they did to Eddie has insulted me. But speaking out of turn to every Tom, Dick and Harry's not going to bring him back."

"Why isn't the murder being investigated by the police?"

He puffed at his cigar. "Who says it isn't?"

Piney was bug-eyed. "The police been here. Axed their questions, wrote down their interpretations."

His desperation filled the air like the cigar smoke, but the memory of Eddie's body would not let her shut up. "The police don't care," she said. "He's just another colored man. Might as well have been a dog got killed for all it means downtown."

Richie spoke. "The police are as puzzled as anyone." His voice was oddly light, almost squeaky, but sharp.

"How could they be puzzled," Arlene said, "when they haven't done anything?"

Piney looked stricken. Richie made a swift, chopping motion with his hand. She saw now that he was not a body-guard or sidekick but the one in charge.

"Angelo, you can leave us."

Lococo motioned Piney out of the room. Richie stared at her for a minute before unbuttoning his jacket, grabbing a chair, and sitting on it backwards, so that his chest rested against the ladderback. Up close she could see that his teeth were bad. He gave her the look most white men, well-intentioned or not, gave her at some point: bloodless, possessive, unabashed. She placed a hand at her neck.

"You're not getting the message, are you?" he said.

"A friend of mine was murdered."

"Like the man said: we understand. You asked who do I think I am. That doesn't matter. What does matter is what I can do. You got that?"

"Yes sir."

"The hurt I can put on a person. Or her family."

Her heart echoed in her head like a steam engine.

"Who's been asking you questions?" he said.

"Nobody."

"If you lie to me, I'll find out."

"I wouldn't lie to you, sir."

"Not even to protect someone?"

"Piney said the police came around here asking questions. Well, no one asked me anything."

He absorbed this comment and wiped his nose with his sleeve. "Where's Virgil Barnes?"

"I wish I knew."

"When did you see him last?"

"Virgil? I never saw him. Eddie did. The night he died, they had planned on meeting up. So Eddie said."

"Him and Sloan were good friends?"

"I don't know about good. They shared a bottle sometimes."

"How about you? What did you share with Sloan?"

"We had a professional relationship."

"I'll bet you did." Casually and coldly he swept his eyes up and down her form.

She did her best to ignore the fear. She thought of Wardell and how he needed her. Richie reached across and plucked at the satin flower on her dress, but it was sewn on, and when it wouldn't disengage he pulled hard. Her dress ripped at the neckline, and the fabric flapped open, exposing her breast. She gasped and covered herself. His mouth tightened as he continued to stare at her bosom.

He threw the flower on the floor and stood quickly, pushing the chair so that it knocked against her knees. "You've known Piney a long time?"

"Yes sir."

"You want to see him stay in business, you keep your mouth shut. *You* want to make a living, you keep your mouth shut."

"Yes sir."

He put his hand on the door knob. She could feel the heat of his stare, his determination, and his anger.

"I'll know if you don't," he said.

After he left, she dropped her head between her knees and vomited on the scuffed wood floor.

13

The Aztec Room was murky after the numbing glare of the late August sun, and Emmett stood blinking at the entrance, hat in hand. The head waiter seated him and left menus. The room smelled of stale cigarette smoke. Unaccompanied women sat at the bar and two swarthy men in sharkskin suits laughed loudly at a table by the window. Not the Muehlebach Hotel, that was for sure.

Ten minutes later Roddy arrived. He wore a striped bottle-green blazer, linen slacks, plaid tie, and saddle shoes. Emmett wore his weekday suit.

Roddy smiled broadly as they shook hands. "Got here ahead of me, I see. What's that you're drinking?"

"Seven-up."

He frowned. "I thought you came from West Bottoms."

He signaled for the waiter, discovered him hovering at his elbow.

"Ted, bring me an old-fashioned."

"Yes, Mr. Hudson."

He took a silver case from his blazer pocket, offered Emmett an English cigarette.

"Don't smoke."

"Strike two."

He snapped shut the case and lit his cigarette. His face was deeply tanned, his teeth large and even. His flat, closely shaven cheeks shone like polished stone and descended to a chin that was solid and confident. Elbow on the table, he held his cigarette high and let his green eyes wander as he spoke. Not the serious figure Emmett had expected. More Clark Gable than Spencer Tracy.

"I was here two weeks ago," Roddy said. "George Foster's thirtieth birthday party. There was a Negro band playing that blew the roof off, let me tell you. George had a good-time girl on each arm, drinking champagne like it was going out of fashion."

He gestured at the piano, shook his head at the memory. The waiter delivered his drink. Following his lead, Emmett ordered prime rib. The women at the bar laughed.

Emmett sipped his soda. This was their meeting? Murder and investigation seemed like the last things on the agenda.

"You're married to Lloyd's daughter, aren't you? Phyllis?"

"Fay."

"Fay, of course. Excuse me. I knew Isabel years ago."

"She was married herself recently."

"So I heard. Mrs. Richard Brewster." He smiled, knocked cigarette ash into a black onyx ash tray. "A girl like Isabel could have done a lot better than Dickie Brewster."

"Dickie's doing all right."

An amused look. "There is no-one more boring than a dull man waiting for an undeserved inheritance. Or more stifling to a bright young woman than having to live with him."

He lifted his glass as if for a toast but drank and said nothing.

"I appreciate you coming," Emmett said. "You're busy, I'm sure."

"To tell you the truth, it's a relief to get away. Government may do its business in Jefferson City, but the place is not what you'd call cosmopolitan. You walk a block from the Capitol and it's corn cob pipes and tattered dungarees."

"Not the best of times for farmers."

Roddy sighed. "No, it isn't. You know, more than half the division's murder cases now are rural. That's what the dust storms did. Robbed farming people of all they had and turned them desperate."

"Some pretty desperate men in the city."

"That's why we're here, Whelan."

Their food arrived and they ate silently for a few minutes. The beef was excellent. Sensing a big tip, the waiters were tactful and attentive.

Roddy glanced sideways and asked, "Where are we at?"

"With the case?"

"What else?"

The swift change in tone disoriented him, and Emmett fumbled for a response. "Ah, Lloyd and his friends said you'd help me."

"And so I will."

"How is it going to work? Will I get access to division records?"

Roddy wiped the corners of his mouth with his napkin. "Emmett, this is not your usual case."

"I know that."

He dropped his voice. "The machine has its fingers in the state pie. Which makes the conventional routes...." He paused, lifted his fork. "This territory we're headed into, you step carefully. We all do."

"I understand."

"So. Where are we at?"

Emmett quietly summarized his work so far. The visit to the morgue. The gathering of documents. The case file. It felt slight.

"Where's the jacket?"

"Don't worry. It's back in bed. Not that there was much to see."

"How'd you get your hands on it?"

Emmett paused. "I have my sources."

"Like I said."

"I know."

Roddy dabbed a piece of bread in his gravy and ate it slowly. He rested his elbows on the table and brought his hands together at the fingertips. "Look," he said softly, "we both know what's going on here. Bob Perkins and his pals are tired of being on the outside. They see an opportunity."

"To get rid of the corruption," Emmett said.

"Among other things. These are businessmen. Their righteousness is, well, double-edged."

"Are you saying they're using me? Or you?"

"Nobody's using anyone. By all means, let's do what we have to to get rid of the rot. The state will love us for it. But let's be smart about it and do it in a way that's self-contained. And deniable. In case things don't go our way. That way we don't get burned. Win or lose, we survive." His eyes had grown hard. "So you've assembled the evidence. Do we have a case or don't we?"

Emmett told Eddie Sloan's story, as he had cast it in his own mind. The soft-spoken man minding his own business. His witness of something sensitive or brutal. The manner of his death.

Roddy listened carefully. "You seem convinced of the scenario."

"You're not?"

"It's plausible."

"Of course it is. It happens all the time. And most of these cases never get solved. Never even get investigated, really."

"Except this time, right?"

"I'm working on it. I'm checking stolen vehicles. Trying to pinpoint the scene of the crime. Looking at potential witnesses."

"You haven't identified the crime scene?"

"Not yet."

Roddy's mouth was flat, the ridges of his cheeks reddened by the wine. He was good. Like Mickey. A step ahead and short on patience. He tapped the table with the ball of his thumb. "What else?"

Aware of a stirring above his head, Emmett glanced up and saw the ceiling fan swinging into motion. "The investigating detective is a guy named Timmons."

"Richie Timmons?"

"The very man. Pretty Boy Floyd's dancing partner after the Union Station massacre. Just happened to be given the Sloan case."

"And given his history…"

"Well, it's worth exploring. Though I don't – "

Emmett looked at the waiters, their hands folded across their aprons, their eyes clear of all anxiety but the mild strain of their job.

"You don't what?" Roddy asked.

Maybe it was recalling Sloan's death. Maybe it was the heat. But he felt queasy, put off by the room's tawdry furnishings, the plates of congealed fat and half-eaten vegetables.

"Are you all right?" Roddy asked.

Emmett cleared his throat. "Say I manage to prove what seems to be true. Say I dig up the evidence and build a case and we take it to the next stage. What's different this time? How can I make it stick when Pendergast owns the state?"

Roddy lit another cigarette, blew smoke out the side of his mouth, and smiled. "That's where I come in."

"I'm listening."

He laid his hands on the table, palms upward. "A change is coming."

"Amen."

"You said you're listening, so listen. Don't underestimate men like Will Hutchins and Charlie Hayes. You think the Perkins brothers seek their company for their wit? They look like crotchety Bull Moosers but they know what's what. They are imperialists. They understand how empires work and they have foreseen the coming of the next great dominion."

"God in his heaven."

"Closer than you know. The federal government."

Emmett snorted. "Those boys hate FDR."

"Of course they do. They're businessmen. But they can see the writing on the wall. Centralization. The regulation of industry. The Treasury stockpiling gold. Some people see socialism. Will and Charlie, they make a virtue of necessity. They see economies of scale. New markets." Roddy's voice had deepened. Nothing like talk of money to stimulate sincerity. "These guys don't make things. They're into banking, insurance, securities. Pure money businesses, mobile and fluid, that can benefit greatly from federal control. As long as you understand and manipulate that control. Look at this fire insurance case your father-in-law is pursuing. Nine million dollars. And the Feds are the key. They've got the dough in escrow."

That voice. Intoxicated by its subject but in complete command.

"What does all this have to do with Eddie Sloan?" Emmett said. "Or Richie Timmons?"

Roddy stubbed out his cigarette with undue force. "The Feds will be Pendergast's downfall. It's inevitable."

"He's stronger than ever."

"The bigger they come. Listen to me. There's been a power shift. Congress has expanded federal jurisdiction. And Pendergast is blinded by greed. He sees federal programs as just another opportunity to skim. He was smart enough to get control of WPA jobs in Missouri, but what did he do? Channeled them to his pals. And made a big mistake."

Roddy's face whole face was arched with intent – eyebrows, cheekbones, upper lip.

"What was that?" Emmett said.

"He hasn't given any of the welfare jobs to Negroes, that's what. Washington is not happy about it. Not happy at all. And it's not enough that he's keeping them poor. Now he's *killing* them as well."

Emmett would not have wanted to face this man in a courtroom. The sound of his voice alone was convincing.

"And if we… if you and I can bring a case to them."

Roddy was nodding like a politician. "An innocent Negro murdered by his supposed protectors, in cahoots with gangsters. A tailor-made *cause célèbre* for the Feds. We'd have the power of the US government behind us. At the right moment in history."

He swiveled in his chair and signaled for the check. He was agitated, like a race horse in the traps, and needed to move.

"As with business," he said, "so with the law. Control and manipulation. Build me a case, Whelan. Build me a case and I'll bring it to the federal attorney. Who just happens to be a friend of mine."

"Maurice Milligan?"

"An honest Irishman." He blinked. "Like you."

"There's a few of us around."

"He's honest and he's smart and he's ambitious. And he remembers his friends."

The head waiter arrived with the check. Roddy paid and they took the elevator to the street. The Saturday afternoon traffic blurred past them. Brickwork and tarmac shimmered in the heat. The sun crashed down on their heads, but Roddy appeared not to notice. Sweat beading his brow, he stood on the sidewalk and touched the lapel of Emmett's jacket.

"Can you imagine how happy the FBI would be to get payback on Richie Timmons? Dillinger they nailed. Baby Face Nelson. Even Pretty Boy Floyd they killed last year in Ohio. But Kansas City has been a brick wall to them. And you, Emmett, you can make it happen. You have the jurisdictional authority. You'd be a national hero."

He peered up the street, took a white handkerchief from his pocket, and wiped his forehead. Newspaper boys warbled the late editions, and Emmett could hear his name in headlines.

"Listen. Laura and I are throwing a party at Mission Hills," Roddy said. "For some charity. An end of summer thing."

"Doesn't feel like the end of summer."

"Well, we can't wait for the weather to turn. Next Friday. Why don't you and... your wife come along. Lloyd will be there and we can follow up. He'll want to hear about your progress first hand."

"Sure."

"I'll have Laura send you an invite. Of course, we'll be talking in the meantime."

Emmett wanted to hear more about national heroics, but Roddy's mind had moved on. He tapped Emmett's forearm. "Build me a case."

He put his hat on and headed up the street in long, loping strides, the tail of his striped blazer flapping in the sunshine.

14

The night sky was the color of a bruise. Pillars of dark cloud bunched along its starless edges. The cab driver talked throughout the journey. Sharecropper from Dekalb County he was, still city-struck. Could have been a distraction, but his history was too close to her own.

They stopped at Alice's to pick up Wardell. He lolled beside her in the back seat as they bounced up Olive Street. The weather threatened. The wind rose. Thunder rumbled from the west. At the house she paid the man with two dollars Piney had thrust into her hand when she left the club. She slid the key into the front-door lock and held her breath.

She took Wardell to her bed. In the sound of his slow breathing she could hear the voices stir. Hadn't heard them in a long while, but no mistaking that sound. The storm grew closer and louder, but the voices rose right along with it. She lay face up, arm around her boy, while lightning flashes revealed a shadfly bumping randomly against the stained ceiling. Sweat dripped from her temples to the pillowcase.

At ten years of age she had woken in the middle of a July night much like this one and instead of the sounds of locusts and wind heard drunken voices and the whinnying of horses.

She shared a bed with her two younger sisters at the rear of their dirt-floor shack a mile outside of Chilhowee. Their mama dragged the three of them from the room and hustled them out the back door. Breaking glass, shouts, a pistol shot.

"Goddamn nigger shacks."

"Throw it over, throw it over!"

Mama whimpered.

"Where's Papa?" Arlene asked.

The night crackled and glowed. From the edge of the aspen grove they saw the sparks stream towards heaven as the men threw anything they could find onto the blaze: farm implements, saddlery, fencing. Their guns flashed in the firelight. Mama prayed.

Papa returned in the morning, his arm broken, his front teeth knocked out, his face badly bloodied. Through drifting smoke and light rain the family trudged across Johnson County fields, past scorched earth and abandoned shacks. At Warrensburg a colored doctor set her father's arm, fed them, and arranged for nighttime transport to Independence. Chilhowee and several other towns, he whispered, had been purged. Homeless for a while, they eventually settled in Raytown. She and Mama worked as domestics and Papa stared at the fire. The war came and with it decent work for colored folk. He got a job in a packing plant but was dead within a month. He was thirty-six years old.

It was a number of years before Arlene learned that her Uncle Selden had been lynched that fiery night for knocking a white man off his horse.

Arlene married Spencer Gray in 1922, in the Baptist church in his home town of Shawnee, Kansas. He played second base for the Monarchs and shoveled coal three days a week in Merriam. Wardell was born two years later. His daddy was proud, hard-working.

When Wardell was a year old, Spencer came home from a road game so badly beaten that she did not recognize his slumped figure, carried to her doorway by two teammates almost as bad themselves. Their bus took a wrong turn south of Independence and stumbled across a Thursday-night Klan meeting. Didn't know what hit them. Three months it took her to nurse him back to health. His body recovered but not his spirit. He stopped working. Often went missing. His mother looked after Wardell so Arlene could clean offices and the grocery store in Shawnee. Good times for the country, she kept hearing, but bad times for her family. She kept waiting for the voices to return.

Spencer played some pick-up ball and tried out for his old position on the Monarchs. Didn't make the cut. Finally he latched on to a traveling club based out of Omaha and stayed away for longer and longer stretches.

By 1930 she reckoned he was gone for good. Wardell needed schooling, so she moved to the city. Slum life was bad, but she was among those like herself. Safety in numbers.

Until now. The man named Richie, and others like him, were out there. With knowledge of her son and his movements. And whether it was him or other white men who had killed Eddie, who wanted to kill Virgil, it didn't matter. They were all the enemy. Even the investigator down from Chicago was a danger. If Richie or Mr. Lococo found out that he was poking around, it was Arlene who would pay.

The voices hissed. She held Wardell close to her and softly sang:

And though this world, with devils filled,
Should threaten to undo us,
We will not fear, for God hath willed
His truth to triumph through us.

Forgiveness? It didn't come into things. Justice? Only a fool would hope for it.

Simply escape. To be left alone, to be granted peace, would be enough. Though she would fight if she had to. They had taken from her all the men in her life. They would take Wardell over her dead body.

15

At lunchtime on Friday Emmett told his secretary that he would not be back that day. After a shave and a trim at the hotel barbershop, he bought a bouquet of zinnias and took a Monarch Cab to the top of Hickory Street in West Bottoms. Stepping around pools of mud and sludge, he walked past the cement factory and down the street to his parents' house. The crash of shunting boxcars came from the switching yard behind the factory. The stink of the stockyards was everywhere.

When his mother answered the door, she stared at him for a moment as if she didn't recognize him and then pulled him into the kitchen by his sleeve.

He kissed her and gave her the flowers. She bunched them in an old coffee can and put the kettle on the stove; took scones and tea from the pantry and butter from the icebox. Every movement was familiar from the days when he sat at this same deal table and ate his porridge before school. Except slower.

"Your arthritis acting up?"

She waved away his question.

He had not visited since early in the summer. The kitchen was stifling. The linoleum was streaked with grease and a broken window above the sink had been covered with torn oilcloth. Flies hovered around the butter. Emmett tugged at his suit cuffs and wrestled with his disgust.

"Has the help been here today?"

She pretended she hadn't heard. He asked again.

"Sure, she was only getting in the way."

"Ma. I went to a lot of trouble to find that woman. She came highly recommended."

"Came highly paid."

"*I* was paying her."

She poured the tea. He refused a scone.

"How long's that window been busted?"

"Not long."

"How come Da hasn't fixed it?"

"Your father has enough to worry about."

They drank their tea and made small talk. It took her a while to remember details. He waited for questions or comments about Fay, but none came.

"I need to look through my old stuff," he said when he was finished. "My books."

"Your what?"

"My books from law school. I put them in boxes and stored them under the stairs."

"That's all cleared out."

"You threw away my *books*?"

"There might be some out back. In the shed."

The back yard was a dump: broken whiskey bottles, rusted bicycle parts, scraps of wood, weeds waist-high. As a kid, he and his older brother Harry had played stickball out here. His dad had kept the place spotless, the ground swept and graveled, his woodworking tools hung on the shed wall as if on store display. Harry had been in Chicago for ten years. He did not come home anymore.

As he searched for his books, he heard the creak of the back door.

"His highness pays a call."

His father's voice was a little too loud, the diction a little too precise. A bad sign.

Emmett stepped from the shed, brushing dust from his suit jacket. "How come you're not at work?"

"I could ask the same of you."

"Half day at the factory?"

His dad went into the house. Emmett followed, and his mother pleaded for peace with her eyes. He had taken a bottle from the cupboard and was pouring whiskey into a teacup. His overalls were stained with dried sweat and old grease.

"You'll join me."

"It's two in the afternoon, Da."

"You know me, son. Never one for watching clocks." He drank the whiskey in a single gulp. "And never one," he croaked, "for letting anyone tell me what to do."

He wiped his mouth and rapped the table with the cup.

"Have a cup of tea, Ned. There's a fresh pot."

He ignored her, staring at Emmett. "Jack Harte told me you were at Billy's. Some big case by the look of it."

"You know, I can't figure out what Fat Jack likes more, drinking himself silly or poking his nose into other people's business."

"He's honest company. Sticks by his friends."

"He hasn't had an honest moment since he got off the boat."

His dad poured another shot. "You have a fucking nerve."

"That so?"

His mother squirmed, fretted with her cardigan.

"You'd think you'd have the decency to let us know."

This comment threw Emmett. His dad had changed the subject mid-conversation. An old ploy.

"Know what?"

His father drank the shot and smiled at Emmett's mother. "Lettin' on he hasn't a clue," he said. "Your mother rang that woman of yours two weeks ago. Invited the pair of you to dinner. Said she'd get back to us and we haven't heard a word since. *That's* what."

Emmett looked at his mother's stricken face. It was true. "Fay hasn't been herself. Since losing the baby."

Nodding righteously, his dad said, "The offer still stands. If she can hold her nose long enough."

"Ned!"

Emmett patted his mother's arm and left. The books could wait.

When he got home, an unfamiliar woman was vacuuming the hallway. He stood in front of her until she turned off the machine.

"Where's Hattie?"

The woman was older, in her fifties at least, with a sad cast of face and a sagging body. She had no idea what he was asking.

"Mrs. Whelan?"

"She upstairs, sir. Dressin' for the party."

It was after seven. Roddy's Mission Hills bash started at eight.

The house had an alien feel, as if he had returned after a long absence. The air had been soured by cigarette smoke and the oak floorboards and newels were dull with French polish and unreflected light. On his way upstairs he heard the clock chime the half hour, eclipsed by the vacuum cleaner restarting. He walked into their bedroom as if onto a stage set.

Fay was sitting on the edge of the bed, dressed and made up, emptying onto the coverlet the contents of a beaded bag and redistributing them among the pockets of a leather clutch.

"You're cutting it a little close, aren't you, darling?" she said without looking at him.

"Who's that downstairs?" he said.

She snapped shut the bag's flap and stood up, smoothing her dress.

"Ophelia," she said.

"Ophelia?"

She examined herself in the full-length mirror. "Ophelia Jackson. Hattie's replacement."

As she spoke she lifted her shoulders, already heightened by the butterfly sleeves of her party dress.

"Hattie's gone?"

"Long gone."

Through the window was the patterned green of their back yard, shaded by black walnut and cherry trees, bordered by clumps of gardenias and irises that were tended Saturdays on Lloyd's nickel.

"I visited my mother this afternoon."

She kept her eyes on her image in the mirror. "Oh? How is she?"

"Same as ever. She told me – actually, my dad told me that they had invited us to dinner. Two weeks ago?"

"Your father was there?"

"I wasn't expecting to see him, but yes, he was."

She moved past him. He caught her arm. She pushed his hand away.

"Did she call you and ask us to dinner?"

"I vaguely recall something like that."

"Why didn't you tell me?"

"Emmett, do you really think we're going to go to your parents for dinner, all things considered? How *was* your father, by the way?"

"It's not a question of whether we go or not. You didn't even tell me. I was embarrassed in front of my mother."

Rubbing her hands briskly, as if ridding them of crumbs, she said, "I'm sure you'll get over it."

She left the room. The vacuum cleaner had been turned off and he heard the tap of her heels on the stairs.

Halfway down she stopped and said in a sing-song voice, "Are we going to this party or aren't we?"

16

L aura Hudson had a way of looking through anyone who was not on her A list. Emmett clearly didn't make the cut.

"It's been *ages*," Laura said, ignoring him and embracing Fay carefully. "Where have you been *hiding*?"

They were standing at the entrance to the country club. Ground staff were lighting Japanese lanterns and carrying fanback chairs onto the lawn. As if in a movie, Laura had floated towards them in a floral-patterned silk gown, her hands and neck dense with jewelry, her hair cut like Claudette Colbert's.

"At the Plaza, of course," Fay said. "Where else?"

"Don't torture me. In Jefferson City the shopping is squalid."

"Poor dear."

"Roddy has to bring me to Chicago once a month. How else would I survive?"

"I *know*."

Fay acknowledged Emmett with the slightest tilt of her head. "You know Emmett. My husband."

"Haven't had the pleasure."

Laura extended a limp hand and gave him the benefit of her full disregard. He could have reminded her that her father had started professional life as a cattle rustler, but why bother? On the south side of Kansas City, money was money.

"I've heard much about you," he said.

"I'm sure," she said, looking away. "Fay, darling, where did you get those *adorable* pumps?"

Laura was a thoroughbred rich bitch, but Fay was in the running. On the ride over, she had refused to speak. More than ever, Emmett was being punished for who he was. The rules had been refined. It wasn't enough that he pursue her father's version of success – he must disown his past as well. Visiting his mother was all right as long as it stayed unmentioned. He had to pretend his family didn't exist.

Roddy strode in from the lounge, his face as red as his cummerbund. He wore a matching bow tie, an unbuttoned white dinner jacket, and black trousers. With a twinge of embarrassment, Emmett remembered that the party was formal. And Fay had said nothing when he came downstairs in his light wool suit.

But Roddy was not looking at him. "Fay, you look splendid. Doesn't she look wonderful, honey?"

Roddy was smooth. He spoke to Fay as if he'd known her for years.

"Ravishing," Laura said.

"You always make an effort for a Hudson," Fay said. After a beat she added, "For a Hudson event."

Laura hooked her arm through Fay's and led her into the English lounge, talking at full throttle.

"Listen to them," Roddy said, frowning. "Couple of yardbirds."

"Roddy, I'm sorry. I forgot it was black tie."

He didn't answer. He moved to the entrance, stuck his head out, and examined the sky with a flare of his nostrils. The front staff watched him attentively. He inspected an ornate barometer hanging in the hallway. "Twenty-nine and falling," he said. "I think this dry spell's finally going to break. And soon."

"Suits me."

Roddy opened his silver case and took out a cigarette. For a moment he looked in the direction the women had gone. "They're saying there's a big one coming in for Labor Day. Down South. Hurricane out at sea, going to hit Florida on Monday."

"Long way from Kansas City."

"Weather systems are all connected. We'll get a change up here as well."

He smoked, hand on his hip. Something was on his mind, and it wasn't the weather.

He snapped his fingers at the doorman, who glided over. "Tell Horace to move the lawn furniture to the verandah. And bring in those paper lanterns. It will be raining within the hour."

"Yes, Mr. Hudson."

He watched the man head off. Without looking at Emmett, he said, "You had a good week?"

"Not bad."

"You can tell me later. Lloyd will want to know." He straightened his tie. "Let's join the fray."

The cream of Kansas City society had assembled beneath the cut-glass chandeliers of the English lounge, chattering, drinking, sizing each other up. All the right families were there: the Perkins, Chathams, and Bridges; the Altmans, Lawsons, and Treadways. Dickie Brewster and his father stood beside the bar, smoking cigars. Henrietta Kincaid fluttered from clique to clique in a pill-box hat, photographer in tow, gathering copy for the *Tattler*.

The men talked business and politics, their faces red from cocktails and the heat. The young women clustered around Laura Hudson, admiring each other's clothes and inspecting the flow of arrivals. These were women of Fay's age. They had all come out together, all married in recent years, and all except Fay and Isabel delivered their first babies. The sole male in the group, Peter Lawson, hovered at the edges, handsome, unmarried, fashionably disheveled. He was laughing at something Laura had said, something wicked and close to home, judging by his tone. Fay glanced Emmett's way and blushed. *That awful bore Peter Lawson.* If she really thought that, would she enjoy his company so much?

"Stands out, doesn't she?"

Lloyd was beside him, ramrod straight, white eyebrows flared like the wings of a gull. Emmett grew flustered at this sudden appearance. He put his soda on the table and offered his hand. Lloyd's wiry body was as still as a cigar-store Indian, but his creased eyes moved from Emmett to Fay and back.

"It's good for her to get out," Emmett said. "All day on her own, and so forth."

"It seems to me," Lloyd said after a few moments, "that she has no problem getting out, as you put it."

The curtains on the room's upper windows stirred. Emmett smelled ozone. Roddy's storm was on the way.

"You know your daughter better than I do, Lloyd."

"Do I?"

Lloyd had a habit of pausing before each remark, a pause that left Emmett feeling judged.

"Roddy said you're looking for an update."

Lloyd fluttered his fingers to mean *not here.* Across the room the laughter grew; Peter Lawson was pretending to chastise the women, and phrases from his banter reached the men like scraps of newspaper in the wind: *not a thing about business... beauty parlors and Bancroft's... all day doing your nails...*

"That man is a fool," Lloyd said under his breath.

The wild eyebrows hiked a notch and his tapered face contracted. He looked like he was about to lead his platoon up San Juan Hill. All he needed was a saber in his hand.

And through Lloyd's eyes Emmett saw that Lawson was flirting with Fay, and that she was flirting back.

"Gentlemen."

It was Roddy, jacket off, bow tie askew.

"I have a room."

As Emmett followed the men out of the lounge, he heard Fay laughing like a schoolgirl.

Roddy led them to a private office behind the reception desk. He cleared a small conference table of papers and set out coasters for their drinks. The room was designed for seclusion: a double-locking door, dark oak-paneled walls, windows high and narrow. From outside came a distant roll of thunder.

Lloyd said, "Fine party, Roddy."

"Hasn't started yet, Mr. Perkins. There's a dance band lined up. And we've got filet mignon and Atlantic salmon coming, with enough champagne to float a cruise ship."

Unimpressed, Lloyd gave Roddy a tight, almost oriental smile. His dress suit was well tailored but cut like a military uniform. Roddy's unjacketed torso was a maroon slash in the subdued room, and his eyes had the glow and blur of a man on his third strong drink. The sparkle of Fay's face as she spoke to Peter Lawson crowded Emmett's mind, but feeling the heat of Lloyd's bearing, he focused his thoughts on the Sloan case.

Though Roddy seemed to have forgotten why they had gathered. "Ordered the bubbly in Chicago."

"Chicago," Lloyd said.

"Importer I know up there, gets it straight from Paris. Passes on the savings to me."

"You traveled to Chicago to buy champagne."

Roddy blinked, picked up his drink, replaced it carefully on the coaster. The room was very warm. "I was in Chicago on business, Lloyd. Criminology convention."

Lloyd nodded. "Learn anything?"

"The FBI demonstrated the Keeler polygraph for us."

"Is this the same machine Lindbergh won't allow used on his staff?"

"Keeler's refined it." Roddy turned to Emmett. "It charts blood pressure, pulse rate, and breathing. And now Keeler's added a galvanograph." He struggled a little with the word but kept going. "It measures sweat gland activity. If someone's lying, they start to sweat."

Roddy was sweating himself in the small, humid room, which had darkened quickly as storm clouds continued to mass. Lloyd got up and turned on the overhead light. Almost immediately it flickered, and a split second later thunder crashed overhead.

Lloyd glanced at the small windows, which were rattling in the growing wind. Roddy sniffed loudly and cleared his throat. "So Emmett," he said, "are we going to need a polygraph?"

"Why would we?"

"For Richie Timmons."

Lloyd looked up sharply. "Who?"

Emmett said, "We have some work to do before we start thinking about polygraphs."

Lloyd shifted in his chair. "Slow down here. What's this about Timmons?"

Emmett expected Lloyd would have been brought up to speed. But Roddy's face was a blank. Something was up. He was not on the ball. As if he were still thinking about the great deal he'd gotten on the champagne.

Emmett summarized the morgue mix-up, the vague reports, the scenario he had built around Eddie's death, and his suspicions about Timmons. Lloyd listened intently. The rain was now whipping the windows in waves, and the wind was hooting.

A knock on the door interrupted. The chief steward told them that a tornado warning had been announced on the radio and that all guests were being advised to shelter in the basement.

"What about dinner?" Roddy asked him.

"Being kept warm, sir. We expect the storm to pass directly and the party to continue on schedule."

The steward closed the door. Roddy pushed his chair back, but Lloyd didn't budge. His forehead was crinkled. "Let me get this straight: this guy Timmons – who we all know is a crook of the first order – is the investigating detective. And you can tell from his reports that he is covering something up?"

"That's my belief, sir."

"So where's your evidence?"

"Well, the reports – "

"Forget the reports. I said *evidence*. You're a prosecutor, presumably you know how to build a goddamn case."

There was a gust of power in the room; like the wind, Lloyd could summon forces that smashed all resistance.

"I'm working on it," Emmett said.

"You're *working* on it? Where did the murder happen? Who found the body? How can you possibly build a case when you haven't been to the scene of the crime?"

At a loss, Emmett stared at the shimmying windows.

"With respect, Emmett," Roddy said, eager to jump on Lloyd's bandwagon, "everything you've told us is old news. What about this week?"

"Well, as you can imagine, there's a lot of tension in the Negro community."

Lloyd raised his eyes to the shadowed ceiling.

"People are wondering why nothing is being done," Emmett said. "If there was some public reassurance, it would go a long way towards calming matters."

"What are you suggesting?" Roddy said.

"You told me the Feds will get involved at the appropriate time. Now you're telling me you met them in Chicago. Why can't we get them in now and get some teeth into this investigation? I feel tied down."

Without rising from his chair, Lloyd was a storm of commotion. His tux front was fit to burst. "No, no, no. Goddamn it, Emmett, out in Oakwood less than two years and already you've lost touch with reality. This is Pendergast's turf. If he gets a whiff of what we're doing, the whole town will shut down on us."

"Any sign of Virgil Barnes?" Roddy asked.

"No. Could be he was killed too, body just hasn't surfaced."

"Who is Virgil Barnes?" Lloyd asked.

"A friend of Sloan's. The two of them, it turns out, were living in the same hotel. He went missing same time Sloan turned up dead."

But Lloyd wasn't listening. "Les Newton tells me someone's been snooping around."

"Well, I have."

"No. Someone else."

After a considered pause, Emmett said, "I hired a PI."

"A *what*?" Roddy said.

Lloyd leaned forward in his chair and thrust a finger into Emmett's chest. "Who is he?"

"An old friend," Emmett said.

"*Who!*"

"Mickey McDermott. I went to school with him. Straight as they come. And for what it's worth, he hates KCPD. With a passion."

Lloyd stood up and paced the room. "Jesus Christ. Why didn't you tell me this?" he said to Roddy.

"I didn't *know*."

"What have you told him?" Lloyd asked Emmett.

"Nothing but what he needs to know."

"Goddamn it, how can you take a risk like this?"

Lloyd turned back to Roddy, who shrugged. Emmett was on his own on this one. Fay's face drifted into Emmett's consciousness like a full moon. Was the whole world going to kick him around? The blood rose in his throat.

"You keep telling me my job is to build a case," he said hotly. "With no help from the city or the Feds. And with no one in county in the know. You think I'm going to do that with paper? There are no paper trails on this one, Lloyd, that's the whole fucking point. If there's a case here, it's in the margins. What falls between the cracks. I got to roll up my sleeves, and I *can't* do it by myself. I have to have someone who knows where the bodies are buried."

Hands on his hips, Lloyd said, "OK, OK. Cool down."

With a crash of thunder, the light blew out.

"Goddamn it, Emmett," Lloyd said in the dark, "you'd better find this Barnes. Last thing we need is another dead nigger." He made his way to the door. "We'll finish this later," he said.

He opened the door, and the steward's flashlight lit up his craggy features. The steward led them around the reception desk, back to the lounge, and down a stairway at the rear of the bar. They made their way along a narrow passageway lined with crates of empty bottles, stacks of folded chairs, and gas canisters. Ahead was laughter and the sound of clinking glasses. The steward's flashlight bounced along the white-washed walls and exposed pipes. Roddy stumbled over a box and cursed. The air smelled of dust and damp.

They came to an open door, and the steward paused. Within was a flicker of light and a murmur of voices. Expecting the party, the men ducked inside.

Black faces stared across the empty space at them, tight mouths ghostly in candlelight. The room went silent. Lloyd cleared his throat. The steward stuck his head in and said, "Just colored in here, gentlemen. Follow me, please."

They continued down the passageway until they reached a large room lit from the back by two Coleman lanterns hanging on the heating pipes. The atmosphere was loud and gay. Laura Hudson had bottles of champagne in both hands and was topping up glasses. Emmett could not see Fay. Or Peter Lawson.

Roddy and Lloyd melted into the crowd. As Emmett's eyes searched the wide, low-ceilinged space, he saw the white staff working the room, Irish and Italians carrying trays of hors d'oeuvres and crustless sandwiches, bottles of wine and spirits. Pouring champagne was the ginger-haired kid who had waited the bar the day of Emmett's meeting with Lloyd's friends. The family name came to him. Garrity. His uncle had run liquor during Prohibition and now delivered beer for Anheuser-Busch. Used to drink with Emmett's dad.

He floated around the room for ten minutes or so, not once seeing Fay. When the lights flickered back on, the crowd groaned with mock disapproval. The stewards snuffed the lanterns and herded everyone back upstairs. Emmett hung back, sick to his stomach.

He felt a tap on his shoulder. It was Fay.

"Where have you been hiding?" she said.

He looked her over. Hair unruly, color high, lipstick freshly applied. Her eyes glittered with sexual energy.

"That's funny," he said, "I was about to ask the same of you."

She drew in her lips and watched the retreating guests. "I've been enjoying myself," she said.

"Yeah?

"Yes. For a change."

She walked away and he followed her to the foot of the stairway. Beneath the smooth silk of her gown, her hips swung back and forth. Rage churned in his chest. She mounted the stairs. More than anything, he wanted to lean forward, grab her by the collar of her expensive dress, and drag her to the floor. But he stayed put, letting her move ahead without him.

He got his breathing under control. His nausea had left him. For the first time in years he wanted a drink. A real drink. He remained in the cool of the basement, happy to be alone.

But he was not. From down the hall came a low, mournful sound. A mix of voices singing something steady and lilting that was the exact opposite of the anger and confusion he felt around his heart. He stood stock still for a moment, listening. He could not make out the words – just the rolling rise and fall of the song. Pulled towards it, he moved down the hallway and came to the room where the Negro employees were riding out the storm. Where they had been herded so that Laura and her friends would not be have to be near black men in the dark.

He edged in to the room. The people were in a circle, heads bowed, singing with their eyes closed and clapping lightly in time with the spiritual:

Nobody knows the trouble I've seen
Nobody knows but Jesus
Nobody knows the trouble I've seen
Glory Hallelujah.

It was like Hattie singing in the kitchen, soft and soulful and from another world. He listened until they finished. They opened their eyes, saw him, and went stiff with fear and suspicion. He backed out of the room like a kid caught where he was not supposed to be and made his way back to the ballroom.

17

Satch was coming. It was for sure. Not to play with the Monarchs, like Jesse said, but to play against them. The greatest pitcher in the world had signed a contract with a mixed-race team in Bismarck, North Dakota. And the Bismarcks were coming to Kansas City.

Satchel Paige. Mannish boy. Upright and lowdown and born to wander. Coming to Municipal Stadium.

On Wardell's bedroom wall was a photo of Satch from *Life* magazine. He was outside a poolroom in Harlem, sitting on the fender of a Buick Roadmaster. Dressed to kill in a pinstripe suit and two-toned leather shoes. About to light a cigarette and looking at the camera like he owned the world. Or a mighty piece of it, anyhow.

"You watch," Jesse's Uncle Josh said. "Two innings left, he'll tell the outfield go sit down."

"Infield, too," Jesse added.

"Then, bang! Six strikeouts."

Wardell and his mama were eating with Jesse's family on their back porch. Arlene had to go to work after supper. Already she looked wore out.

"When's this game?" she asked.

"Next Saturday. Quincy Johnson, he's getting tickets for us."

Jesse's dad shook a rib bone at his brother. "Don't be counting on stunts like that, Josh. Monarchs ain't no exhibition team."

"Listen to your daddy, Jesse. Local pride be messin' with his judgement. We talkin' 'bout *Satch*."

Jesse's mother gave the men her Sunday frown. Same look she gave Josh when he showed his hip flask. "This North Dakota team," she said.

"Yes, Alice?"

"The club is – am I right? – integrated."

In-te-gra-ted. She said the word like it was dangerous.

"Not a lot of colored folk up that direction," Josh said, winking at Wardell. "Got to make do with lesser talent."

Lester licked barbecue sauce from his fingers. He said to his wife, "Some doors are opening, honey. Thought you might welcome that."

Alice stood, starting clearing dishes. "All for open doors, I am. But open too quick and they liable to hit you in the face."

Arlene said to Wardell, "Maybe going to this game isn't such a good idea."

"What?"

Shaking her head, Arlene followed Alice into the kitchen. His fingers still in the air, Lester glanced sideways at Wardell.

"What they worried about?" Josh said, low-toned.

"Oh, you know," Lester said. "Where there's white folk, there's trouble."

"Well, that may be so," Josh said. "But she can't be serious. Keep the boy at home? With Satch comin'?"

Before supper Wardell and Jesse had snuck out of the house and walked to Eighteenth and Vine. Arlene was cleaning at the Plaza and Alice was giving a music lesson. The boys hung outside Street's Hotel, hoping to meet some of the ballplayers.

The corner was quiet in the afternoon heat. Under an awning at Fox's Bar, four musicians played cards and drank beer. The boys sidled up.

"If it ain't Alice's kid," one of the men said without looking up from his cards. "The one with the teeny-weeny pecker."

The other men laughed.

"That ain't true," Jesse said.

"That a fact? You gonna prove us wrong, son?"

Jesse wiped his nose and sneered but said nothing. Wardell smelled something stronger than beer and stepped back.

"You Arlene's boy?" another man said to Wardell.

"Yes sir."

"How your mama doin'?"

"All right."

"Who's playing with her now?"

"Phineas," said a fat man with a toothpick in his mouth. "Phineas Jordan."

Cards flew back and forth.

"This Phineas, he play a little jelly roll?"

More laughter. On the street, two dogs were nosing each other's privates.

"Eddie played, we know that."

"Oh yeah."

Squinting in the sun, Wardell glanced at a passing streetcar. The white driver gave him a nasty stare, and he looked away. Taped to the inside of the bar window was a photograph of Eddie Sloan, with black around the edges. The picture was all over the district. Eddie wore a collar and tie and a soft hat. Wardell tried to remember him from the days when he would visit. But he couldn't line up his memory with the photo.

"Satchel Paige is coming to Kansas City," Jesse said.

The fat man took the toothpick from his mouth and drank his beer. "When Jesus come again, boy, you feel free to let me know. Otherwise, we appreciate you let us get on with our game."

The barkeep came to the door. He wore a white apron and had his sleeves rolled. He pointed at the boys. "You peanuts get movin', you hear?"

That night Wardell's mama carried him into the house from the taxi. He lay in bed and listened to her move around the kitchen. It was like part of his brain was in dreamland, but another part watching her.

She stayed up later every night. She wasn't crying anymore, but sometimes there was no noise from the kitchen for a long time. Just when he thought she was in bed, her heard her walk across the plank floor or shift dishes in the sink.

Sometimes she brought him to her bed in the middle of the night. But she didn't say the words she used to, the comforting things. Her body was still all soft and warm, but when she held him close, it was like she was thinking of something else. He wanted to ask her: is this how it's going to be from now on?

On their way home from Jesse's, he had told her that he wanted to see Satchel Paige pitch more than anything else in the world. She squeezed his hand and said nothing.

Tonight she didn't come to his room. He woke after she was in bed. The locusts were loud as a buzzsaw. Moonlight poured into the room and turned the floor and the walls blue.

He stared at Satch's picture. Everything about him was cool: the look in his eyes, the way he held his hands to light a cigarette, the hat tilted back on his head. If Wardell could see the man on the ballfield, all would be well. Satch would make things right. His hesitation wind-up, his screwball and whipsy-dipsy-do, his high-step kick. See him on the field and shout his name, like the old women shouted out the Lord's in church. That would drive away the ghosts.

No doubt.

18

Tension in the district was running high. Arlene could feel it. The weather stayed hot and folks stayed edgy. Storekeepers cleared the sidewalks of layabouts and country boys. Cops on the beat were quick with the bully club. Musicians and other night people peered over their shoulders.

Eddie's picture remained in the windows of local businesses, and church and newspaper kept calling for the city to solve the murder. But Reverend Jones and Bill Carter tended to a parlor view of politics. A daytime outlook. Arlene knew that things were different on the street, especially after the sun went down.

You could push white folks only so far. Take this baseball game on Saturday. Eighteenth Street had bunting draped across the storefronts and pennants fluttering from the telephone poles. Chauncy Downes and his Rinky Dinks played hot tunes on a bandstand outside the Gem Theater. And the local boys were talking about whether Cool Papa Bell could get a hit off Satchel Paige or if Bullet Rogan would play. But underneath the holiday buzz was trouble. A lot of white people didn't take to the idea of a mixed-race team playing in Kansas City. There were rumors of marches and pickets and extra police.

But the buzz got louder. The game was the social highlight of the year and everyone in the district was going. The saloons and gambling halls were roaring, and other businesses were closing for the day. Folks were coming from as far as Minneapolis. Cal Watkins had reserved a dozen seats on the third-base line, and Wardell and Jesse were like a couple of jumping beans. Even Alice was getting into the spirit. And Arlene wasn't going to let her son go without her. So she claimed a ticket and thought about what to wear. Monarchs games were always a fashion parade.

Game day was glorious – warm, dry, breezy. The Bismarcks' bus sat outside Street's Hotel, surrounded by autograph hounds and overdressed young women. In the morning Arlene stood beside the bus with Wardell for an hour while he waited for Paige to show. He did not. They returned to Lester and Alice's house for lunch and then headed to the stadium in a car laid on by Cal.

"Now this," Lester said as they were driven along the riverfront, "is what I call traveling in *style*."

"No riff-raff in here," Josh said.

Alice said, "Glad to hear it."

The women had spoken over lunch about the need for the district to show its better side at the game. White folks would be watching, and roughneck fans who drank corn liquor under the stands and cursed at the other team would be an embarrassment, even a danger.

Josh held to a different view. He was a heavyset man, with cheeks like a chipmunk, a grizzled mustache, and a scar on his chin from a long-ago brawl. All his life he had worked in a meat-packing plant in West Bottoms, where he was now a foreman, high as a colored man could go.

"Riff-raff and police," Josh said. "It's all the same."

Lester said, "Police got the guns."

Arlene didn't like this turn in the talk. She had seen Josh nipping at the hip flask before getting into the car.

"Few of the boys drink a little bootleg," Josh said, "and the womenfolk all upset. Meantime the police and who know who keep whalin' on our ass."

"*Josh*," Alice said.

"And where's all this reform I keep hearing about? All this bullshine about what Washington gon' do for us colored? We can't even apply for federal jobs."

Lester glanced at the boys, sitting in the back between their mothers. "OK, Josh. That's enough on that subject."

The driver dropped them off at the entrance to the stadium. The place was hopping. Scalpers barked like carnies. The hotel women sashayed past men with teeth bright as cufflinks. Smells of grilled sausage, roasted nuts, cold beer. On top of the eastside wall was the Monarchs' maroon flag with its gold-stitched legend – WORLD'S COLORED CHAMPIONS.

"Best baseball team in the world," Josh said to the boys. "And Satch on the mound. What more could you ask for?"

In the parking lot were buses with license plates from Missouri, Kansas, Oklahoma, and Arkansas. In front of one bus, a quartet sang:

Is you is or is you ain't my baby
The way you acting lately makes me doubt
You is still my baby, baby, baby
Seems my flame in your heart done gone out

The good mood dipped as they approached the turnstiles and saw the protestors: women in dowdy frocks and men in short-sleeved shirts and straw hats. White, all of them, and middle-aged, holding hand-lettered signs that said *No to Integration* and *Races Don't Mix*. The game crowd kept their distance, creating a no man's land of hard-packed dirt littered with candy bar wrappers and cigarette butts where the police strolled, blue-black and slot-mouthed, their badges glinting in the sun.

Inside the park they met Leonora and Cal, who bought the boys scorecards and root beer. They made their way to their seats, five rows up from the dazzling infield. The grass was cut to perfection; the basepaths were smooth as a highway. A groundskeeper paced the white canvas fence bordering the outfield, checking the stakes and tightening the guylines.

"Gonna be a sell-out," Lester said. "Eighteen thousand. At least."

But his voice was strained.

"Look," Josh said. "They got a rope up."

The whole way round the ballpark, the police had roped off the first two rows of seats, where kids usually gathered to shout at the players and snare foul balls.

"They got a nerve," Lester said.

"Check *this* out."

The police detail filed onto the field, two abreast, and took up positions in front of the empty rows. In the cheap seats, country boys in overalls and low hats jeered.

"Since when the police been runnin' Monarchs games?" Josh said. Hands on his hips, he hung his head like a bulldog. "Ain't seen *nothin'* like this before."

"Sit down, Josh," Cal said.

Arlene made Wardell sit beside her and clasped his hand.

"It's a shame, Cal," Josh said.

"I know. But what are we going to do? Let's just watch the game."

Josh paced back and forth, glaring at the cops until Alice lost her patience and told him to stop being a fool, he was asking for trouble. As she spoke, the Monarchs sprinted from the home dugout and fanned onto the field. The crowd whistled and stomped. The players took their positions and went through their warm-ups. Several of the Bismarcks popped up from their dugout, jogging up and down the lines and tossing loosely in the bullpen. The fans rubbernecked, looking for Satch. But he was going to make them wait.

He stayed out of sight until the bottom of the first. Two hits for the visitors in the top half of the inning but no runs. When a double play retired the side, the crowd held its breath. The sky expanded and the infield grass brightened. For a minute the police seemed to disappear. After a long wait Satch emerged from the dugout, loose-limbed and game-faced, tugging the bill of his cap as he made his way to the mound. The crowd erupted in a huge cheer. He slapped his leg with his mitt and looked at the sky, ignoring the uproar. All eyes on the man. The beanpole frame. The freakishly long arms. Even the cops had turned around to look.

Arlene watched Wardell. He sat bolt upright, eyes fixed on his hero, right hand softly socking the palm of his mitt. Satch tossed his first warm-up. It popped in the catcher's glove like the snap of a bull whip, and Wardell gasped. When Satch scuffed the mound and tossed the rosin bag behind him, Wardell's lips parted with a soundless cheer. When he smoked the first batter on three pitches – Newt Allen, Cal said, shaking his head, Newt Allen struck out looking – Wardell laughed. Drunk, the boy sounded. Leroy Taylor managed to foul off a couple pitches, but he too fanned. And when the third batter, Big Bomb Brown, struck out swinging, Wardell rose from his seat, leaned forward and, as Satch strutted back to the dugout with his finger pointed at the sky, held his opened mitt out as if asking his hero to fire one his way. Arlene thought of Spencer, husband and second-baseman, who should have been here, beside his boy. Who last shared her bed seven years ago. Then Eddie, who had always said that baseball was like jazz. Her men, taken by the world. Who was going to stop Wardell from being taken? A ballplayer?

Satch pitched perfect but was pulled after four innings, the better to rest his arm for the Bismarcks' next barnstorming stop. So Monarchs fans got all they wished for – Satch in full flow *and* a victory, 3-2 when Bullet Rogan smacked a two-run homer in the ninth. In the euphoria that followed, Arlene lost her grip on Wardell. Hemmed in by the surging crowd, she felt him wriggle away and cried out so sharply that Cal put his arm around her shoulders and told her that he and Jesse were only going to the locker-room door to get Satch's autograph. Josh would be with them.

As they made their way to the exit, a drunk in his hog-killing clothes somehow slipped past the police cordon and capered onto the field, shouting and waving a crushed hat. Two cops chased him, but he dodged their tackles and ran across the infield, where he stopped near the pitcher's mound, hooting and breathless. The boys in the cheap seats cheered. The cops caught up with him and their billyclubs flew high, coming down on his bare head with a crack. Arlene's stomach turned at the sound. The departing crowd paused as one, saw the man slump to the grass, and then pushed hard for the exits.

The smell of blood was in the air, of bad liquor and adrenaline. The boys in the bleachers lingered, scowling at the gathered cops, who were bunched together in the infield, batons raised. Arlene's blood beat in her ears. Wardell, she had to find Wardell.

An empty bottle flew from the bleachers. Then a piece of two-by-four. The grumbling turned to shouting, more bottles flew, and the cops rushed the seats. There was mayhem. Yelling. Crashing. Gunfire. Arlene clawed desperately at the people in front of her. Clawed as if buried alive.

Outside the ballpark was chaos. Men with bloody hands and faces dragged others too broken up to walk, laying them along the sidewalk. Alice and Leonora went over to help. Men were taking off their shirts and ripping them into strips for bandages. Monarch cabs appeared from the 22nd Street rank to take the injured to the hospital.

Arlene ran up and down the stretch of boardwalk in front of the ticket windows, shouting Wardell's name. Lester chased her and grabbed her arm. "Arlene, come over here. With us."

"*Wardell.*"

"Don't worry. Josh is with him. Come on over now."

After a few minutes Jesse emerged from the mob. Josh followed, pale and limping, his jacket torn.

"Where's Wardell?" Arlene said.

Josh looked confused. His face was the color of wet ashes. "He isn't with you?"

"Oh my God, Cal, where is he? Where's my baby?"

Cal held her. He spoke in low tones to Josh. Lester was on his tiptoes, peering through the smoke. Beyond the fleeing fans and injured bodies were knots of tense white men, hefting weapons of all descriptions.

"Wardell!" Arlene shouted.

"He said he was going back to you," Josh said. "I told him stop, but he kept going."

Arlene broke from Cal and ran to the west entrance. A man with a shotgun stood in front of the turnstile. He had a brutal mouth and a cast to his eye.

"My boy's in there."

The man spat at her feet and hitched at the gun.

"I said, my son's in there."

"Well, that's his funeral, ain't it?"

"He's a child. I have to get him out."

His stray eye made it hard to tell where he was looking. She moved to pass him, and he barred her way. His breath was sour and metallic.

"I have to – "

He struck her in the breast with the gunstock. She staggered back and fell to the dust. He looked at her as at a wounded animal. Cal and Lester, who had followed her over, helped her up.

"*Wardell!*" she cried.

"You boys better get that bitch out of here right quick."

Cal was breathing hard and his face was dark. "I want to speak to the man in charge," he said to the guard.

"You *what?*"

"Who's heading up this operation?"

"Listen to me, you dumb nigger, *I'm* the man in charge."

Cal tried to grab the gun but slipped and fell to the ground. The man stepped on Cal's hand and aimed the shotgun at his head. The women screamed.

"Hey. You there. Put that gun down."

Several uniformed policemen approached, led by a man in a seersucker suit and a slouch hat. Wardell was at his side.

"Mama!"

He ran to her and she clutched him like a life buoy. He was unscratched.

"I got the autograph," he whispered.

The man who had rescued him, and rescued Cal, looked familiar. He had bad skin and a crooked mouth and an air of command.

"Take that goddamn thing off him," he said to the cops, "before he ups and kills somebody."

The cops took the guy's shotgun and led him away. The rescuer wiped his mouth with a handkerchief and peered at Arlene. "You the singer?"

"Yes sir."

He pointed at Wardell. "And *that's* your son."

Arlene nodded. Then, with a shudder, she recognized the man. It was Richie. Mr. Lococo's boss. And no gangster, after all.

Richie pointed at Cal and said to Wardell, "Go on over there, boy."

Wardell held her arm tightly. "Go ahead, honey," she said softly. "Do what the man says."

"This woman was attacked," Cal said. "And I was assaulted."

Richie removed his hat, exposing small eyes and thinning hair. "I would think you'd want to quit while you're ahead," he said to Cal. "Take these kids and head on home."

"He clubbed her with the barrel of his gun."

"You have a problem I suggest you file a complaint at the station."

Cal stared, thumbs looped through his suspenders. His hair was mussed and there was a lump above his eye.

"C'mon Cal," Arlene said softly. "Let's go."

As she pulled him away, Richie crooked a finger. "No. You stay."

"Arlene."

"It's all right, Cal. I'll be with you directly."

Cal and the others moved off but stayed where they could see her.

"This doesn't look good," Richie said.

"What's that?"

"First I hear the dead piano player's a friend of yours. Now looky here – the kid who found the body is yours. I'm asking myself: is this a coincidence?"

"We just came to the ballgame. He loves baseball."

"Forget about the ballgame. Why didn't you tell me about your kid? At the club?"

"I didn't know you knew who he was. I didn't even know you're a policeman."

He set his teeth and pushed his face so close she could smell his bad breath. "What did I tell you? If you lie to me, I'll find out."

"I didn't lie."

"That boy there could get himself some real trouble, running around unsupervised. Talking about what he mighta found."

"He doesn't talk about it."

"How do you know?"

"He doesn't. And I don't. We're trying to forget all that."

He sized her up, sucked at his bad teeth. Reaching out, he lifted her chin with a finger. "I'd hate to think what might happen to the boy," he said, "if his tongue get the better of him."

She nodded. Blood from her wound stained her shirt. He pointed at her breast and said, "You want to get that looked at."

He loped off. She searched out Wardell. The sky was full of smoke and sirens.

19

E mmett heard about the riot on Saturday evening. After an afternoon at the office chasing empty leads, he stopped in O'Toole's for a soda. Red Blaney leaned against the bar, his face slurred with drink.

"More funerals in niggertown."

"What do you mean?" Emmett said.

"The colored game today. Crowd went apeshit and the cops had to bust a few heads."

"There were people killed?"

Blaney blinked at his beer, lost his train of thought.

"What happened?"

A small guy in a cloth cap piped up, "Cops were escorting some geechie from the field and the crowd went bananas. Three dead."

"Negroes?"

"So I heard."

"Who – players, fans?"

"No idea. They were shot, anyhow." He drank deeply from his beer. "Fuckin' appleheads."

Through the smoke and noise Emmett saw his reflection in the mirror behind the bar. Strangled by collar and tie, his face was shiny and flushed, like a slab of corned beef. Holed up in his office, out of touch. Even the stewbums in the gutter knew more than he did.

When he could get no more scoop in O'Toole's, he crossed the street to Hanlon's. Nothing there either, so he bit the bullet and walked the half mile to Billy Christie's. No sign of his dad, but at the bar was the usual crowd: Jem Boyle, Joxer Martin, Fat Jack Harte. Firemen and rivermen and party hacks. Fat Jack's voice, high-toned and sarcastic, rode the high surf of a Saturday night. Emmett made sure not to look his way.

He found Mickey in a snug with a bunch of guys from the tanneries. The stink was monumental. Emmett pulled him aside.

"What's this about killings at the stadium?"

Mickey shrugged. "You tell me. I been in here since lunchtime."

"If you've been here, you know more than I do. What happened?"

Blood streaked the whites of Mickey's eyes. Dandruff powdered his shoulders. He nodded towards the bar. "Why don't you ask Fat Jack's boys? They were probably in on the action."

"Wake up, Mickey."

"I'm off duty."

"The fuck you are."

Mickey listed, and Emmett stilled him with a hand to the chest. A funk of tannic acid, stale porter, and roughcut Virginia rose from him. The deep fog of daytime drinking.

"A fucking donnybrook," Mickey said, rubbing his eyes. "That's my understanding."

"How did it start?"

"You know how these things go. Mixed race team comes in from North Dakota, and your know-nothing types have a conniption. Words, tempers. Police step in."

"I hear three dead."

"Could be."

Emmett felt eyes on him. He turned and caught the sharp end of Jem Boyle's glare before he swiveled away.

"Listen to me, Mickey. Shit like this is going to turn the colored district upside down. Like our job isn't hard enough already. You got to get off your can and get out there. Find out what happened. The word on the street."

"OK."

"Call me at home tomorrow."

"Sunday?"

"You doing anything more interesting?"

"Not a question of what I'm doing. Nothing going on of a Sunday."

"All the easier to dig below the surface."

Mickey swayed, steadied himself with a palm to the wall. "Buy me a drink, Emmo."

"Ask Fat Jack. I gotta run."

He turned to go.

"Emmo."

"Yeah."

Mickey's smile showed yellow teeth and pale gums. "Saw your better half today."

"That right?"

"Swanning out of the Westport Hotel. To the nines."

Emmett spat on the floor. "Just do your fucking job, Mick."

KCPD didn't like county boys nosing around, but after dark Emmett chanced a visit to headquarters. He figured he could blend into the chaos. He was right. The place was in crisis mode: telephones ringing off the hook, duty cops shouting, uniformed cops clattering in and out of the paneled muster room looking grim and ready to rumble.

The death toll from the stadium stood at four – all Negroes – but the casualty on police minds was Officer Lawrence J. O'Neill, a baby-faced rookie thumped on the head with a crowbar while on duty outside the visitor's locker-room. He lay unconscious in the trauma ward of St. Luke's, attended to by his father and three brothers, all cops themselves. The top brain guy in Missouri was on his way from St. Louis.

Emmett looked for a foothold in the swirl and found it in Ben McKenna, a young cop from the old neighborhood.

"Curfew in the colored section," he told Emmett. "Everyone off the streets by eight o'clock."

"Club owners can't be happy about that."

"The chief's worried we could have another Tulsa. It's for the niggers' own good."

"I'll bet."

"We got double duty on every beat."

"What happened, Ben?"

The kid shook his head. "Larry was just standing there, guarding the visitor's locker-room. Bunch of nigger boys come running down the corridor and crack him open with an iron bar."

"I heard there were four men killed."

Ben leaned close, top lip lifted in a savage sneer. "We'll find these fuckers, Emmett. Heads will roll. Mark my words."

Emmett went to the press room but ducked back when he saw two reporters from the *Star* who knew him. Among the uniforms were a few city suits, shifty-eyed and dark around the mouth. No doubt waiting for Charlie Carrollo's boys to turn up. The curfew was going to hit the mob bosses where it hurt. Which meant the machine would suffer and Pendergast's boys would want action. Shit flows downhill. The worker bees were in for a bad time.

A tall man in corduroy approached, pad and pencil in hand. Emmett tried to slip past, but he blocked the way. "I saw you in the press room, sir. Can I ask you a few questions?"

"I'm not with the force."

"Oh? And, ah, who are you?"

"A curious bystander."

"Very much, if I may say, very much like myself. Yes. I'm down from Chicago, from the *Tribune*. Leo Pruitt." He extended a pale hand, and Emmett had no choice but to shake it. His skin was dry and warm. "A bad turn of events, don't you think?"

"I wouldn't know," Emmett said.

"You're from Kansas City? A native?"

"You could say that."

"Then perhaps you could, ah, tell me this. I'm working on a story for the *Trib*, you see. On the murder of a Negro named Edward Sloan."

Emmett let his gaze drift across the room. No one was listening. "You're doing a story on the Sloan murder?"

"For the *Tribune*, yes. The way our paper sees it, the stadium riot is not a, ah, an isolated incident. The Sloan murder creating tension in, ah, the Negro community. And so forth."

The man blinked and pushed his thick-lensed glasses up his nose.

"Well, maybe I can help you," Emmett said. "What have you found out so far?"

"Ah, let me see." He flipped through the pad. "There's an associated case, I believe. The disappearance of a Virgil Barnes."

"That's right."

"I say disappearance, but to the best of my knowledge a missing person's report has not been filed."

"Filed here? At the police station?"

"Yes."

"If you were given access to a KCPD missing person's report, Mr. Pruitt, it would be a first in my experience. Reporters must be more privileged in Chicago."

Pruitt sniffed and went back to his pad. "You have, ah, any idea where this Virgil Barnes might be?"

"Can't say that I do."

"You're familiar with the Friendship Brotherhood?"

"The what?"

"Fraternal organization for Negroes. Barnes and Sloan both belonged is my understanding."

Emmett noticed the man's footwear, heavy work boots rimmed at the soles and heels with dried mud. "How long have you been in Kansas City, Mr. Pruitt?"

Before the man could answer, there was a loud commotion at the front door. Two uniforms dragged a young colored man across the polished marble, yelling and kicking him as he covered his head with his arms. Pruitt had his glasses off and was staring at the scene, eyes scrunched up. As they approached the duty desk, one of the cops tore the man's hat from his head and punched him in the face.

Pruitt put his pad in his jacket pocket. "I'd better see what's going on here."

"Wait a minute," Emmett said. "This Friendship Brotherhood."

But he had already melted into the turmoil.

Mickey called Emmett at home the next day. He was raspy with hangover, but he'd done his legwork.

"A bloodbath, Emmo. Not just the dead – the colored hospital is overflowing. They ran out of beds and they've got the injured laying in the halls."

An annoying click on the line cut across his words.

"How'd it start?"

"Depends on who you ask. The cops say they were clearing the field of troublemakers when country niggers attacked them with clubs and iron bars. The colored I talked to said the cops hit first."

"Does it matter?"

"Well, yeah. You know, there's pictures of Eddie Sloan everywhere. In the stores and bars. The barbershop. The kind with a black border and words from the bible underneath."

"There'll be more of those now."

Emmett was sitting in a leather chair in his den, drinking lemonade. Through the open window he could see Fay watering the flowers. She wore a yellow sundress, and one of the shoulder straps had slid down her arm, downy in the afternoon light.

"I was in headquarters last night," he said. "They're baying for blood on account of what happened to Larry O'Neill."

"Larry's a good man."

"They were all good men, I'll bet."

Mickey blew loudly into the receiver. "What a mess."

Fay glanced over her shoulder, her face sour. *Swanning out of the Westport Hotel.* She moved out of his view.

"Guess who was in the ballpark when all this happened?" Mickey said.

"Tell me."

"Richie T."

"You're shitting me."

"I am not."

The click again on the line, muddying the last phrase.

"Do you know why was he there?"

"Well, he is a detective-in-charge. But get this – I got a look at the roster for the day, and he was not on the detail."

Emmett stood up. Outside, the fading hydrangea glistened, freshly watered. The leaves on the cherry tree were just beginning to yellow. Like Fay's dress. Where had she gone? The hose lay coiled in the grass, still spouting.

"He was out there stirring things up," Emmett said.

"Why would he do that?"

"Think about it. If he's, you know… *involved*, then this whole shitstorm would suit him."

Mickey coughed so roughly Emmett held the receiver away from his ear. "C'mon, Emmo. Why would he start something where his own men would get hurt?"

"*One* cop down. Small price to pay." Emmett tried to get above the facts, to frame the big picture. "Listen, Mick. We have to follow this up. Timmons has every reason to make this riot happen."

"Emmo, Emmo." Mickey's voice was worn. "You're doing this ass-backwards, and you know it. Motive. Start with motive."

"Why else would he be there? Think about it."

Mickey sighed. "Stop asking me to think. I'm pooped."

"I've got another lead for you. Have you heard of the Friendship Brotherhood?"

"No," Mickey said.

"Some kind of Negro lodge. Apparently Sloan and Virgil Barnes were both members, and it was a small organization."

"You got it."

"And another thing. There's a reporter from Chicago nosing around. Guy named Leo Pruitt who claims to be doing a story on Sloan's killing. See if you can find out where he's staying, how long he's been around, so forth."

Outside the window was pure suburban Sunday: sprinklers hissing and the smell of cut grass. Sunlight dappled and maudlin. Then the click on the phone again, sharp and irregular.

Emmett had a sudden, clarifying fear. "Let's get off the line," he said.

"What's the matter?"

"Come by my office tomorrow. After five."

He hung up and stared at the telephone. Could it be? He scrambled back through the conversation. The scenarios suggested, the names mentioned. Not good. The Feds were the guys with the technology, but more likely it was Pendergast's boys. The guy was in total control of his patch.

He heard a rustle. Fay stood in the doorway.

"How long have you been there?" he said.

She had her hands on either jamb, one bare foot lifted behind her. Through the cotton sundress he could see the outline of her body. Her face was cold and blank.

"If it isn't Sherlock Holmes," she said.

"What's that supposed to mean?"

She shrugged. "Sounded like high drama on the phone."

"I'd appreciate it if you didn't eavesdrop."

"Eavesdrop? The dogs in the street could hear what you were saying."

Her voice was like bad weather.

"I'm doing what you said you wanted me to do. Looking into a case that's important to *us*, remember? What your dad asked."

"Good boy."

"Fuck you, Fay."

For a moment her face lost the dull sheen of mockery and flashed bright with anger. But she recovered. "I love it when you talk dirty."

He pushed his chair back and gathered his notes. Without looking up, he said, "I heard you were at the Westport yesterday."

"Is that what you heard? So it's more than murder you're investigating."

"What were you doing there?"

She bared her teeth. "I could tell you I had an appointment with Henrietta Kincaid. I could tell you the Nelson Gallery patrons were holding their monthly meeting. I could say I was shopping downtown and simply *dying* for a cold drink."

"You don't shop downtown."

She plucked at the material of her dress so that the hem lifted, exposing a softness of leg. "Bought this in Fields. Their fall sale."

"Stop it, Fay. Please stop it."

"Just answering your question. Be careful what you ask."

He gripped the desk.

"I have work to do," he said.

"I'm sure you do."

She held his gaze with purpose before walking away lightly on bare feet. He watched her hips sway down the hallway, the hem of her dress twitching.

20

First day back at grammar school, Wardell sat next to Jesse. Usual spot in the third row. Same classroom, same old desk with the stained inkpot, same broken windows patched with brown paper.

But he felt different. He was in the sixth grade. The teacher was a man, first time ever. Mr. Lewis wore glasses and a bow tie and had a tiny mustache. He wrote each student's name on the blackboard and passed out schoolbooks. The books were hand-me-downs from white schools and had the old signatures on the first page: Otto Schrier, Max Larsen, Albert Reeves. Cross them out, Mr. Lewis said, and write in your own name.

On Sunday, nobody in the district had left home, except to go to church. No women or children were allowed anywhere without a man. Jesse's Uncle Josh moved in with Wardell and his mother for the curfew hours. He slept on a camp bed in the kitchen. The boys hoped that school would stay closed, but Reverend Jones decided to open on Monday. Monarch cabs brought the children back and forth to school. They weren't doing much business anyway.

From the get-go, Jesse pestered Wardell. "You got it?" he whispered.

Wardell nodded.

"Show me."

"No."

"Go on."

"I said no."

Mr. Lewis paused in the aisle.

"You sayin' no 'cause you ain't got it."

"Do too."

"No you ain't."

Wardell felt in his pocket for the piece of paper. It wasn't there. He twisted in his desk and saw it on the floor. He reached through the seat slats and picked it up. Mr. Lewis stood above him.

"What's your name, son?"

"Wardell Gray, sir."

"What's that you got there, Wardell?"

"Nothing, sir."

"Awful lot of discussion over nothing, wouldn't you say? Give it up."

Wardell handed him the slip of paper. Mr. Lewis squinted and pushed out his lower lip. "What is this?"

"Autograph, sir."

"Who I think it is?"

"Satchel Paige, sir."

"What I say!" Jesse shouted.

The classroom stirred. "Y'all quiet down, now," Mr, Lewis said. He looked at the signature like it was a thousand-dollar bill. "How long have you had this?"

"Since Saturday."

"You were at the Monarchs game?"

"Yes sir."

He handed back the paper. "Put that away. Later we can all talk about what happened on Saturday. How we must conduct ourselves during this difficult time."

At recess the boys clustered around Wardell. They wanted to see the signing. These were the rough boys, with torn knickers and socks one-up one-down. Usually they teased him. Today he was the man.

"Tell 'em, Wardell. Tell 'em about Satch."

But he couldn't tell them anything. The memory was like a loud noise that drowned out his own voice. Satch cocking an eyebrow and licking the pencil tip. Jewbaby Floyd massaging Satch's shoulder while he signed. Satch asking Wardell to spell his name.

"You play ball, Wardell?"

"Yes sir."

"Pitcher?"

"Yes sir."

"You call me Satch, you hear. What's your money pitch?"

"My what?"

"Gots to have a money pitch. The one that get you out of trouble."

"You have trouble, Satch?"

Satch. The name was like honey on his lips.

"Wardell, all God's children know trouble. Don't you ever forget it."

Satch handed him the autograph and pencil. A man in a white shirt and suspenders came into the locker-room. He held his hat in his hand and hopped from one foot to the other. "We got to get out to the bus."

There was shouting outside the door. The man waved his hat at Wardell and some other kids, like he was herding sheep. "Go on now, all of you. Out you go."

He'd lost Jesse and Uncle Josh. Or they lost him. Outside the locker-room, ballplayers and stadium folk ran back and forth. A policeman stood guard, hand on his holster. He told Wardell to scoot. As he ran down the corridor, country boys came hollering, waving clubs and bricks. He ducked into an equipment room.

The room was dark. He felt his way across and found another door that opened onto a cinder track behind the outfield fence. There was gunfire. He ran along the track until he found an opening in the canvas and crawled through. His head bumped into someone's legs. The man hauled him to his feet.

"What the hell you doing here?"

"Nothin'."

"Goddamn it! Richie, look what crawled out of the woodwork."

He shoved Wardell towards a man in a light blue suit. His jacket was wet at the armpits and his hat pulled low on his face. This man dragged him to a break in the canvas and pushed him back onto the track.

"Where'd you come from?"

The voice was familiar.

"Nowhere, sir."

The man held him by the chin. "You again?"

Wardell shook his head.

"Stop blubbering, boy. What are doing down here?"

"Ain't doin' nothing', sir."

The man gripped harder. "Tell me."

"I saw Satch. I done got his autograph."

He waved the piece of paper. The men let go of his face and examined the signature.

"You remember me?"

Wardell nodded.

"You remember what I told you?"

"Yes sir."

"OK, boy, let's find your people."

When he tried to tell his schoolmates about Satch, it was like the man in the blue suit held him back.

All God's children know trouble.

"Go on, Wardell," Jesse said. "You tell 'em."

The rough boys pressed in on him. Across the playground Mr. Lewis stood in the doorway, arms folded. He was looking past the boys and his face was dark. Wardell looked in the same direction and saw a long black car behind the broken picket fence. Two white men got out. They wore derby hats and dark overcoats buttoned tight across the chest. One of them had a beard.

The clean-shaven man kicked two loose posts from the fence. They passed through the gap and towards the group of schoolboys. Mr. Lewis made a little strangled sound and ran across the schoolyard. One of the men cut him off. The other said, "Which of you kids is Wardell Gray?"

The boys pointed him out. The man dragged him by the arm to the car. A third man was behind the wheel. The engine was running and smoke puffed from the exhaust pipes. He threw Wardell into the back seat and sat beside him. The car smelled like a tavern. Mr. Lewis shouted, but Wardell could not make out the words. The man with the beard raised his hand and hit Mr. Lewis in the face with something shiny. He fell to the ground. The man ran to the car and jumped into the front passenger seat.

They drove off with a spray of dirt. Wardell scrambled up and looked out the back window. As the man pulled him back he saw his schoolmates milling around like small animals. Mr. Lewis lay in the middle of them like a pile of dirt.

21

The weather had turned. After Labor Day, the heat lifted, the pressure rose, and cooling breezes flowed down from the north. Fay put away her sandals and summer whites and drifted in and out of the house in clothes that Emmett hadn't seen before: leather jacket and flared skirt, tight black dress with a scalloped collar, crested blazer and flannel slacks. Something about her make-up had changed; her eyes were darker, her lips more pronounced.

Anger could roll in like a fog, blinding him. Treat it like a case, he told himself. Gather evidence. Create a record. Build a narrative.

She was out of the house most of the day, and her schedule was always different. It would be easy to carve out an hour or two that couldn't be traced. Easy, too, to find a place. Even respectable downtown hotels did a brisk afternoon trade in married couples named Jones or Williams, who arrived at different times without bags and left by separate exits.

She tracked his movements, he knew that. Not that it was hard. He was a person of routine. His court appearances were a matter of public record. He had stopped noting appointments in his home diary, but Fay had Ophelia phone his secretary several times a day with useless information and unnecessary requests. And he could not pretend he wasn't in his office. It would look suspicious and would change nothing anyway.

But the facts were never just facts.

He imagined her infidelity. The scenes were as clear in his mind as Eddie Sloan's killing: dressing carefully to be undressed; orchestrating meetings that appeared accidental; food left untouched, drinks nervously consumed; quickened breathing, loosened silk and lace, stifled cries in curtained rooms. Everything she denied him, she gave, freely and fully, to another man.

Sometimes, without warning, his whole body would burn with jealousy. The things about her that had once enraptured him – the curve of her lower back, the feel of her thigh, the catch in her breath before she moaned her pleasure – stung him unbearably when he remembered them. Peter Lawson, that hawk-nosed son of a bitch with his dim-witted mug and family fortune on the shelf, kept popping into his head. He pictured beating him bloody in a rage as pure as any orgasm. Or maybe it was one of the married guys, Joe Lister or Bill Treadway or Alton Parrish. She had known these men since girlhood. They could move in and out of her company without suspicion, screened by friendship and reputable standing, happy to provide her with excitement and escape. Emmett imagined the cold joy of shoving the barrel of a nickel-plated .38 under their chins.

But the fantasies were a distraction. The man, whoever he was, wasn't the problem. And Emmett was a prosecutor, schooled in legal recourse and rules of evidence.

Proof, he needed proof.

The mood in the colored district was ugly. Though curfew didn't apply until nightfall, cops kept an eye on the streets all day and didn't allow any groups to gather, especially young men. Business was light. Eighteenth Street had none of its usual gaiety, no music from the barrooms, closed doors and muted lights. In the residential areas, idle men glared from the safety of porches. An eerie quiet lay over everything.

"This way," Mickey said.

He led Emmett down a narrow dirt street lined with unpainted shacks and broken fencing. Soon they were in a warren of sagging chickenwire, piles of debris, and slum dwellings stacked three high. The stink of sewage and the sound of a baby crying.

They were headed to the Friendship Brotherhood.

"Down *here*?" Emmett said.

"This is the cross street. The office is on Cleveland."

"How'd you find it?"

Mickey's limp was noticeably worse. A light wind ruffled his dirty hair. Above, the sky was the color of mud.

"It wasn't easy. No record in City Hall, and my colored CIs, they're gone underground since the curfew. But church registers lists fraternal affiliations. Emmanuel Baptist had an address."

At the next intersection Mickey stopped and checked the paper. "This is it."

The two-story brick building looked like a foreclosed bank, with a wooden sign that said *Bibb Funeral Home*. The windows were dusty and backed by ramshackle blinds. Broken gutters hung above a water-stained façade.

"Not much better," Emmett said.

"Don't forget where we are."

They knocked on the door. No answer. Across the street, a little girl in an organdy dress stared at them from a collapsing porch.

Mickey rubbed dirt from a window and peered inside. "Someone's in there," he said.

He rapped on the window and motioned with his fingers.

"Hey," Emmett said. "Look."

Taped to the inside of the window were pictures of four men – two photographs and two pen-and-ink drawings – with their names in Gothic script beneath the legend *In Memoriam: 9/7/35.*

An old man in a serge suit opened the door. "Thought you was local boys up to no good." He laughed nervously, flashing a row of gold teeth. "All the peoples round here on edge, so to speak. Hear a rap on the door, we don't know who be causin' trouble, you know what I'm sayin'?"

"We have a few questions we'd like to ask you," Emmett said.

With a limp so broad it made Mickey look nimble, the man led them through a tiny chapel to a paper-strewn office at the rear of the parlor.

He sat behind a desk and said, "How can I help you gentlemen?"

"Is this the headquarters of the Friendship Brotherhood?"

He pointed at the ceiling. "Second floor."

"How do you get up there?" Mickey said.

"Stairway out back. Near where we stack the coffins."

"You got a key?"

"It's open."

"Is anyone up there right now?"

The man cocked an eye. "They meet on Tuesdays. Eight o'clock. Nobody tell you?"

"Who would tell me?"

"Whoever it was sent you."

Emmett nodded at Mickey, who slipped out the back door. They heard him climb the stairs.

The man licked his lips. "What he doin'?"

"Just having a look around."

"Nothin' up there but a table and a bunch of chairs."

Emmett sat on the edge of the desk. "Who do you think sent us?"

The man smelled of wintergreen and old tobacco. He pushed himself away from the desk and sharpened his gaze. "How would I know?"

Emmett stared him down.

"I make my payments regular," the man said. "I ain't no fool."

"What's your name?"

"Charles Bibb."

The ceiling creaked as Mickey walked around. "Mr. Bibb, what's your connection with the lodge?"

"No connection. They just rent the space."

"Did you know Eddie Sloan and Virgil Barnes?"

"Same as everybody in the district."

"They were members."

"So I believe."

A raw, chemical smell tainted the air. Emmett felt the presence of corpses. "I take it you arranged the funeral for Sloan."

"Sloan and the four boys from Saturday." He paused. "Funerals was yesterday. Ain't but one parlor in the district."

"Let's talk about Sloan for now. Was Barnes at his funeral?"

"No sir, he was not. Virgil Barnes ain't been seen in these parts since the day Eddie gone missin'."

"Is that a coincidence, do you think?"

"I reckon I don't know."

"And both of them Friendship men."

"Like I said, I's just the landlord. There ain't been no meetings up there since Eddie Sloan's passin'."

"Are you worried?"

Bibb opened a canister of snuff and placed a pinch behind his lower lip. "You a colored in this town, Mister, you always worried. Mess of peoples think what happen out at the stadium some kind of cause to go all *militant* and such. Talkin' white *an'* colored. Law abidin' folk like myself, yessir, we worried. No doubt."

"What did you tell the police?"

"About what?"

"Sloan and Barnes."

"Didn't tell 'em nothin'. They didn't ask."

"Nobody came poking around?"

"No sir."

Bibb's face had glazed over. He was hiding something, but he wasn't going to open up. Not now.

Emmett asked him anyway. "What do you think happened to Barnes?"

"It's a mystery."

"You sure about that?"

"Only knows what I read in the papers."

Mickey returned, a sheaf of papers in his hand, and nodded at Emmett. Bibb leaned to his right and spat into a tin can.

Emmett laid his card on the desk. "You knew him, so I guess you'd like to see justice served. You remember anything, anything else comes up, give me a call."

Bibb did not look at the card.

As they were leaving, Emmett asked, "You own the building?"

"Free and clear," Bibb said.

"And you're paying the man his due every week."

Bibb kept his face blank.

"Tell me this," Emmett said. "If you thought I was collecting juice, why were you expecting me to arrive on a meeting night?"

"I don't follow you."

"No, I'm sure you don't."

In the car Emmett stared ahead, silently. Mickey lit a cigarette and sputtered into a fit of coughing that brought tears to his eyes.

"Jesus, Mick. You OK?"

Mickey waved away his concern.

"Bibb," Emmett said. "He's holding back."

"He's scared. They're all scared around here."

Emmett pointed at the papers. "What did you find?"

"I don't know. I just grabbed whatever I could."

They leafed through the pile: receipts, lists of names, meeting minutes, rules and regulations, all written longhand in flowing script.

Emmett slid them into his briefcase. "I'll go through these later."

"Look at those guys," Mickey said, blowing smoke out the window. On the corner of Eighteenth and Vine were four older men in cloth caps and white shirts and ties. They stood with legs set wide and hands on their hips, carefully watching the flow of cars and pedestrians. They were spaced out widely enough not to be seen to be fraternizing.

"Business owners," Emmett said. "Keeping an eye on things. The last thing they want is trouble."

"Then why do they all have those pictures in their windows?"

"Are you saying they can't honor their dead?"

"Whole place feels like a tinderbox to me."

"Well, Richie T has a lot to answer for."

Mickey flicked his cigarette butt out the window. "You still thinking that's a plausible scenario?"

Emmett started the car and drove off. "I'm working with what we have. I'm working off the evidence, which so far is pretty slim."

"Doing my best," Mickey said.

"It's been three weeks. What do we have?"

Mickey ticked off the dead leads on his fingers. "Barnes vanished into thin air, stolen cars that were routine thefts, nobody seeing nothing from the trains, and the vice district shut down. What am I supposed to do?"

"What about Timmons?"

"What about him? Everybody I ask knows he's in with the gangs and nobody wants to talk about it. It's a Kansas City secret."

A goods truck swerved in front of him and Emmett hit the horn. The image of Fay in bed with another man pushed its way into his mind.

"And what about the crime scene?"

Mickey spread his hands. "What do you expect? I'm doing this all by myself."

"That's what I'm paying you for."

"We got seven, eight lines of enquiry going here. Every little detail buried six feet deep by the machine. And I'm on my own."

By now Lloyd had expected a case against Timmons, a stream of detail and influence that pointed at Pendergast. But Lloyd was a corporate lawyer. He knew nothing about the blind alleys of criminal investigation. The slow construction of a case, the elimination of reasonable doubt, the vagaries of evidence.

"If we don't have a crime scene," Emmett said, "we don't have jackshit. That's what it comes down to."

"What am I going to do, Emmo, comb ten miles of shoreline?"

"I'm under some pressure to show results."

Mickey raised his eyebrows. "Some things you can't rush."

"I know."

Pulling up to a traffic light, Emmett accidentally bumped the horn, and they both jumped.

Staring straight ahead Mickey said, "I need some money."

"For what? Hooch?"

Mickey rolled down the window and spat into the street. "What I spend my salary on is my business. This is for expenses. You need a blow by blow?"

"How much?"

"Fifty."

While Mickey looked away, Emmett took a bankroll from his pocket and peeled off some bills. In just this way he had gone to Lloyd three days ago, squirming while the old man stooped at his safe, glancing over his shoulder as he fingered the combination.

He handed the money to Mickey, who did a quick count. "There's a hundred here."

"Yeah." Emmett stuffed the roll back in his pocket.

"This a big tip or you going to enlighten me?"

The light turned green and Emmett gunned the Packard. The road grew suddenly smoother as they left the Negro district and approached the high buildings of downtown.

"I want you to follow someone," he said.

22

B y the time Emmett arrived at his office on Wednesday morning, Lloyd and Roddy had left two messages each. His secretary, Mrs. Johnson, gave him their numbers, along with his schedule of appointments for the day. She also reminded him that she was leaving the office at eleven-fifteen to attend the wedding of her niece in Overland Park.

His work lay piled on his desk: litigation briefs, claims adjuster reports, summaries of appeals pending, a grand jury proceeding awaiting analysis. After the stadium riot and declaration of curfew, the Attorney General's office had requested a special report on the crisis from Harold Fleming, the Jackson County Prosecutor, who had passed the work on to his assistants. Emmett had not been this busy since his first year out of law school.

But he pushed the work aside. And ignored the phone messages. On the green baize of his desktop he spread the paperwork Mickey had retrieved from the Friendship Brotherhood office. For a half hour he sorted through the documents, comparing, sifting, isolating what he thought might have something to tell him.

Mrs. Johnson buzzed. "Mr. Hudson on the telephone."

"Tell him I'm in a meeting."

Most of the Friendship Brotherhood material was useless. One list of names, however, had check marks beside three members – Virgil Barnes, Edward Sloan, and Rube Gilmore – and a corresponding column of dates. A rota of some sort. There was also a 1935 calendar with red X marks penciled though a range of days over the previous months, including August 13, the day leading up to Sloan's death.

Mrs. Johnson came into his office without knocking. "Mr. Hudson is unavailable for the rest of today, but he asked you to meet him tomorrow afternoon at the Kansas City Club."

"Thank you."

"And Mrs. Whelan called."

"You didn't put it through?"

"I was going to, and then she said she had to go. Said she'd call back later."

She stood before his desk, hands crossed in front of her skirt.

"Is there something else, Mrs. Johnson?"

"There's a group in the lobby. They asked to see you and I told them you were busy, but they insist. They will not move. I've had the porter speak to them, but they will not move."

"How long have they been there?"

She checked her watch.

"Thirty-five minutes."

"What do they want?"

"I have no idea." She looked out the window.

"They're colored."

"Is that why you didn't tell me they were here?"

"They don't have an appointment."

"Send them in."

He returned the Friendship Brotherhood documents to his briefcase. Mrs. Johnson showed the men into his office. He greeted the two he recognized: Calvin Watkins, a clothing-store owner and prominent district booster, and Lucious Jones, a dark-skinned Baptist minister with a dramatic voice and a poorly disguised hatred of white people. The third man wore a hound's-tooth-check jacket and an open-neck shirt with enormous, winged lapels.

"William Carter," the man said, shaking Emmett's hand.

"With the *Call*?"

"That's right."

Emmett sat them in front of the big window and offered them coffee. They refused.

"Mr. Whelan," Watkins said, "we don't lightly impose upon your time. We know you are a busy man."

"I'm sorry about the delay. I didn't know you were here until a few minutes ago."

"This is a bad time for Negro folk," Reverend Jones said brusquely. "There are those in our community who have suffered in all innocence and whose patience grows thin."

Watkins raised a hand. "What Lucious means, Mr. Whelan, is that those among us who want stability and good relations have grave concern."

"The man knows what I mean," Jones said.

"I do know," Emmett said. "I've been in the…district. Felt the tension. Curfew's never a good thing, never saw the sense of it myself."

"We're not here about the curfew."

"About what, then?"

"A personal crisis."

"But why come to me?"

"You tried Philip Sweeney," Carter said.

Jones pointed at Emmett. "The policeman who killed an innocent Negro boy," he said.

"I know, Reverend. It was my case."

"You have a reputation for integrity," Watkins said softly. "And we need some help."

Emmett spread his hands.

"We have a situation," Jones said, "a very unpleasant situation. So bad is it that, although it is of the utmost local concern, Mr. Carter has had to refrain from making any mention of the affair in his newspaper."

"Keeping in mind," Carter said, "what's been happening."

"So, what is it?"

"A friend of mine," Watkins said, "a woman in our neighborhood, has had her boy abducted."

"What? Here in Kansas City?"

"That's what the man said."

"Kidnapped?"

"Whatever word you want to use, Mr. Whelan."

"I haven't heard anything about a kidnapping. Who is it?"

"The mother's name is Arlene Gray," Jones said. "An upstanding woman of the district and one of the finest singers in my church."

"She also," Watkins said carefully, "sings at the Sunset Club on Twelfth Street."

"Where Eddie Sloan played piano?"

The question surprised the visitors.

"And no one has gone to the police?"

The three men frowned in unison.

"OK," Emmett said. "Stupid question. Tell me what happened."

The boy had been snatched the day before from his school playground, in the middle of the morning. A teacher who had seen the grab and intervened had been pistol-whipped and was in Douglass Hospital recovering from concussion and a broken cheekbone. He'd told Carter that the boy had been pushed into the back seat of a late-model black Lincoln sedan with whitewalls and a broken taillight. Two white men in dark topcoats and derby hats. Plus a driver.

"This teacher remembers a lot for a guy who was beaned," Emmett said.

"Nathan Lewis had his eyes open," Jones said. "Everyone among us needs be vigilant, especially since the events of Saturday."

"We've tried to keep the whole thing private," Watkins said, "for the safety of all concerned. For the safety of the district. But the boys and girls on that playground told their parents. Naturally. So word has gotten out. We have our hotheads like everywhere else. There are a few veterans from the war who have taken up positions outside the hospital."

"Bodyguards, they call themselves," Carter said.

"Others talking about violent action. Openly talking. We don't want another Tulsa. We want something done, Mr. Whelan, before these vigilantes react."

"Not that anyone could blame them," Jones said.

Watkins shook his head. "Our investigator tells us that the boy cannot be traced."

"Investigator?"

"Investigations. The mother is beside herself, of course. You have to help us."

Emmett stood up and walked to the window. "What can I do? I'm a prosecutor, not a detective."

"You are a neutral party in a racist town."

Emmett waved away the description and watched the silent traffic ten floors below. From here, the city was all light and peace. "Have you heard anything from the kidnappers."

"No."

"Any idea of motive?"

The men didn't answer.

"Well?"

"This is the boy," Watkins said slowly, "who found Eddie Sloan's body."

Emmett turned from the window. "You know who found the body? And you haven't told the police?"

"Oh, we told the police, all right," Watkins said. "Damn fool thing to do, but we told them. And Wardell brought them there."

"The singer's son, *he* was the one?"

"Yes."

"Ah. Are you sure you men don't want some coffee?"

Emmett opened his office door, but Mrs. Johnson had left for the wedding. His outer office was empty. He picked up pen and paper from his desk and sat down again. He took down the details: the boy's name and address, the time of the abduction, the names of his teacher and the school. He asked if he could speak to the mother.

"I don't think that's a good idea," Watkins said, "and I don't think it would help, anyway."

"How about some of the other kids who were there?"

"We can arrange that."

They were all silent for a while.

Carter finally spoke, looking at his hands. "Mr. Whelan, if anything happens to this boy…."

Reverend Jones raised his hand as if on the pulpit. "Crimes that go unpunished shatter the very fabric of society. They lead to other crimes and ultimately to an all-consuming chaos. And it will be the Negro folk that suffer, not the prosperous Anglo-Saxon in his comfortable house."

"Lucious," Watkins said.

"I'll look into it," Emmett said, "I promise you that. I'll see what I can do."

The men got up to leave. Emmett said, "By the way, what can any of you tell me about the Friendship Brotherhood?"

They looked at each other. "Why do you ask?" Carter said.

"Another case I'm involved in."

"Not a serious organization," Watkins said. "Not in this town anyway. And I don't think the KC branch's been functional for quite some time now. Isn't that right, Bill?"

"I have no idea."

More silence.

"OK," Emmett said. "Thank you. I'll be in touch."

23

She sat at the window all day and all night, rocking in her hard chair and staring through the warped glass. Two men guarded the front porch and one the rear. They were always sober and formally dressed. Every four hours a new team of guards arrived. Members of Reverend Jones's First Baptist congregation. None of them spoke to her. They touched their hats, nodded, took up their posts. In the daytime they sometimes read to one another from the bible. Mostly they also sat and stared.

Food held no interest for her. She left the chair only to use the privy or get a glass of water. Sometimes fell asleep in the chair, but always woke abruptly after a few minutes. She hated these naps because waking was like nightmare. Her back was always sore, but she took a peculiar comfort from the pain. Suffering might help bring back her boy.

She stared south, down Olive Street. There was a spot in the road past which her vision was blocked by the edge of the house. Her eyes stay fixed on this blank triangle of dust and debris for hours at a time. During the afternoon, the shadow of a telephone pole crossed this patch like the blade of a sun dial, marking time and parceling out her pain. Once or twice a day some kid would emerge from the blocked view, kicking a can or pushing a hoop, and her breath would seize and her muscles clench as if she'd been thrown from a cliff.

Still, she stared.

At night she prayed. At first she tried direct communication with the Lord, but the rawness of her message was too much, so she took refuge in passages from the bible and old hymns.

> *Yea, though I walk through the valley of the shadow of death,*
> *I will fear no evil;*
> *For thou art with me;*
> *Thy rod and thy staff, they comfort me.*

But comfort was thin, and often she lost track of the words and found herself sobbing while she clutched the arms of her chair and stared at the dry road through a smear of tears.

On the afternoon of the second day, Cal and Leonora came to the house with a plate of fried chicken, biscuits, and a bottle of cold buttermilk.

Cal sat close to her and whispered, "Parks spent all night searching the North End for the car. He has contacts in Chicago with expertise in… these situations. He's waiting to hear from them." When she didn't answer he continued, "And we also went to the county. Some men there who might be able to help."

"White men," she said.

He put a hand on her arm. "There's a curfew, Arlene. You know that. Lucious's men, even that's a risk."

After they had left, Arlene offered the food to the guards. They refused to take it until she'd insisted several times. The sound of them eating drifted from the porch. The food loosened their tongues; they spoke of the curfew, of the church, of the funerals for the men killed in the riot. She was probably the only person in the district who had not attended those funerals.

Returning from the kitchen, she passed Wardell's room and caught a glimpse of his magazine pictures and baseball memorabilia. Back in her chair, she saw a dog zig-zagging up the street with a dead chicken in its jaws.

24

Emmett was not a member of the Kansas City Club,
but he had been there as Lloyd's guest once or twice.
During the boom, six orchestras had played in the fourteen-
story building, including a dance band on the roof garden,
and the club kitchens could serve a six-course dinner to
a thousand guests in less than two hours. These days, the
Depression made it more elite than ever. The tone was polished hardwood and art deco glass, the membership rich
and reactionary.

"Mr. Hudson is in suite 822, sir. If you'd like to wait in the
library I'll let him know you're here."

The 822 was a club within a club, known for its stiff
drinks and serious poker. If Roddy was in a session, he could
be a while. Emmett took a copy of the *Star* from the newspaper rack and brought it to a leather armchair by the window.
In the distance, smoke rose from the Negro district. Closer
to hand were the County Courthouse, City Hall and, just
beyond them, the soiled redbrick façade of the Schumann
Hotel.

He scanned the headlines but couldn't concentrate.
In his jacket pocket was a surveillance report Mickey had
delivered that morning. He had read it so often he knew it
by heart.

11:55 am – Departed Oakwood house and drove north on Prospect
12:37 – Left car at Morello's Garage on Walnut and took taxicab to corner of McGee and Seventh Ave
12:56 – Entered Schumann's Hotel
2:17 – Departed Schumann's Hotel, hailed taxicab
2:31 – Arrived Morello's, collected car
2:39 – Drove south on Prospect
2:57 – Stopped at Piggly Wiggly grocery store on 57th
3:21 pm – Arrived Oakwood house

The numbers played in his head: 12:56 to 2:17. An hour and twenty-one minutes. The rear of the hotel was visible from Emmett's office. At one-thirty yesterday afternoon he had been eating a sandwich at his desk and, for all he knew, staring as he chewed at its tarred roof and curtained windows. The hotel did not have a bar or restaurant. It had little daytime traffic. In spite of its central location, it was as safe a place as any for a tryst. As long as you weren't being tailed.

"Emmett."

It was Roddy, out from his poker session quicker than expected.

"You rescued me," he said with a wince. "Down thirty bucks, and Roy Bartell was on a roll. The guy doesn't touch a drop, but he has the waiters freshening our bourbon every five minutes."

Roddy led him to the President's Bar, where he ordered himself a cocktail and Emmett a soda. They took their drinks to a quiet table in the corner.

"Since when have you stopped returning telephone calls?" Roddy asked. His face was flushed and the knot of his tie was crooked. Before Emmett could answer, he added, "Lloyd isn't happy."

"Is that right?"

"He wants evidence."

"Don't we all."

Roddy bared his teeth. "Not all of us have been tasked with finding it."

"I'm doing my best."

"So far your best isn't good enough."

Roddy's voice was frayed and his tone brittle. There was none of the bonhomie of their Aztec lunch.

Emmett set his drink on the tabletop.

12:56 – Entered Schumann's Hotel.

2:17 – Departed Schumann's Hotel, hailed taxicab.

An hour and twenty-one minutes.

"Actually, I do have some news," Emmett said. "Sloan and Virgil Barnes were both members of a local fraternal association. And I found out Richie Timmons was present at the riot on Saturday."

Roddy raised a palm. "What about the crime scene?"

"I've got a clear lead."

"After a month on the case I expect more from you than leads. There are four more Negroes dead. From what I hear, their deaths could be related to the Sloan killing."

"Who's telling you that?"

"How many more colored have to get murdered before you get anywhere? Before you even identify the crime scene? And meantime Lloyd and I can't get you on the phone, even though your secretary is telling us you're in the goddamn office."

Roddy lit a small cigar with trembling fingers and dropped the spent match in the ashtray.

Hand in his pocket, Emmett fingered Mickey's surveillance report gingerly, as if it might singe his fingers.

"I'm on the crime scene. I've found the kid who led the cops to Sloan's body."

Roddy waved his hand in front of Emmett's face. "Keep your voice down. What kid?"

"A Negro kid who goes to Crispus Attucks Grammar School. Found the body on the riverbank. His people brought the police in – which they regret. Whole thing went underground as soon as the cops were involved."

"Was it Timmons?"

"I would think so."

"Is the kid prepared to testify?"

"I haven't talked to him."

"Why not?"

"I'm still working on it."

"What the hell does that mean?"

"It appears he's been abducted."

Roddy blinked and stared, as if he hadn't heard, then tapped his cigar above the ashtray. "My God, Whelan, you do have a way of complicating matters, don't you?"

"It's not me who's doing the complicating. Obviously, I'm not the only one who knows that *he* knows something important."

"*Jesus!*" Roddy hissed, slapping the table so that Emmett's drink spilled. "Abducted? By who?"

Emmett had made discreet enquiries at police headquarters, the *Star*, in the neighborhood. Nobody had heard anything about a kidnapping. He'd checked the latest court filings and probed the clerks for any gossip. No word there, either. Mickey was on the case but hadn't turned up anything.

It all pointed one way.

"If I were to guess," Emmett said slowly, "I'd say Timmons."

"It's always guesswork with you, isn't it? Anyone can *guess*, Whelan."

The worst of this dressing-down was that Roddy was right. Any investigator worth his job would have turned these leads into something concrete by now. But most investigators had a bunch of flatfeet at their disposal, a fully equipped lab, access to records.

"Lloyd tells me you're racking up the expenses," Roddy said. "Where's all this money *going*?"

On his way to meet Roddy, Mickey had stopped at the Schumann and slipped the day clerk ten bucks to show him the daily register. There was an entry at one o'clock the day before for a Mr. and Mrs. Radcliffe. No other details. After some grilling, the clerk admitted he had been working at that time. But he claimed not to recognize a photograph of Fay. He was, he said, "no good with faces."

Roddy's face was dark with daytime drink and anger. "I'm going to say this one more time. We have a small window here. If the Feds don't get what they need from us, they'll go elsewhere. Maurice Milligan did not get to be federal attorney by waiting for others to build his cases. Word is he has Pendergast on income tax evasion, and it's only a matter of time before the Boss falls."

"So why does he need Timmons?"

"He doesn't need Timmons," Roddy snapped, "*you* do. Do you think Lloyd and his pals will be happy with Pendergast in the clink for three to five on a tax rap? Out on good behavior in twenty months? For God's sake, Whelan, his organization is murdering innocent men." He stubbed the cigar violently in the ashtray. "And if you don't deliver the goods, you'll be prosecuting drunks and wops on your two-bit county salary for the rest of your life."

The country-club reserve had completely fallen away. Flushed and twisted, he straightened his tie, stood up, and bolted down the rest of his drink. "We will not have this conversation again. You've got to shit or get off the pot. I don't care whose family you're married into."

He returned to his game.

Emmett fingered the report.

2:57 – Stopped at Piggly Wiggly grocery store on 57 th

As Emmett drove home, a black Plymouth appeared in the rear view, the third time since leaving the club. He pulled over to the side of the road and let it pass. A woman driver. He sat, listening to the engine idle, thinking of the clicks on the phone. He rejoined the road and headed home. After ten minutes he passed the Piggly Wiggly.

Since the riot, he and Mickey had stopped using the phone. So when Mickey slid the report on Fay across Emmett's desk that morning, it had been a surprise.

"So what next?" he'd said.

Mickey coughed into a dirty handkerchief. "What do I do next – that what you're asking?"

"Yes."

"It depends."

"On what?"

"On what you want."

Emmett stood and crossed the room. He stayed away from the window. He didn't want Mickey thinking he was looking down at the Schumann. "I want to know."

Mickey's tone was dry, ultra-careful. "Know more than you know already?"

"All I know is she was in a hotel."

"For an hour."

And twenty-one minutes.

Emmett picked up an ashtray and threw it hard at the window. The crack was almighty but the blow only chipped the glass.

Mickey jumped to his feet. "Jesus Christ, Emmo."

Emmett strode across the room and thrust his face at Mickey, so close he could smell the stale whiskey on his breath. "Proof," he said savagely. "I want proof!"

"What – photographs?"

He had turned away. "Don't talk about it, Mick. Just fucking do it."

25

"Not the only one. Lot of them boys needed money."

"All of them."

"Well, yes, all. You could be right about that. But what would they do to get it? How far would they go?"

Something about the men's voices made Arlene pause. Whispery. Careful. She had come in from the front porch to get herself a glass of water. Her legs were heavy and her head foggy. But the tone of these words blew the mist clean away.

Piney was sitting on the back steps with Jake Barlow, another club manager, drinking beer and smoking. They had come over to offer moral support. Were on a break.

"Take Eddie," Jake said.

"Eddie worked for me."

"Yes, he did. So you know how much he was taking home. Or wasn't."

"Nobody takin' *nothin'* home right now."

The men were right there, a few feet away. The kitchen window was open and the smoke from their cigarettes drifted through the torn screen. Arlene stood at the sink, as still as a scared deer.

"When the man come to Eddie and ask he want a job, what you think he said?"

"What my boys do after hours their own business."

"Where he went after hours done got him killed."

"Keep your voice down," Piney said. "You *guess* it did."

"Be an educated guess."

"Eddie kept his eyes open. He was a smart individual."

"Some folk say he a little *too* smart."

She crept back to the front porch. The floor of her house was like a ship's deck in a storm. Out front her pine rocker creaked in the light wind. The sun beat down on the empty street like the worst kind of bad luck.

In the distance was the sound of a marching band. For a week, the only music in the district had been funeral marches. Behind closed doors was a dark sickness waiting to spill onto the dirt streets. Everything she knew was unraveling.

Where he went after hours. She had always thought her house was where he went. So who was he working for? Why hadn't he told her? The last night, as it had so many times, replayed itself in her mind. Their parting words.

I'm not inclined.

Well, then, don't bother. Don't bother on my account.

Tomorrow night be better. Our customary evening.

You rather spend time with Virgil than me then you go right ahead. See if I care.

Well, he did care. Cared enough not to tell her what might be dangerous for her to know. To let her think he was thoughtless.

No one she had ever met had been more thoughtful.

She collapsed in the rocker and covered her face with her hands. Was that why Wardell was taken? Because of Eddie needing a little extra cash?

From the back steps came sounds of laughter.

26

Emmett had a street kid run into Billy Christie's and give it the once over. It was eleven-thirty on Monday morning, the saloon's slowest time of the week. He retreated to the other side of the street and waited in a dusty doorway. A harsh sun shone through thin cloud, warming the shoulders of his dark suitcoat and draping the faded buildings in shadowless light.

The kid came out. "He's there."

"By himself?"

"He's reading the paper. In a booth at the back."

He gave the kid a nickel and went inside. Fat Jack Harte had a copy of the *Journal* spread across the table, open to the sports section. A half-drunk pint of Guinness sat beside his left hand.

As Emmett approached, the big man peered sourly above half-moon reading glasses, the tangled white hairs of his eyebrows inching upwards.

Emmett signaled to the barman. "Two pints, Larry."

Fat Jack drained his pint, cleared his throat, and spat between his thick legs into the sawdust. "Well," he said gruffly, "look who's falling off the wagon."

Emmett shrugged.

"Seeing the light, counselor?" Fat Jack said.

He settled in opposite and crossed his hands on the table. Behind the bar a radio was tuned to "Amos 'n' Andy". "I need some advice, Jack."

Jack folded the newspaper and wedged it into the space between his leg and the wall. "Begob, how the mighty have fallen."

"Is that how you greet another Irishman?"

"Fuck off, Sonny Boy."

The saloon door swung wide and Redser Malone stumbled in, moist-lipped and blinking, and made his way to the bar. "Look," Emmett said. "I know there's no love lost between us, but you've been good to my old man."

"Still good to him."

"Well, he needs all the help he can get these days."

"That he does. From every quarter."

Larry brought the pints and set them on the table. Emmett watched the porter settle. God, how he used to love this stuff. Two years since his last drink. Maybe that's why things went so wrong with Fay. Him trying to be someone he wasn't.

"Sláinte, Jack," he said, drinking deeply and licking the foam from his lip.

Fat Jack left his pint where it was.

"Word on the street," Emmett said with a level voice, "is that a colored boy was kidnapped from his schoolyard. A week ago today."

"I would have thought the street was silent from ten floors up."

"You should come up and visit some time. It's a hell of a view."

"I prefer ground level."

Redser loudly ordered a ball of malt and a chaser, then waved stiffly in their direction. Jack ignored him. "I'm asking myself," Emmett said, "who would want to kidnap a Negro boy in broad daylight? And why?"

"Why indeed."

"Unless he knows something."

"I thought you were here to ask for advice, not to blather on like a niggerlover."

Jack's eye had a shine to it. Nothing pleased him more than letting fly with insults.

Emmett lifted and resettled his glass. "A few years ago my old man told me about the time you went to Ireland."

"Did he, now?" Jack said.

"He said you sold your business and gave all the proceeds to the Irish Republican Brotherhood. That you were in Dublin for a year."

Jack drank from the fresh pint. "I'll tell you one thing for nothing: there were no niggers in Dublin."

"No? I would have thought there were. I would've thought that was why you coughed up the dough."

"Well, now, there's the difference between us."

"Whatever the difference, I know that if this kid isn't back in his home within a few days then all hell is going to break loose in this town. These people don't like being kept down any more than we Irish do."

Jack spat again on the floor. "I don't need any history lessons from the likes of you," he said. "This town was built by the sweat and blood of men like your father. It's run by those who know when to talk and when to raise the sword. It will not be intimidated by a few niggers who think that just because they saw a month's worth of action in France they know how to fight a battle."

Jack's face was rough and sagging, with deep creases and fleshy lips that shaped words as if they were spitballs.

"I wish I had your confidence."

"You should wish you had a lot more. You should wish you still lived where people know the value of friendship and a man's word." He jerked his chin up. His mouth was flecked with spittle. "Like your old man."

"Leave me and my old man out of it," Emmett said quietly. "And name one person who doubts my word."

Jack smiled, cradling his pint. "You want advice, I'll give you some: tell that tupenny sidekick you have working for you to keep his mouth shut. The whole goddamned police department knows he's snooping around. The boy never could hold his drink." He pointed at Emmett's near-empty glass. "You'll have another," he said.

Emmett's head was swimming with the unfamiliar buzz. "I won't," he said, rising.

"No, I don't suppose you will."

Jack shouted for another pint, donned his reading glasses, and respread the newspaper on the table as if he were alone.

As Emmett walked out he heard Jack say, scarcely audible, "Danny Farrell. Department of Child Welfare."

When he looked back, Jack was mouthing the words of a sports story, his forefinger gliding beneath the type like a schoolboy's.

Farrell's office was a windowless cube on the ground floor of the old City Hall, where the smaller cogs in the machine toiled. He was white-haired and stooped, with pale, shaking hands dense with liver spots. Like any Pendergast appointee, he had no time for outsiders.

Emmett started low key, giving him plenty of opportunity to bluff himself into a corner. At first he was evasive and aloof. Emmett kept prodding. It wasn't long before Farrell lost his temper.

"How would I know?" he snapped.

"Like I said, a boy has been abducted."

"And like I told *you*, that's a matter for the police."

"Of course it is," Emmett said, slowly showing his hand, "and the Missouri Statutes stipulate that all crimes involving minors get reported to your department within twenty-four hours."

He leaned sideways in his chair, sizing up Emmett's suit and wingtips. "Where'd you say you were from?"

"I didn't."

"Charlie Johnson send you down here?"

Emmett waited for a moment and said, "The last time I saw Charlie Johnson was at his indictment."

Farrell shuffled some papers. His sleeves were rolled in the heat of the office and the loose skin of his elbows looked parched and painful. "Could be the file's still on its way over."

"Danny." Emmett reached across the desk and smacked the riffling papers to the desk. Farrell wouldn't look him in the eye. "The incident happened a week ago."

"I don't know anything about it," Farrell said.

"Maybe you'd like to come down to the courthouse and tell Harry Fleming just exactly what it is you don't know."

Farrell's hands were all over the place: picking lint from his clothes, smoothing his tie, rubbing his badly shaven chin. "Why don't I make a call," he said.

"Yeah. Why don't you."

While he was out, Emmett scanned the papers on the desk – all routine forms from charitable organizations and adoption agencies. The desk drawers were empty except for a half pint of whiskey and a dirty glass. Emmett loosened his collar; the room was so close his upper lip had beaded in sweat.

Farrell returned and said stiffly, "Seems like there was something of a mix-up. A boy answering to your description has been at Nolan Farms since last Tuesday."

"Is that right?"

"A runaway, so I've been told."

"What are we going to do about it?"

He checked his watch. "I'll order a car."

Nolan Farms was a reformatory ten miles east of the city on the grounds of an old Spanish mission. It was where the soft cases were sent and included a dairy farm where the boys worked part-time and a school run by priests. Not a bad place, as such places went.

On the way out Emmett sat in front, beside the driver. The sun had penetrated the dirty clouds and lit the brown hills with shafts like church light. Farrell chattered nervously behind him. "It's easy to lose track of these kids. With the curfew and such, they get picked up and brought in and passed from pillar to post. Maybe they see things down the station that a kid shouldn't see. Anyhow, when you go to process them, they clam up. Can't remember their own names, never mind where they live. Too damn scared to talk."

"Are you telling me that Wardell Gray was picked up on a curfew violation?"

"Could be – if it's him. Or maybe he was truant."

"He was taken from his school playground. During *recess*."

"Runaway. That's what the report says."

Emmett waved impatiently. "Who was the arresting officer?"

"That seems to be unclear."

"Is there anything that isn't unclear?"

Farrell stared out the window at the passing cottonwoods. "People have no idea," he muttered. "No idea at all."

The reformatory superintendent met them at the entrance. Another machine functionary and jumpy as a colt. His teeth were stained yellow and his eyes flicked back and forth as he spoke.

"I'm going to need a release form," he said. "Signed by the proper authority."

"Farrell here will sign," Emmett said.

"No can do. City staff can only release boys in cases where there is a legal guardian on record."

"Wardell Gray has a legal guardian. His mother, I believe that would be."

"Not on the record."

"Why hasn't she been contacted?"

The super looked at Farrell, who shrugged. They both knew the bind they were in. Let the kid go and there would be hell to pay at City Hall. But stonewalling would be worse.

"Bring the kid here," Emmett said.

The super did not move or speak. Farrell was looking out the window, letting the guy twist in the wind. They could hear the dairy cows lowing.

"Listen," Emmett said. "Either I leave here with the kid or I leave with you."

"Me?"

"The County Prosecutor will need you to explain why I've returned empty-handed."

The super left and returned five minutes later with a young priest and the boy, who was light-skinned, with a large, round forehead, frightened eyes, and closely cropped hair. He clutched the priest's hand and was breathing quickly.

Emmett hunkered down and looked the kid in the eye. "Wardell," he said.

"He hasn't spoken since he arrived here," the priest said. His pale Irish eyes glanced from Wardell to the super.

"Give us some privacy," Emmett said to the other men.

"This is highly irregular," the super said.

Emmett stared him down, and the two men left.

As soon as they were gone, the priest spoke to Wardell and had him sit in the most comfortable chair in the room. "He does not have the most pleasant associations with this office," he said to Emmett in an Irish accent.

"I'm here to bring him home," Emmett said. He smiled at Wardell. "Back to his mother."

The blankness in Wardell's face did not change.

"Hasn't said a word?"

"The odd remark to myself. Never when the boss is around."

"About who brought him here, or what happened?"

The priest shook his head. "Nothing like that."

Wardell was picking at the ragged skin around his fingernails.

"How would you like to take a ride, Father?"

The priest nodded in the direction of where the super had gone.

"Don't worry about him," Emmett said.

27

The car ran smooth over the blacktop. Wardell silently named the trees as they passed. Sycamore and cypress. Hackberry, hickory, honey locust. And towering high in the low sun, his favorites, the yellow-leaved cottonwoods. Father Houlihan told him these names. Taught him how to milk a cow, too.

Behind the trees was a field of corn stubble. "Look over there," Father Houlihan said, pointing.

A gasoline tractor pulled a flatbed wagon. Closer in, a Negro field hand stared at the car. He held an axe in his hands.

"It's mostly horses they'd be using in this area," the priest said in his funny voice.

Mr. Whelan smoothed his hair with his hand and said, "Nice to see someone prospering, dust bowl and all."

After a while they could see the city in the distance. Wardell's belly went all funny, like had to go to the privy. His hands shook. Father Houlihan reached across the seat and touched his arm.

"Your mother's waiting for you," the priest said.

"Yes sir."

He watched the landscape whiz by. The hills moved up and down in a blur. In his mind, someone was running through the trees, keeping up with the car. Up and over the hills he went. Nothing could stop him. Not fences or ditches or groves of trees. Wardell watched him and his stomach felt better. The runner turned his head and winked at him. It was Satch, Satchel Paige, strong and fast and in control.

Mr. Whelan and Mr. Watkins went into the parlor and shut the door behind them. Mrs. Watkins took Wardell into the kitchen. She petted him and made funny noises and her eyes were shiny. Father Houlihan sat at the table.

"Would you like some coffee, Reverend? Or perhaps some lemonade?"

"I'm grand, Mrs. Watkins. But maybe the boy would like some."

She bent over and kissed Wardell. All kind of smells came off her: perfume and soap and powder. Not the simple smell of his mama.

"Who gave you these clothes?" she asked him, straightening the cotton vest he wore.

"The clothes he arrived in are over there," the priest said, pointing at a paper bag near the door. "What he's wearing is what we gave him."

Mrs. Watkins pulled at her dress and shook her head. Wardell hunched on the wooden chair, his hands between his knees.

"He's been properly cared for," Father Houlihan said. "Fed well and kept clean."

Tears ran down her cheeks. "Why?" she said.

He lifted his hands. It was like he was going to cry too. "I didn't know. Isn't that right, Wardell?"

Wardell said nothing.

The door to the kitchen opened and the men walked in. Mr. Watkins had put on his jacket and Mr. Whelan had his hand on his shoulder.

"It's up to his mother," Mr. Watkins said.

"But you can put in a good word."

"I could."

Mr. Whelan shook Wardell's hand. His face was serious and scrunched up, like he was going to make a speech. But all he said was good-bye. The priest touched his hair and gave him a picture of St. Theresa.

After they were gone, Mr. Watkins stood at the kitchen window for a long time, staring into the street. The grandfather clock in the sitting room chimed five times.

He took his gold watch from his jacket pocket and reset the time. "What are you waiting for?" his wife said to him.

He took his handkerchief from his pocket and used it to pat Wardell's face.

"C'mon, son," he said. "Let's take you home to your mama."

28

When the curfew lifted, it was like a break in a heat-wave. Suddenly the district was loose and cool and full of life. Street vendors shouting, crap games in the alley-ways, games of pinochle under the hotel awnings. Kids hawking newspapers, shoe-shine stands doing brisk business, the stores and sidewalks packed with people who had been holed up scared. The Monarch cabs were running again. Big John Creach dug a barbecue pit behind the Negro Veteran's Club on Cherry Street and cooked up short ribs and pulled pork and turkey sausage. All you could eat. Everybody welcome. It was like all the year's holidays rolled into one.

And the music – the clubs had reopened and were making up for lost time. Twelfth and Eighteenth Streets were rocking: jazz and blues, swing and boogie-woogie; the Boulevard Lounge and the Cherry Blossom and the Reno Club. Saxophones riffing like a freight train, hot trumpet licks. "Tiger Rag" and "Nagasaki" and "West End Blues". The clickety-clack of tap dancers. Beer and whiskey flowing like the Missouri River. Bill Basie and Bennie Moten in a battle of the bands and Christine Buckner dancing like a dervish, urged on by wild drumming and the call of the brass section. And nothing closing until after the sun came up.

Emmett could sense it from downtown. The whole city was loosy-goosy. But he was worried. The good times were a little too good. A little too Mardis Gras. Underneath the gaiety nothing had changed. The dead were dead, the injured nursed their wounds, murder remained unsolved. Wardell was back home, his mama back at work, but no word from Cal Watkins. Emmett couldn't blame him for not trusting a white man, but the kid had information. The kind of information that could break this case open. Was it the mother? Was she getting in the way? Emmett decided to visit the Sunset Club and find out for himself.

He'd never been in the Negro district after dark. He was surprised at the energy, the neon buzz and the sensual music. Women in low-cut dresses and boas smiled from doorways, the smell of marijuana drifted from back alleys. No sign of any cops, but plenty of Palm Beach suits and two-tone shoes and felt fedoras. And even a few white guys from downtown offices who had gone from work to the saloons and now drifted to the district looking for a little action.

As he entered the Sunset, he scanned the tables for anyone who might know him. The room smelled of barbecued meat and cheap liquor. He took a seat at the rear, ordered a drink, and set his hat on the chair beside him. There were gaps between the floorboards and a blue haze of tobacco smoke. Onstage, a dance band blared the end of a tune as a chorus line of dancers shook their hips at the hooting audience and shimmied off to the dressing room.

The musicians followed the dancers, leaving the stage empty. He was the only white person in the club. He kept his head low in the sudden quiet and sipped his drink. In his Brooks Brothers suit and striped tie he felt naked.

"Mr. Whelan, that you?"

Hattie Renfroe had stopped at his table, purse dangling from her forearm and lips twitching like she was trying not to smile. She was dolled up: a floral-print dress with the hemline above the knee, heels, heavy make-up, and conked hair. Behind her stood a callow man in an oversized suit and a soft hat. He looked at the floor and slouched like someone forever at his girl's beck and call.

"Why hello, Hattie."

She put a hand on her hip and let the smile break wide. "Of all people." She tilted her head at her consort. "This here Hence."

Hence touched his hat, eyes still averted. He leaned forward and whispered.

"Whiskey and soda," she said, and he glided away.

"I thought you didn't listen to the devil's music, Hattie."

She draped her wrist over the chairback and thrust out a hip. "Never said I did and never said I didn't."

Though he kept his eye from wandering, he was aware of the cling of her dress and the sheen of her stockings.

She looked at the whiskey glass in his hand. "Look like *you* want to listen to it," she said.

He pushed his drink from side to side. Back on the sauce since his pint with Fat Jack. What difference did it make?

"I seem to remember you singing the blues once in a while," he said.

"Maybe you talk to Piney Brown, get me an audition."

"Who's Piney Brown?"

"The manager here."

"And what makes you think he'd listen to me?"

"You important."

The tables were filling up with neighborhood folks in their Friday-night finery. A few of them looked Emmett's way. Hattie checked on Hence, who was gabbing with the bartender.

"Where are you working now?" he asked.

"Who said I was workin'?"

She lost the smile. He searched for something else to say and came up with nothing.

"How M's. Whelan?" she said at last.

"Oh, she's fine, I guess."

"That so?"

Stone-faced, she walked off abruptly, just as a piano player took his seat and started playing. Emmett watched the stretch of her legs. At the bar, she grabbed Hence's arm and leaned into him, moving her hips in time with the music.

The piano man played three or four tunes solo. The music had a church tinge, not the barrelhouse that had accompanied the dancers. Most of the audience stopped chattering and listened. Once in a while the bartender would shout, a blues bark that extended a musical phrase and got the tables murmuring. Emmett tapped his foot and watched Hattie. She sat at a table near the stage. Her dress had ridden up her thigh and Hence had a hand on her knee.

By the time the singer appeared, the house was full. Arlene Gray stepped elegantly on the stage and approached the microphone, one hand moving in time with the music, the other resting against the curve of her hip. There was warm applause. Light-skinned and full-figured, she wore a black, strapless sheath with sequins that sparkled in the house lights.

She looked like a diva, but her voice was delicate, almost shy. She opened with "Willow Weep for Me". Six years ago, when he was courting Fay, it had been the torch song for a generation. Irene Taylor had the hit, a big, show-stopping number with orchestral flourishes and quavering grace notes. But Arlene Gray's version was low-key and off-center. She sang as if speaking to her audience, and the phrases moved gently and rhythmically, like the sound of lapping waves.

Whisper to the wind and say that love has sinned
Left my heart a-breaking, and making a moan
Murmur to the night to hide its starry light
So none will see me sighing and crying all alone.

The sad music washed over him. Unused to whiskey, he grew maudlin. He thought of Fay. A lost cause. Solving the case wasn't going to make any difference. It would land him the job with her old man and make him a shitload of dough, but none of that mattered. She might stay with him for what he could give her, but she hated something inside of him. Something that wasn't going to change.

He drank his whiskey. Let Mickey get the dirt on her. Let him find out the worst.

At the end of the set he moved unsteadily to the bar. He ordered a double. The bartender was brisk but deferent. He wiped the counter with a cloth and set the drink on a beermat.

"She's something, huh?" Emmett said.

"Yes sir. M's. Gray, she know how to sing."

The man was broadshouldered and muscular. He continued polishing the bar, waiting for Emmett to speak.

"Do me a favor."

"Yes sir."

"Tell Piney Brown I want to see him."

After a few minutes, the manager approached. He had a heavy limp, gnarled hands, and a puckered mouth. "If you from Charlie, I paid at seven o'clock. Like usual."

"I'm not from Charlie."

Piney licked his lips. He was missing several teeth. "How 'bout another one of those." He pointed at Emmett's glass. "On the house."

Emmett shook his head. "Nice music tonight."

"Thank you, sir."

"This singer, she been with you long?"

Piney put his hands on the counter. "Arlene, she been around a good spell. She the house act."

"Where is she now?"

"Havin' a break."

"I'd like to talk to her."

Piney leaned close. "This 'bout Mr. Lococo?"

"I just want to talk to Arlene Gray, Piney. I'm not from anybody."

They passed through a bead curtain to a back booth. Arlene and the piano player were eating chicken.

"Phineas," Piney said. "You mind?"

Still chewing, the piano player lifted his plate and left. Emmett slid into his place. Piney hung over the table like a waiter. "I'll get me a chair."

"Just leave us on our own," Emmett said.

Piney slowly moved off. Arlene's knife and fork were still poised over her plate; she laid them down, took her napkin from her lap, and wiped the corners of her mouth.

"Can I get you a drink?" Emmett asked.

She shook her head. She was as elegant in this grimy booth as she was on stage. Her broad face was poised and careful. Her hair was tied back tight, and big, looping rings hung from her ears. Large eyes and high cheekbones and fine skin.

"Mrs. Gray, I'm a prosecutor with Jackson County."

"I'm working this evening, sir. And I'm back on in ten minutes."

She spoke as she sang: clearly and without affect, with a little rasp at the edge of her voice.

"Your singing is wonderful," he said.

A glass smashed somewhere near the bar, and Arlene cocked her head, as if hearing a baby's cry. "You didn't come here to ask me about my singing."

"No, I didn't. But I don't mind telling you, I was moved."

When he wouldn't give in to her stare, she poked at her food. "I sang in church when I was a girl. Only training I ever had."

Emmett could see where Wardell got his wary eyes and full features.

"I'm the man who brought your boy to Cal Watkins," he said.

She looked up sharply and drew her elbows in close to her sides. "You're Mr. Whelan?"

"That's right."

"I suppose I should thank you."

But her eyes weren't grateful. They looked caught in the headlights.

"I'm not looking for thanks," he said. "I just want to ask a question or two."

She pushed the unfinished food aside and leaned back in her seat. "About what?"

"Well," Emmett said, "how do you like your new piano player?"

"My new piano player?"

"Yes. Phineas."

"I like him fine."

"How does he compare with Eddie Sloan?"

She leaned out of the booth and lifted her bag from the floor. The dress was cut low at the back and its sequined waist strained across her hips as she bent over. Taking a pack of smokes from her bag, she shook one loose and lit up. "I've told all I know."

"Told who?"

"The police."

"I'm not the police."

"So who are you then?" she said.

"Like I said, assistant county prosecutor."

"You didn't say 'assistant'."

"No, I guess I didn't."

She blew smoke sideways. She look more annoyed now than scared. "Phineas is good. But it will be a while before we have the thing I had with Eddie. We played together three years."

"Since Eddie left, has anything unusual happened?"

"He didn't leave. He was murdered."

"Of course. That's why I'm here."

"I was told this is a city case."

"Cross-jurisdictional."

"Fancy word."

"Something tells me you know what it means."

She drew fiercely on her cigarette, and the coal flared beneath her flashing eyes. "Mr. Whelan, I appreciate you found my son. I do. But what makes you think you know what I know?"

He shrugged.

"What I know," she said, "is that no-one is doing a damn thing to find Eddie's killers. What I know is, my son went missing for a week, and when he was returned to me I got no explanation as to why he was gone."

"What did Calvin tell you?"

"Cal Watkins is an old friend of mine," she said, waving her cigarette, "and he does care for my boy. But he's got bigger things on his mind just now."

He brought his hands together and set them on the table, as if in prayer. He needed her confidence. "Police were involved in what happened to Wardell, Mrs. Gray. You must know that, too. Maybe they didn't snatch him, but they were involved. They think he knows something, and they wanted him where they could keep an eye on him."

"He doesn't know anything."

Piney hovered at the bead curtain. Arlene turned in her seat. "You go on and sell your drinks, Piney. I'll come out when I'm ready."

He left. Arlene stubbed her cigarette in the ashtray. Her face was the color of cold oatmeal. "Like I said all along, the boy's got nothing to do with any of this."

"To who?"

"What?"

"Like you said all along to who?"

She coughed into her hand and slid towards the edge of her seat. "I have to get back to work."

He put his hand on her arm. "Mrs. Gray. I need Wardell to show me where he found the body."

"No. Absolutely not."

"Listen to me. At the ballgame, at the riot, your son was attracting attention. From the wrong people. Who found out that you're his mother and that you played with Eddie Sloan."

Her head was thrown back and her face wide open, like a frightened horse. She was gnawing her lower lip.

"I don't know what was said to you," Emmett said. "But the man who brought your son back to you that day is a dangerous man."

"How is he dangerous?"

He just looked at her.

She slumped in the seat, a hand to her breastbone.

Phineas had started warming the crowd, playing a little boogie-woogie to open the second set. Arlene rubbed her forehead with the tips of her fingers.

"If Wardell can help me, it could make all the difference."

"He cannot," she snapped.

Something told him to take a risk. "Richie Timmons," he said. She flinched.

"He found your boy."

"Maybe so."

"I don't need you to confirm it," he said. "It's a fact. And it's a fact that he's the investigating officer on Eddie's case."

"Oh, Lord." She closed her eyes and shook her head.

"And if I'm going to investigate him," Emmett said, "I'm going to need to find the crime scene."

She stared blankly at the curtain, her fingers worrying the edge of the table.

Piney parted the beads again. "Don't make no never mind to me, Arlene, but we got customers out there."

"I'm coming, Piney."

She stuffed her cigarettes back in her bag, slid out from her seat. Straightened her dress. So beautiful and yet so forlorn. As he had with Wardell, Emmett felt a strong desire to comfort her.

"Arlene," Emmett said, looking up at her, "there's no place to hide on this one."

"Ain't no way," she said as if to herself, and left him.

He stayed in the booth for a long minute and then followed her out. She was not on stage and not in the wings. Piney had also disappeared.

Phineas's boogie-woogie had reached a fever pitch and the joint was jumping. Emmett pushed his way to the bar and gave his card to the bartender, making him promise to pass it on to Arlene. As he left the club, he saw Hattie and Hence bent double as they jitterbugged wildly on the gapped floorboards.

29

The schools reopened, but Arlene did not send Wardell. Mornings, she sat on the back porch and watched him while he played in the yard. After lunch she kept him in the house, reading to him and teaching him arithmetic. Alice spelled her on the nights she sang, and on Wednesdays, when she cleaned at the Plaza. Otherwise the boy was not out of her sight.

He had changed. For no reason, he would take her by the hand, scanning the sky and humming tunelessly. He bit the inside of his cheek until his spit was bloody. He shouted in his sleep. For the first time since he was four years old, he wet the bed.

He hadn't told her what had happened. She hadn't asked. When he did speak, it was always about baseball. He studied the box scores of old games and copied them into a notebook. After his lessons with her, he listened to games on the radio, sitting by the kitchen window and smoothing Satchel Paige's autograph on the tabletop.

Since his return she had cleaned compulsively, but she couldn't rid the house of the smells and stains of the last month. She still had a pain in her ribs from where the man had hit her with the shotgun stock. It hurt when she sang and hurt when she knelt to scrub the kitchen floor.

"You all right, Mama?"

"I'm all right."

"Can I go to Jesse's?"

"Read your magazine, child."

The days had grown cooler, but something hot and menacing hovered in the house. She put away the bucket and brush, went to her room, and sat on the bed. She had bathed in the tin tub that morning but felt dirty again.

"Wardell?"

"Yes, Mama?"

"Come here, son."

In the top drawer of her deal dresser was Emmett Whelan's card. Three or four times she had taken it out, intending to throw it away, but the sober typeface and simple telephone number gave her pause. The card was like the man: formal and direct.

Wardell stood in the doorway. She extended her arms, and he came to her.

"I love you, baby."

"Yes, Mama."

On Sunday she took her son to church. Not to Lucious Jones's First Baptist, but to Emmanuel, where Eddie used to play. She hadn't been in a while.

It was like going home. The pastor greeted her at the doorway. The church was packed with folks in their Sunday finery. Women fanned themselves with prayer books, and the usher winked at Wardell as he directed them to seats in a middle pew. The choir wore blue robes and sang "Rock of Ages" and "Just a Closer Walk with Thee". The new organ player was the music teacher at the Crispus Attucks school, who wore reading glasses that slipped to the end of her nose.

The pastor chose the twenty-third psalm as his text, and when he preached his voice boomed like a tenor saxophone.

The choir and congregation shouted out their responses until the whole church trembled with tongues and swayed with the holy spirit.

> The world is *full* of the pathways of evil (*yes, Jesus*) and only the *Lord* can shepherd us to safety (*amen*)... and we will encounter, listen to me now, we will encounter a *multitude* of perils (*tha's right*), but the *righteous* among us, (*oh yeah*), the righteous will know the *wolf* be always with an eye on the flock (*watch it, now*)...the wolf, he always among us...but we keep, yes we do, we keep our trust in *Jesus* (*Alleluia!*)...we keep our trust in the *Lord*.

The organ swirled around the preacher's words. Arlene raised an arm and waved it through the air in time with the sermon, just as she had as a little girl. With her other arm she held Wardell close. As the preacher hit his stride, members of the congregation shouted and sang and testified, and several of them went to the front of the church and marched back and forth, overcome with the word of the Lord.

The pastor turned to the choir and lifted his arms and led them in "Shall We Gather at the River":

> *Soon we'll reach the shining river*
> *Soon our pilgrimage will cease*
> *Soon our happy heart will quiver*
> *With the melody of peace.*

Arlene's eyes clouded with tears, and the blue of the singers' robes mixed with the colors of the hats and dresses of the women in the congregation. The music cradled her in its rhythms. The song gave her something that her singing in the club did not, and she sang along in a strong voice as she had as a little girl in Raytown, when the world was simple and the path ahead of her was straight and clear.

In the morning she dropped Wardell at Alice's and caught a streetcar to Eighteenth and Vine. The stores were open but the streets were quiet. Several shops had black crepe paper bordering their windows. Eddie's picture hung in the ticket booth of the Gem Theater, beside line drawings and photographs of the four men who had been killed at the ballgame.

The awnings were down at Fox's Bar, and she ordered a glass of Royal Crown Cola and sat outside. Early as it was, four men were already playing canasta at a table out front. The click of the cards and the men's low banter were soothing, but from time to time she caught them eyeing her.

After half an hour Piney came limping up the street. Without noticing her he stopped at the game. "Which of you niggers is cleanin' up?" he said.

"You wants to know, you gots to play."

"We too small change for Piney. I had his money, all my troubles be over."

They spoke without looking at him, the cards flying. As the dealer gathered a trick he nodded Arlene's way. Piney saw her and straightened. "Hey girl, what you doin' here?"

"Look like she waitin' for you," the dealer said.

They moved inside, and she sat with Piney while he drank a cup of coffee.

"I need to use the phone," she said.

"Can't wait until tonight?"

"No."

There were extra furrows in Piney's face: between his eyebrows, below the corners of his mouth. "This got to do with that police come round the club on Friday?"

"He wasn't police."

"Weren't there to listen to you sing."

"I don't know about that."

Piney shook his head and signaled for the check.

It took forty minutes to walk the six blocks to the club. Everyone on Vine knew Piney. The talk was about lost business, the lifting of the curfew, the weather. No talk of the killings. Folks avoided her gaze.

She had never been to the club in the morning and was taken aback by the stale smells and cold neon tubing. Piney unlocked the office door and stood there as she entered.

"I'll need some privacy," she said.

"Seem like these days you be needin' a mess of things."

But he shuffled to the bar. She closed the door and for a long time sat beside the phone. Finally she took the card from her purse and dialled. It was several minutes before she got Whelan on the line.

"Yes, Mrs. Gray, of course. What can I do for you?"

"Wardell."

"What's that?"

"I'd like you to talk to him."

30

"Are you sure you remember?"

"Yes sir."

"Near an underpass?"

"A what?"

"A place where you can drive under the railroad tracks."

"Can't drive. Only walk"

Emmett drove along Route 9, on the way to Riverfront Road. A Sunday. Less traffic and less chance of being seen.

Wardell sat in the passenger seat, answering questions in a monotone and biting his thumbnail.

"You can relax, you know. I'm here to help."

"Yes sir."

They pulled into the parking lot of a greasy spoon called The Blue Lite. Mickey's Nash was in the far corner and Emmett parked beside it.

"You wait here," he said to Wardell. "I won't be long."

The boy nodded.

Emmett found Mickey in a dim booth, eating a bowl of chili with saltines and drinking a Pabst.

"Where's the kid?"

"In the car," Emmett said. "I'm not so dumb I'd try to bring him in here. Hurry up, let's go."

"Sit down. I haven't eaten all day."

The diner was dirty and stifling. Emmett sat where he could see the car through the window. He ordered coffee while Mickey spooned chili into his mouth. He was bloodshot and unshaven, his clothes wrinkled.

"This the real deal?"

"I think so," Emmett said. "Says he knows."

"It's a long stretch."

"Said it's near an underpass. One of those access cutaways is my guess."

"That'll help."

The waitress poured his coffee, slopping some on the stained Formica.

"How about you," Emmett said, "any progress?"

"On what front?"

Emmett didn't like the way he hiked his eyebrows. "Those Friendship Brotherhood papers."

Mickey took a swig of beer and wiped his mouth with his sleeve. "The list of names looks like some kind of schedule. Put it up to the calendar with the days ticked off and, you know, they match almost exactly. At first I figured it was a list of responsibilities or maybe some benevolent activity."

"And now?"

"Hold your horses. If you remember, there were three names ticked off on the list – Sloan, Virgil Barnes, and a Rube Gilmore. I tracked Gilmore down out the turnpike."

"In Kansas?"

"Shawnee. Staying with his mother. He was scared shitless when I found him. Thought I was a cop."

"What did he tell you?"

"Nothing that made sense. But when I mentioned Sloan or Barnes he shit himself. Anyhow, when I got back I had my contact poke around headquarters to see if he had a rap sheet. Another strike out, but guess what? His name turns up on a list of contractors for the department. Seems he did some driving or deliveries. There were dockets with his name for jobs going back two years. I dug deeper and sure enough, Barnes had dockets in there, too."

"What about Sloan?"

"No. But my guess is the Friendship Brotherhood had some sort of deal with the cops, making collections or doing number runs in the district."

"Not so unusual."

"Wait for it. Several of the dockets match the dates on the Brotherhood schedule. And what cop do you think signed off on them?"

"Richie T."

"Got it in one."

Outside, a delivery truck pulled up, blocking Emmett's view of his car. "I'd like to talk to this guy Gilmore."

Mickey frowned. "If he sticks around."

"Where would he go?"

"Wherever Barnes went."

"You think he knows anything about Barnes?"

"Nothing he's going to tell us. I gave him a grilling and he didn't budge."

Emmett heard a rustling beside him.

"Mister."

It was Wardell, gaping and fidgety. The cook had come out from behind the counter and was looking at him, hands on his hips.

Emmett ushered him through the quiet diner while Mickey settled the bill. Wardell's head floated fragilely on his thin neck, and the outline of his shoulder blades was visible through his shirt. Emmett had to refrain from placing a hand on his back. The cook watched them all the way.

Back at the car, Emmett hunkered down to Wardell's level and said, "Don't you know you're not allowed in there?"

"I never been here before, sir."

"You don't have to call me 'sir'. I'm Mr. Whelan."

"Yes sir."

Wardell's eyes were alert. He had the signs of an attentive mother: a sweet smell, clean clothes, good manners. When Emmett picked him up at six o'clock, as agreed, at the entrance to the Municipal Auditorium, Arlene was standing behind him, with her arms around his neck.

"I'm not sure about this," she had said after Wardell was in the car.

"All I'm doing is driving him out there, getting a look at the place, and driving back. Won't see anybody except my associate."

"Nine o'clock."

"At the latest."

She had stooped and waved at Wardell, who raised his hand shyly behind the glass. As Emmett moved around to the driver's side, her eyes gave him a little flicker of appeal, so like a look of longing that his heart had jumped.

Mickey emerged from the diner and they took his car. He was about to turn onto Riverfront Road when Wardell said, "No sir."

"No what?"

Wardell pointed. "Cross the bridge."

"You sure about that?"

"Yes sir."

Mickey looked at Emmett. "North side of the river."

"County case after all."

They crossed the bridge and drove west. Ahead the sun was sinking like a ship, reflected in the muddy expanse of the Missouri. They passed an abandoned gas station. The air was cool and earthy, riverbank air. Along the road was a badly strung wire fence, an old windmill or two, and regular underpasses that gave access to the shore paths. Wardell pointed at the second one. "Tha's it."

A dirt road led to the base of the underpass. A tower of railway ties and a pile of gravel blocked further vehicle access. Mickey pulled up short and got out. The dead end was a hardpan of dried mud, and there were tire tracks and footprints on both sides of the road.

Mickey crouched and examined one side, then the other. He pointed at the ruts on the left. "Wide tire tracks and shallow treads. This was a big car, a few years old. While on that side – " he pointed across the road " – we have brand new tires. Goodyear G-3s, I happen to know. Standard issue on new Speedwagons."

"Police vehicle."

"Two of them, over there. Standard unit, I'd say, and a wagon to take the body. And the footprints look like police brogans."

"The tracks could be from anybody. At any time over the last month."

Mickey smiled. "You noticed the weather lately?"

"Hot."

"Hot and dry. I checked Met records. We had one storm on Labor Day. Which petered out, if you remember. Before that, the last rainfall was on the thirteenth."

"Day of the murder."

"Half inch. This place was a mudbath that night and the ground's been hardening ever since. These prints are from the night of the murder, no question. The big wheels are probably the killers. Large sedan would be my guess. These here from the next day, when the cops and the body boys arrived."

Emmett was itching to get to the scene, but he waited while Mickey took casts of the tire and boot prints.

When he was finished, they fetched Wardell from the car and squeezed past the pile of ties and through the underpass. The boy led them eastwards along the shore path. Cattails swayed in the light breeze and the river surface hummed with insects. The dry spell had dropped the water level a foot or two, and lengths of driftwood reached from cracked clay like the arms of drowning men.

After a hundred yards or so, Wardell pointed at a patch of disturbed earth and matted prairie grass halfway up the railway bank. The sun had set fully, and they beheld the scene in pale twilight.

"Looks like a body dump to me," Emmett said.

"Oh, it's the place, all right."

A goods train passed and hooted a greeting. They hid their faces behind their hats.

"Wardell," Emmett said, "you sit on that log over there. We'll be a few minutes."

"It's gettin' dark."

"You'll be all right, son. We're right over here."

They combed the site and found some cotton fibers and a frayed shoelace. Two black buttons. More footprints, both shoes and brogans. No blood or hair, however. Nothing except the shoeprints that couldn't have been left by the cops. Emmett had hoped for more.

Then, as the light was failing, Mickey said, "Bingo!"

Using a twig he pried a cartridge case from the ground and handed it to Emmett: a .38HV caked in river clay. Too grimed for prints but highly matchable should the opportunity arise. He felt the cold metal on his fingertips, imagined a muzzle flash, the smell of gunpowder.

Mickey circled the flattened grass, examining angles. "What do you think?" He assumed a gunman's pose with his back to the river. "Shooter's standing like so, right?"

"So why'd he empty the cylinder?"

"To reload. Had one bullet in the chamber for the hit and popped him a second time to make sure."

Emmett looked at the city lights twinkling in the distance. At Wardell's silhouette in the dusk.

"It's a cover-up," Mickey said. "Either that or unbelievable incompetence."

"Looks like it, doesn't it?"

"There's too much here. And we're supposed to believe that nobody downtown knew anything about the scene."

"Joe Healy said the body was delivered to the county morgue by mistake."

"No mistake. It *was* county."

"But think about it – Timmons would know that the county morgue wouldn't be surprised by unfamiliar faces. Coulda been anyone dropped off the body. Then he claims it's city later. After the dust settles."

"And he's pocketed the slugs."

"Whole thing set up to make sure nobody followed up," Emmett said. "Timmons."

Mickey held out his arms in the dying light, summarizing. "Couple of goons do the business with the full knowledge of the police. Next day the kid here finds the body. His people call it in, someone in HQ gives Timmons the tip, and he heads out to the river with a few trusted lieutenants. They clean up the mess, drop the body off at the wrong morgue, file a fuzzy report."

"And Timmons scares the shit out of the kid and his mother so they won't talk."

Mickey gathered the evidence. The fibers, the shoelace and buttons, the tire mud and footprints. Emmett had a lab guy who could give them the once over. And the cartridge case. If it led to a weapon, he could get a line on the hitmen and start the trace back to Timmons.

When it was all packed up, Emmett looked out over the water, listening to the gurgle of the current. Swallows or bats swooped from a raised bank upriver and disappeared into the thickening darkness. Broken light on the surface.

"We gonna hang around here all night?" Mickey said.

"Wardell," Emmett shouted. "Let's go."

As they approached the underpass, they heard voices. Sabers of light flashed behind the gravel pile. So as not to surprise, Mickey shouted, "Hey there, coming through!"

Three men in straw hats and work clothes stood beside Mickey's Nash. Behind them was a flatbed truck with its engine running. Empty bushel baskets were stacked against the cab. Two of the men held flashlights, and the third cradled a shotgun in the crook of his arm.

"This your car?" said the man with the gun.

"'Fraid so," Mickey said. "Couldn't interest you in it, could I? Give you a sweet deal."

Wardell had dropped back and Emmett motioned him to stand beside him. One of the men shone a light in his face, and Wardell lifted a hand before his eyes.

"Thought you might be Union Pacific boys," one of the unarmed men said. He pointed at the stack of ties. "Come down here in July, dump these here logs. Ain't seen 'em since."

"They do this up and down the line," Mickey said. His voice was louder and brighter than it should have been. "Got some system going where they have different crews for drop-off and construction."

The men were hawk-nosed and hollow-cheeked and unshaven. The flashlight beams hopped from Wardell to Emmett to Mickey. Settled again on Wardell. "What you doin' here, boy?"

"He's with us," Emmett said.

"That a fact?"

"Yes, it is."

The man with the shotgun hiked it up to waist level.

"What's a nigger boy doin' hanging around with a couple of dudes?"

Mickey laughed. "I look like a dude to you?"

"You don't look like no nigger kid's old man."

The man with the gun stepped forward and, using the barrel, edged Wardell away from Emmett. Wardell whimpered.

"You shut up, boy." Then to Mickey and Emmett: "You faggots gonna tell us what's goin' on?"

"I'm going to take my billfold from my pocket," Emmett said.

"No you ain't."

"Show you my ID. I'm Assistant County Prosecutor for Jackson County."

"And I'm Babe Ruth."

One of the other men took his hat off. "Let him get the ID, Clem."

The gunman wavered. "OK, let's see it," he said. "Do it slow."

Emmett took his billfold from his pocket and drew out his ID and held it up.

"Shine a light, Billy." He peered at the card.

"I assume you have a permit for that weapon," Emmett said.

"How do I know this ain't forged."

"Don't be an idiot, Clem," one of the men said. "Back off."

The man spat on the ground and retreated.

"Come over here," Emmett said to Wardell.

The boy stood behind Emmett.

"We ain't up to cause no trouble," the other man said. "If you're a lawman, you know the kind of things goin' on down here."

"Well, you can leave us now," Emmett said.

The men got into the truck and drove off. They watched its broken taillight disappear over the rise.

"You went easy on them," Mickey said.

"I'm not taking any chances with a double-barrel Winchester. Besides, we got bigger fish to fry."

"I got their tag number. I'll run it through Motor Vehicles in the morning."

Wardell was looking back towards the river and sucking his thumb.

31

Emmett woke from a deep sleep to a steady ringing. He was alone in the bed. It was dark. The radium dials on the alarm clock said three-thirty. Monday. A work day.

He drifted back to sleep and dreamt he was in a jazz club. Across the room Fay was serving drinks and flirting with the customers. She smiled at him and it was somehow critical that he go over to her. But he couldn't move. A saxophone wailed in his ear. Wailed and wailed.

The saxophone call turned into more ringing. It was the phone in the living room. As he descended the stairs, he remembered falling asleep without knowing where Fay was.

It was Mickey, talking garbage. He was drunk.

"Whoa, Mickey, whoa. Where are you?"

"Out 'n' 'bout."

"Have you been home?"

"Runners."

"What?"

"The niggers. Runners for Timmons."

"What are you talking about?"

"Numbers or booze. Then see something they're not spose to."

"Right."

"So he has them… you know. Popped."

Not what Emmett wanted to hear said over the phone.

"Mickey, go home and go to bed."

"Been workin', Emmo."

"Good man. Get some sleep."

"Lab. Registry. Other places."

"Meet me at Treacey's at eleven. Can you do that? I'll buy you a cup of coffee."

"We'll nail that asshole, Emmo."

"I know we will."

"Know who I'm talkin' 'bout. Get the pictures and fuck him up good."

"That's enough, Mick. Get some shut-eye."

He went through the house, turning lights on and off. Her car was not in the garage.

He sat in his leather chair in the living room, at an angle that gave him a view of the front door. He waited. The birds came to life. The windows slowly brightened. At five-thirty, the paper boy flashed by on his bike, followed by a thump on the porch. He made coffee and paged through the *Star*. At six he shaved and dressed and left for the office.

Mrs. Johnson spent an hour trying to get through to Roddy's office at the capitol, only to find out that he was in Kansas City. Emmett left a message at the club.

He called home. No answer. He unlocked his desk drawer and took out a 1935 calendar. For the last month he'd been keeping track. A small red x in the corner meant that Fay had not been at the house when he returned from work. A blue tick marked calls Ophelia made to check his whereabouts. And a date circled in black meant she had been to a hotel. Four days circled so far, two Tuesdays and two Thursdays. Calls from Ophelia at noon on each of those mornings.

He had not asked Mickey about photographs. Hadn't the guts.

Mrs. Johnson buzzed. "Mr. Hudson on the line."

Roddy was gruff and direct. Emmett didn't want to use the phone to update him, but Roddy insisted. He told him about the crime scene being on the north bank, the gathered evidence, his theory on the morgue delivery. His contact at the lab. Roddy said nothing until Emmett laid down his trump card. The cartridge case.

"Ah," Roddy said. "What kind?"

".38HV."

"So it matches the slugs."

"Well, if you remember, the slugs went missing. But the coroner had recorded the bullet type."

A pause.

"Well then," Roddy said slowly, "it *could* match the slugs."

Emmett worked to stay a step ahead. "You're saying we need a weapon."

"Or similar shells you can tie to a suspect. Conclusively."

"We have an edge," Emmett said. "They're distinctively marked."

"All cases are." Roddy sounded preoccupied. "It's hard to believe that both the killers and the cops didn't find it. That they didn't make it their *business* to find it."

Outside his office door Emmett heard voices raised.

"Whole thing happened in darkness. And the riverbank was a swamp. It was raining pitchforks that day."

"So?"

"So the shell sank into the mud. And it wouldn't have been easy to find the next day, either, especially if someone was in a hurry."

"OK. But what we need now is proof."

Roddy seemed to be waiting for Emmett to solve the case over the phone, there and then. The ruckus outside the door grew louder. A woman shouting. Was it Fay?

"The weapon."

"Or other shells," Roddy said. "Where does our man shoot? Think about that. Does he belong to a gun club?"

"I'll find out."

"You do that."

The door flew open and Arlene Gray swept in. Her face was crumpled with anger. Mrs. Johnson following like a gundog.

He raised a hand and pointed at the receiver. Arlene folded her arms across her chest and glared.

"Something going on there?" Roddy asked.

"I have to go."

"Well, you have your marching orders. Call me when you hear from the lab. I'm staying in town for the time being."

Emmett hung up and came out from behind his desk. "What's wrong?"

"What's *wrong*?"

"I tried, Mr. Whelan."

"That's all right, Mrs. Johnson."

Emmett stared at Mrs. Johnson until she left the room.

"This is a county law office, Mrs. Gray."

Her lips trembled. Her hair clips had loosened and stray coils fell across her eyes. "Is that right?"

"As it happened, you interrupted a conversation I was having with someone who can help you."

"Had about all the help I ever need, thank you. Wardell told me about last night."

"He did great, Mrs. Gray. He's a smart kid."

"I said, he *told me*."

"Why don't you sit down. I'll get some coffee."

She didn't move. "You promised he wouldn't see anyone. Except your associate."

"The guys at the car, is that who you're talking about? Couple of farmers poking around."

"*Farmers?* They threatened my boy. With a gun."

"There was never any real threat. I don't even think it was loaded."

Her voice flew high. Her singer's voice, frantic but controlled. "Cracker points a shotgun at my son and you don't think to *mention* it?"

"I didn't want to alarm you."

"Lot worse things than being alarmed. You be colored in this town ten seconds, sir, and you know *that*."

She raised her arm as if shielding her eyes from the sun and rubbed her forehead with the back of her hand. A stricken look fell across her face and she swayed.

Emmett helped her to a chair.

"My baby. My poor baby."

"Mrs. Gray, it's all right."

She was crying. He gave her his handkerchief and touched her bare forearm. Her skin was soft. She wore a delicate perfume.

"It's OK," he whispered.

"Oh no, it isn't, Mr. Whelan."

Feelings stirred in him that were tangled and soulful and beyond shame. He touched her again, soothed her, and his heart thundered.

She wiped her eyes. "I'm taking him away from here. I have family in Columbia."

"Isn't he in school?"

"Oh, listen to the man. The boy's in *danger*."

She examined her shoes as if they were pinching her feet then stood up. She straightened her dress. He was aware of her stomach, her breasts, her hips.

"I'm sorry," she said, "you're right. It was wrong to come here like this."

"No, no. Please stay. I can arrange protection for Wardell."

Her eyes flashed but she calmed herself. "He's best watched over by his kinfolk."

"I just want to help."

"Do you? Then leave him alone. And me."

She left as quickly as she'd arrived. Outside his office, Mrs. Johnson shook her head and checked the hallway to see if anyone had overheard.

He walked down Baltimore Avenue in the late-September sunshine, past the Muehlebach Hotel, the legal and accounting firms, the shoe shops and haberdashers, the men in red aprons setting up their lunch wagons. Business back at full tilt after the droop of summer. The skies above broad and clear and deep blue.

Emmett was running chronologies in his head and doing his best not to think about his wife. Or Arlene Gray. The way her dress clung to her body. The plea for help in her eyes.

He reached Treacey's café just after eleven. Mickey hadn't arrived, so he sat at the counter and ordered an iced tea. A trolley car clanged past. Boys shouted headlines of the second editions. Hoover Dam Opened. Howard Hughes Breaks Speed Record.

Emmett took a small black notebook from his jacket pocket and reviewed a timeline he'd drawn, beginning with the murder on August 14, through to the riot three weeks later, and up to the present. On other pages he had written an expense sheet and a checklist of tasks for Mickey and himself, including labwork and follow-up on leads.

He could find a safe house for Arlene and Wardell. Or he could offer to drive the boy to Columbia.

The next time he looked at his watch it was eleven-thirty. It was not like Mickey to be late, even if hungover. And Emmett was impatient. He needed to know that the evidence was in the lab. Maybe Mickey got the hour wrong or was delayed at forensics. Or maybe he was still in bed. He waited another fifteen minutes and headed for the McDermott house, where Mickey had been living since being dropped from the force.

The family lived in the heart of West Bottoms, beside the cement factory and only a few blocks from Emmett's parents' house. A smart bungalow with a picket fence and a St. Brigid's cross above the lintel. Fresh-painted yearly. As he opened the gate, the factory whistle wailed its lunchtime blast.

It took a while for Mickey's mother to answer the door. She peered through the screen. "Emmett, is it you?"

"Hello, Mrs. Mac."

She opened the screen door. "You're here for herself, I suppose."

"I'm looking for Mickey."

"Come in, come in. She'll be delighted."

"She?"

"Your mother."

Emmett followed her into the kitchen. His mom sat at the table. On the table was a teapot in its cosy, cups and saucers, cream buns.

He kissed his mom. "Nice surprise," he said.

"I'll make a fresh pot," Mrs. Mac said.

She refilled the kettle and set it on the hob and lit the gas. Emmett's mom gripped his arm. Her face was sallow, with dark bags under her eyes and patches of scaly red skin beneath her temples.

Something was wrong.

"Are you all right, Ma?"

"What sort of business are you up to with that son of mine?" Mrs. Mac said. "Claimed you had him on a job last night. Haven't seen him since."

"He's not in bed?"

"Ah now, Emmett. He's not *that* bad."

"I was supposed to meet him at eleven. He doesn't miss appointments."

"Does he not? News to me."

"He does his best."

She waved a hand, as if clearing cobwebs from the air. "Ah, he's had a hard time of it, there's no denying. Losing his job, the bad knee, the drink."

His mother's silence was like an axe in the air. She still clutched his arm and stared at the quartet of pictures hanging above the stove: the Sacred Heart, Pope Pius XI, Mickey in his baseball and police uniforms.

The kettle hissed. The women exchanged a glance.

"You'll need to excuse me for a moment," Mrs. Mac said, and left the kitchen.

His mom rose from her seat and turned off the flame beneath the kettle.

"You'll have a cup," she said.

"What's going on?"

She faced him squarely. "I've been staying here. With Nell."

"Staying? You mean living here?"

She nodded.

"Is he that bad?"

She emptied the teapot, warmed it with water from the kettle, and spooned in the tea.

"Ma. What is it?"

"He was let go."

"When?"

"Weeks now. He'd already been sacked when you saw him the last day. I kept waiting for him to tell you."

"And he's drinking."

"More than ever."

"Hard to imagine it could be more."

She filled the teapot and set it on the table to draw. She sat and folded her hands on her lap.

"He hasn't been… you know. To you."

"He was never that way," she said. "Not physically, anyhow. But he's an awful tongue on him. And he's night and day in the pub."

"I don't see him in Billy Christie's."

"He'd be ashamed to show his face there. He goes to the shebeens near the tannery. Where he gets the money for it I've no idea. Oh, Emmett, I just couldn't put up with it. So I asked Nell."

"Mickey never said a word."

"I told him not to. And it's only been a few days."

She poured the tea. The spout of the teapot rattled against the lip of the cup. Below the table, so she couldn't see, he took a hundred dollars from his wallet. Through the open window came the shouts of workers headed home for lunch and the grinding gears of passing trucks.

"The stories about the old country," he said. "That fairy tale about the will."

"The farm was never going to be his. But he couldn't let go."

"Talking about county Mayo like it's across the state line. Like the whole business was yesterday. How did Harry put it? 'Second-son syndrome'."

"You never suffered from that."

"No?"

"No, Emmett, you didn't. Other things, maybe, but not that."

The small kitchen, with its religious pictures and smells of gas and bacon grease, was the right scale for him today. Maybe for always. Alone in the house in Oakwood last night, waiting for the dawn to scatter his despair, he had felt like a lost child.

"Ma. About Fay."

She raised a hand. "I don't want to talk about that."

"I'm not asking you to talk. I just want to say that it's not as simple as it might seem. Like you and Da."

"Ah, there's nothing simple in this life, Emmett. You don't have to tell that to an old woman."

There was a loud rap at the door.

"Should I?"

"Nell will get it."

He reached across and pressed the money into her hand. He gripped her fist so she couldn't see how much it was.

"Now, Emmett."

Before he could answer, Mrs. Mac appeared in the doorway. A slip of paper drooped from her hand.

"It's Mickey," she said.

"What?"

Her face was like chalk.

"He's in St. Luke's."

32

Mickey was in the surgical recovery ward. The ward sister brought Emmett to his bed.

He wouldn't have recognized him. His face was puffy and discolored, his left eye swollen shut. His hair was matted with blood. He had a fractured collarbone, two broken teeth, and ten stitches in his neck. His leg was in traction.

"Jesus, Mick. What happened?"

"What the fuck do you think?"

The soft-voiced sister suddenly turned tough. "*Language.*"

"Sorry, sister."

He fell into a coughing fit. She lifted his head, gave him a sip of water, wiped his mouth with a towel. He groaned. Above his head was a crucifix.

"You're not to excite him," she said to Emmett. "He needs his rest."

"How can I rest, rigged up like this?"

Mickey's words were as mangled as his body. Emmett examined the system of pulleys and weights that suspended his leg. "You really need this get-up? It's like you're being tortured."

"If he doesn't have the traction," sister said, "he'll end up deformed."

"I'm already deformed."

"He's a lucky man. The police said he could have been killed."

"The *police?*"

"Hey, sister, how about doing your rounds."

Beyond her wimple Emmett could see the fair curve of her cheek, long lashes, a healthy color. Like Fay used to look. "Ten minutes," she said to Emmett. "Then he's having his lunch."

"I'm not hungry. But I could use a drink."

"I don't think that would be a very good idea, Michael, do you?"

She gathered her skirts and left the ward.

"Why do the nicest broads become nuns?" Mickey said.

"The cops were around?"

"Don't worry. I didn't tell them jackshit. Did you bring it?"

"Bring what?"

"A pint. I told them to make sure Mr. Beam came with you."

"The message didn't get through."

"Goddamn nurses. I'm parched."

"Mickey, talk to me. What happened?"

He coughed again, and Emmett gave him water. The damage to his face was severe. Clouds of purple and yellow spreading beneath his skin. Lips split and clotted. The bad eye like a rotten plum.

"After I left you last night I went to Union Station and took care of some business. On the way home I stopped in at Billy Christie's. Had a couple of pops with the boys."

"What boys?"

"No one you'd know and no one that matters. Anyhow, I left at closing. Then kind of a blank patch. Did I call you?"

"Three-thirty."

"That late? Jesus. On my way home, anyhow, and two guys jumped me from behind. On Grand. They had brass knucks and a crowbar. Crowbar did the damage."

"Did you get a look at them? Did they say anything?"

"Not a word. And it was dark. But they knew what they were doing."

"Could've been plug-uglies looking to roll you."

"They rifled my wallet but left the money. These guys were looking for something else. Or sending a message."

With his good arm Mickey tried to shift his position. Another groan.

"And you think it was the cops," Emmett said.

"Who else?"

"Like you always ask me: why? They beat you up at night and then come here in the morning asking questions. I don't get it."

"It's a big department. Right hand doesn't necessarily know what the left's doing. But if they weren't cops, they were on the city payroll, Emmo, believe me. Probably looking for the shell."

"How would they know about it?"

"How do they know anything?"

Emmett had to ask. "Did they find it?"

Mickey raised his good eyebrow. "That all you're worried about?"

"Hey, I'm sick about this."

"Another reason to nail the bastard, right?"

"Mickey, that shell could make our case. Where is it?"

"That's why I went to Union Station. I packed up everything from the scene and left it in a locker there. Idea was to go to the lab this morning." He nodded at a drawer beside the bed. "The key is in my pants pocket. Take it before the sweet sister gets back. Her bite is worse than her bark."

The pants were limp and blood-stained. He got the key.

"I'll get everything to the lab this afternoon," Emmett said. "Who do I see?"

"Go to the basement of the Sharp Building. Ask for Leo Gilligan. Don't give the stuff to anybody else. Tell him what's what – I didn't have time to label the items."

"What about you?"

"What about me?"

"I'll get you some protection."

"Emmo, I'm safe. They got me where they want me. Now it's up to you. Did you follow up with the Brotherhood?"

"Not yet."

"Let's say the shell leads to who we think it does. You still need a motive."

"Not necessarily."

"Goddamn it, Emmo, you're a prosecutor. And aren't you curious?"

"If he did this to you, I just want to get him."

"Then go to the Brotherhood. Figure out what those guys were doing for Richie T."

"Your Ma's not too happy. I wouldn't let her come."

"Tell her I'm fine. And get me that goddamn pint. Actually, make it a quart." Mickey winced and squirmed. "Call the nurse, Emmo."

"What's the matter?"

"The dope they got me on gives me the shits. *Call the nurse.*"

The sister arrived just in time.

Emmett slipped out of the ward and found a public phone. No answer at the house. Of course, she could've been standing in the hallway, listening to the ring, guessing it was him. It was ten days since she'd said a word to him. Spoke to Ophelia in a bright voice, gabbed on the phone to her friends to beat the band, but acted as if he wasn't there.

After sitting in his chair for hours in the dark that morning, waiting for her, he had returned to the bedroom and searched her closet, secretary, dresser. At first he was careful to put everything back in its place. Then he a found locket he had given her, inscribed with the date of their engagement and the words *To Fay, with all my Love.* He fell into a rage, throwing her scarves and negligee about the room and spilling the contents of her purses and hatboxes onto the bed. More clothes than she could wear in a year. Perfumes and ointments, silks and lace, earrings and bracelets. Sitting on the floor, surrounded by her underwear, he buried his face in her stockings, then tore them into pieces scattered them throughout the house.

If she had come home, that was what she faced. Did he really want to talk to her?

Walking back to the ward, he passed the sister carrying the bedpan down the corridor. Outside, the wail of an approaching siren. Shouts and the shuffle of feet.

Mickey lay panting in the bed. His tongue lolled. The ward stunk to the rafters.

"You OK, pal?" Emmett said.

"Couldn't be better."

"I gotta go."

"Hang on a minute. There's one other thing."

"What's that?"

Gingerly, Mickey touched his swollen lip. "There's a few other things in Union Station. Including a roll of film."

"What I think it is?"

"You'll have to get it developed. But it will tell you what you want to know."

"What do I want to know?"

"The truth."

Emmett grabbed him roughly, and Mickey howled in pain.

"Goddamn it, Emmo!"

"Who is it?" he hissed.

"I don't know."

"Don't lie to me, Mick."

"I didn't take the pictures."

"Who did?"

"Nobody who knows you and nobody who cares. A guy from out of town."

Emmett let go of him so that he fell back. The pulleys rattled and Mickey groaned more loudly than ever.

The sister returned. "Time's up, Mr. Whelan. You'll have to go."

"Get 'em developed," Mickey whispered.

33

Colored had a special waiting room. Same as at the movie house and the ballpark. It was at the back of the station, and the door was next to the ramp where the buses sat with their engines running. Clouds of exhaust puffed into the room. There were no windows. People coughed and waved away the flies.

Wardell and his mama had waited in line for an hour. The man behind the window bars wore a hat with a green brim and no crown. His bald head stuck through. He told them that they couldn't buy tickets to Columbia until all the white folks had theirs. He gave them a piece of paper and said to go to the waiting room until they knew if there were enough seats.

His mama led him to the corner. Wardell carried a satchel of schoolbooks and a cowhide suitcase. At the bottom of the case, beneath his knickers and vests, was his baseball mitt. His mama wore her black wool dress and a hat with a feather in it. She spread a square of newspaper on the bench and gave him a biscuit with honey, slices of apple, and a bottle of warm milk. Opposite sat an old woman with a lump on her neck the size of an orange. He stared at the lump until his mama poked him in the ribs. He ate the apple slices and rubbed his forehead on her velvet collar. He tried not to think about where they were going and how she would leave him in the morning.

They got the last two seats, at the very back. They were the only black folks on the bus. The leather on the seats was torn and springs poked through the rips. There was a bad smell. The man sitting in front of them grumbled and spat on the floor and called them dirty niggers. Wardell's mama held her head up and stared straight ahead.

The bus left Troost Street and passed through downtown and into the nice neighborhoods. The houses had huge lawns and tall trees and statues of black jockeys beside the mailboxes. Then the countryside. Cows and windmills and clumps of trees at the edge of wheatfields. Wardell thought he saw the farm where the rough men had brought him and his stomach felt sick. But it turned out to be a different farm.

After an hour or so the bus stopped at the train station in Odessa and sat there for a long time. Thunder rumbled overhead. Two women got on the bus, and the driver shouted something that Wardell didn't understand. Then he came down the back.

"You listenin'?" he said to Wardell's mama. "You and the boy have to get off here."

"We're going to Columbia."

"Did I ask where you were going, gal?"

"No sir."

"Go on and get your butts off this bus before there's trouble."

They stood in the rain outside the tiny stationhouse. The next bus to Columbia was in four hours. Wardell lifted his suitcase and followed his mama up the street. There was a fancy building that his mama said was the opera house and a big piece of stone with names of dead men carved on it. Wardell asked her who the dead men were, but his mama didn't answer.

At the post office, a man in a blue uniform stopped them. "We're closing shortly."

"I need to send a telegram," Arlene said.

"I said we're closing."

A white couple stepped around them and went in.

"Is there a Western Union in town?"

"Oak Grove," he said, and closed the door in her face.

"Where's Oak Grove, mama?"

She didn't say, and he followed her back to the station-house. He had to pee, but there were no colored toilets. They were not allowed to use the waiting room, so they crossed the road and stood beneath an elm tree.

Wardell's clothes were wet and his side hurt. "I have to go."

"Shh."

"Mama!"

But then she began to shift from one foot to the other. After a while she told him to hide the suitcase behind the tree. She brought him to a field of high grass beyond the railroad tracks. After he went she told him to stay where she could see him but to look away. He heard the rustle of her clothes and a long hiss. He didn't look at her directly, but he could tell she was squatting, and for no reason he could work out he felt ashamed.

When they got back to the elm tree, a pick-up truck was parked outside the stationhouse. Two men sat in the cab. It was getting darker and Wardell saw their cigarette coals glowing beneath the brims of their hats. His mama told him not to get the suitcase and not to look at the men. The streetlamps came on and the rain stopped.

After a while a man in a suit and tie and shiny black shoes stopped as he was walking by. "What are you doing here?"

"We're just waiting, sir."

"Waiting for what?"

"The bus to Columbia."

He checked his watch. "The next bus doesn't leave until nine o'clock."

"Yes sir."

He put his hands on his hips and examined them. Then he looked at the stationhouse and the men in the truck. He stared at them until the engine started and the truck moved slowly up the main street.

His face was wrinkled and serious. "Do you have any bags?" he said.

"Behind the tree," Arlene said.

He nodded at Wardell. "Go get them. Then come with me."

He spoke to the man in the station and brought them to the waiting room. After a few minutes a woman brought them bowls of soup and dark bread. The nice man gave Wardell's mama two dollars and told her that if there was any trouble she should tell the stationmaster to call him. Mr. Matthews, he said. To tell him to call Mr. Matthews.

Then he left and his mama started crying. She didn't stop until the bus arrived two hours later.

They got to Columbia after midnight. The streetcars had stopped running, and Charlotte didn't have a telephone, so they walked to her house.

Charlotte opened the door before they knocked. "Arlene, honey, I was worried to death."

The women hugged. Charlotte's husband, Alvin, carried Wardell's suitcase to his room at the back of the house. There were dark stains on his overalls.

"You bring your mitt?"

"Mama told me not to."

"But did you bring it?"

"Yes sir."

Alvin laughed and poked him in the chest with a finger.

"Uncle Alvin, how long I got to stay here?"

"Long as you want. We gonna have a real good time."

His mama was in the kitchen with Charlotte. She had started up crying again.

"Now that's enough of that," Alvin said. "Charlotte, what about that chicken you got goin'?"

He sat Wardell at the table and poured him a glass of milk. Charlotte fussed at the counter and his mama left the room.

"What we need here," Alvin said, "is a little music. You think so, Wardell?"

He turned on the big Philco in the corner and fiddled with the dials. A scratchy voice came from the speaker. "*And now, ladies and gentlemen and listeners, live, from the famous Savoy Ballroom in New York City, the Count Basie Orchestra.*"

The music started, a big band sound like they played on Eighteenth Street. Alvin grinned and tapped his foot. The singer started. A woman singer, like his mama, but with a funny, gravelly voice. Charlotte hummed along with the tune.

When Wardell looked up next, his mama was standing in the kitchen doorway. Softly, she sang along with the lyrics.

The way you hold your knife
The way we danced till three
The way you changed my life
Oh no, they can't take that away from me!

"That a new singer, Arlene?" Alvin asked. "Ain't heard that voice before."

His mama wiped the tears from her eyes. "That's Lady Day," she said. "That's Billie Holiday."

34

On Monday afternoon, Emmett picked up the evidence from the Union Station locker and delivered it to Leo Gilligan. He handed over everything except the roll of film, explaining each item in as much detail as he could. The next day he returned to the lab. The metal film canister sat unopened in his inside jacket pocket, pressing against his ribs like the muzzle of a gun.

Leo brought him to a coffee shop across the street from the Sharp Building. He was a fussy man with a thin mustache, close-bitten fingernails, and oily hair. He stirred three heaping spoonfuls of sugar into his coffee. On his left pinkie he wore a gold signet ring.

"I don't have a report for you," he said. "I could generate one, but it wouldn't mean anything. Michael told me not to log any of the evidence, so legally it does not exist."

"Did you keep benchnotes?"

He admitted he had. "But that doesn't change the status of the evidence."

"Let's worry about that later," Emmett said. "What can you tell me?"

"I can make some concrete observations. The shoelace fragment contained some dried blood. O positive, which I believe matches the victim's. Though don't forget that it's the most common type in the country. Thirty-seven percent of all red-blooded Americans." He smiled and sipped his coffee. "The tire tracks come from two different days. The second day, after the mud had dried some, they're all from police vehicles. The first day's tracks were tougher to reconstruct, but eventually I nailed them. Firestone A11s, standard issue on Dodge sedans from 1930 to '32. The shoeprints likewise. Second day, cops; first day, high quality leather brogues. Men with some dough."

Leo had bad breath. Emmett leaned back. "Do you always call him Michael?"

"That's how he was introduced to me."

Emmett didn't like that Leo knew so much about the case. He wondered what Mickey saw in the guy to inspire trust. "What else?"

"On the other clothing items, not much. The fibers are cotton, dyed green. The button you found is hardwood, probably from a man's suit jacket. Couple snappy dressers, sure, but not enough evidence to trace anything. Even if I had all the lab equipment in Chicago."

"What about the shell?"

"Cartridge case. 'Shell' is shotgun terminology."

"Whatever."

Leo stirred more sugar into his coffee. "Here, Mr. Whelan, is where you have a real lead. As you know, the cartridge is a .38HV, which can only be fired from a 38/44 – a .38 Special, to use the vernacular. Smith & Wesson only began manufacturing this firearm five years ago, and I wouldn't say there are too many in Kansas City. The standard-issue duty weapon for KC police is a regular .38, so the heavy duty model that fired this cartridge was probably owned by a criminal."

"Or a detective."

"A few detectives carry the Special, yes. Thing is, because they're relatively new, the individual characteristics left on bullets and cases tend to be more distinctive than those fired by an older piece."

"Which makes a match easier."

"I don't even need the gun. If you can get me another case which you know was used by the same piece, thirty seconds under the microscope will confirm a match. Though I have a feeling I'm telling you something you already know."

Leo smiled, but his eyes were nervous. The science was over. So what was next?

"What can you tell me that I don't already know?" Emmett asked.

Leo asked for more coffee and waited until the waitress had refilled his cup. Sweat dotted his hairline. He stared at the swirling surface and said, "Mickey hasn't paid me yet."

"Really?"

"He was supposed to meet me yesterday with the funds."

"How much does he owe you?"

"Two hundred."

"Two *hundred*?"

"You can ask him. It's what we agreed."

Leo bit his lower lip. Slowly, Emmett took his billfold from his pocket and counted off five twenties. "Here's half," he said. "The rest when we're done."

Leo folded the notes and put them in his shirt pocket. "Criminals," he said, "I can't help you with. Strange as it may seem, I know very little about that world. But most detectives on the force shoot at the Paseo Gun Club, near Fairyland Park. They tend to have their own bays, so linking a cartridge case with a specific individual should be straight-forward."

Emmett's palms were sweating. He was close and he knew it. Good old Mickey. He had known who to go to.

Laying a dollar on the table, Emmett stood and put on his jacket. The film canister pressed against his chest. "You develop film?" he asked.

"Of course."

Leo finished his coffee, licked his lips, and wiped his mustache and moist brow with a napkin.

"OK," Emmett said. "Good to know."

When he'd opened the locker at Union Station, Emmett found something that Mickey hadn't mentioned. Lying between the cigar box of evidence and the roll of film, wrapped in brown paper and twine-tied like a birthday present, was an Army-model Colt .45. Silver-blue and well-oiled. Loaded. Looking over his shoulder, he examined it, surprised at its heft. The serial number on the cylinder had been filed off, though the bottom of the barrel was stamped UNITED STATES PROPERTY. Unregistered and unlicensed, clearly. Also in the wrapping were ten magazines of ACP cartridges and a wire cleaning brush.

He'd put the gun and ammunition in his Packard. As he drove away from the meeting with Gilligan, he sensed its presence in the trunk. Was that why he felt so bulked up? So in control? At the crime scene, gazing out across the water at the lights of Pendergast's kingdom, Emmett had smelled the power and arrogance of City Hall, drifting across the Missouri like stink off the stockyards. Men so sure of what they could get away with that they killed even the most innocent with impunity. Pendergast trusted few, but he trusted Timmons. And now Emmett felt the balance slowly tilting. He had justice on his side. He had evidence. And he had an untraceable semi-automatic pistol.

He drove to the Paseo Gun Club. At reception was a burly ex-cop with a flat, menacing face. Emmett recognized him from the old neighborhood.

"How you doing?" Emmett said.

The man shrugged.

"I want to shoot a few rounds."

"You a member?"

"No."

The guy eyed Emmett's jacket and striped tie. "We got a few public bays."

"How much?

"Four bits an hour plus ten cents a target."

"OK."

"I'll need a five-buck deposit and a look at your license. Where's your piece?"

"In the car."

The guy leaned on the counter with his knuckles and raised his shoulders. His eyes were like bullet holes in a roadsign. He wasn't in this job for nothing. He would know a rogue piece if he saw one and know what to say to its owner.

Maguire, Emmett remembered. Mulberry Street. Beside the gravel pit. "You're Joe Maguire's brother, right?"

The guy frowned, trying to place him.

"Emmett Whelan. I was with Joe in St. Jerome's."

"You the prosecutor?"

"Yeah. County."

Maguire moved some papers from the counter to a desk behind him. "Take bay three," he said. "The kid will set you up with a target."

Emmett held out a five-dollar bill. Maguire raised a hand. "On the house."

He had not fired a weapon since his Army days in Fort Riley fifteen years ago. Back then he had been a decent shot, better than average with a Springfield rifle. His gun sergeant had recommended him for field artillery training, though he'd lost interest and ended up in the Signal Corps. But shooting, his sergeant always said, was like riding a bike. Once you know how, you won't fall off.

A kid showed Emmett his bay, gave him earplugs, and pinned a fresh target to the corkboard wall. He gave the kid a nickel and told him to stick around. There were no other customers in the public area. Behind a riveted metal door marked PRIVATE came the thud of regular fire. Emmett removed the magazine from the stock, rubbed the action with a chamois, and reloaded. For a long time he tried out different stances – one hand or two; feet shoulder width apart or left foot forward – and squinted down the sights with either eye. Then, fumbling at times with the action but without interruption, he fired the full magazine – seven rounds. The muzzle noise was huge. The kid whistled and Maguire shot a glance from behind the counter. The air reeked of black powder and his arm and shoulder stung from the recoil.

Emmett felt like he was floating. His head buzzed with the echo. He wanted to curse and roar and shake the pistol like a drunken bandolero.

"Not so good, Mister."

The kid laid the target before him. They stared at it. Not the shredded mess he expected: only one slug had found the cardboard, and it was way off center.

"Maybe you want to slow it down a little," the kid said.

"Yeah."

"One good thing, though."

"What's that?"

"Don't need to buy a new target."

He stopped the session after using up five magazines. By the end he was finding the target more often than not. He decided that firing a handgun was tougher than shooting a rifle. And more thrilling. Definitely more thrilling.

The kid cleaned up the bay and took a shoebox from behind the counter. He wiped down the Colt and set it in the box beside the unused magazines. Emmett asked him to carry it out to the car. Beside the open trunk he handed the kid the five bucks Maguire had refused. He gaped at it.

"Put it in your pocket," Emmett said, "before anybody sees."

"Yes sir."

"What's your name?"

"Henry."

"Henry what?"

"Henry Conway."

"Your dad's name Henry too?"

"My uncle. My dad's dead."

Emmett tapped the kid's shoulder. "Tell me something, Henry – who uses the private bays?"

"Today?"

"Any day."

"Different guys."

"You know them?"

"Most, yeah."

"After you clean up, what do you do with the shells?"

"I sort them for Ned, and he sells them to a scrap dealer."

Emmett assessed the kid's face: snub nose, poor teeth, dirty hair that fell in front of his eyes. Ten years old, at most. A scar on his chin and a collar three sizes too large. He could see him sleeping in a small room with three or four older brothers, running to Billy Christie's for a bucket of beer for his uncle. Kid like this might know the meaning of discretion. Certainly knew the meaning of a buck.

"Richie T," Emmett said.

Henry nodded.

"Has his own private bay, right?"

"He does."

"When does he come in?"

"Couple times a week."

"Get me two of his shells and I've got another ten bucks for you."

"Which gun? Uses a couple."

".38 Special. Think you can do that and keep quiet about it?"

"Like eatin' pie."

Emmett slammed the trunk. Across the street was a derelict drugstore with a dark alleyway beside it. He pointed. "Meet you over there next Friday. This time."

The kid nodded and sprinted back to the club.

That night Emmett cut the engine as he approached his house and glided to a stop beneath the spreading oak across the street. He slumped in the seat and listened to the cooling engine tick in the gloom. A light wind ruffled the oak leaves, and their vague, spiked shadows danced across the hood of the car.

He surveyed the house. A crowd of moths fluttered around the porchlight. The kitchen and sitting room lights were off.

She wasn't home. He knew what she was up to. At night, she stayed at her parents' house or with friends. When he was at work, she came by the house. Piece by piece, she removed her good furniture, her jewelry, her papers. When it suited, she would announce it was over. Would she sue him for divorce? Would she have the gall?

He had no idea what she told her parents. He had waited for Lloyd to raise the subject, but she likely hadn't told him the truth. Yet how could she pretend that all was well?

He waited. In his lap was the Colt, reloaded. One sweaty hand gripped the gun's checked-wood stock. The other held a pint of Irish whiskey. In his imagination he saw her return. She entered through the garage door, turning on the lights, fussing in the kitchen, going to the bedroom. He gave her enough time to get undressed. He got out of the car and slipped quietly through the front door. Shoes off, he climbed the stairs in the dark. He heard her moving about the room. He edged into their bedroom. She sat at her vanity in her negligee, brushing her hair. She saw him in the mirror and her arm stopped mid-motion. He raised the muzzle of the Colt. Her green eyes widened, and the mole beneath her left eye pulsed like a star.

Who was he kidding? She wasn't there. And even if she was, it wasn't her he wanted to shoot.

35

The next morning Emmett told Mrs. Johnson to hold his calls. He locked his office door and sifted through his law books until he found the Missouri Divorce Statutes. For an hour, he drank coffee and read about authorized motions, petitions for dissolution, disposition of property and debts. It was like being back in law school, except that stray phrases stuck like a bone in the throat. Mental cruelty. Alienation of affections. Injured party. Every statute tinged by the language of violence.

After a while the words lost their meaning, but their sounds lingered like a bad dream. He had not slept the night before, sitting in the car until after three, finishing the whiskey, tossing and turning the rest of the night in his stale bed. Losing focus, he sat at his desk, rubbing his eyes. His head ached. His shoulder was sore from the recoil of the Colt. He sniffed his fingers for traces of powder.

At noon he called the house.

"She done gone," Ophelia said.

"So she was home when you arrived."

"At home?"

"Yes. She was in the house when you got there."

Silence.

"Ophelia – was she there when you came to work this morning?"

"Course she was, Mr. Whelan. Where else she be?"

"Did she say where she was going?"

"No, sir. She never do."

Half an hour later he was huddled in a doorway across the street from the Schumann Hotel, a borrowed hat pulled low over his eyes. His teeth chattered. His shirt was soaked at the armpits. Yet he felt on the edge of a breakthrough. The street wheeled with activity, but he had a clear view of the hotel's front door. People came and went. Businessmen. Delivery boys. A couple or two. But no Fay. An hour he stood there. An hour and a half.

At two o'clock he went to the Muehlebach Hotel for lunch.

He drank two stiff bourbons while he waited for his steak. By the time it arrived he'd lost his appetite. Another drink. The restaurant glittered and tilted and popped with random squeaks of sound. As he picked at his food, Lloyd Perkins arrived with a group of gray-haired men in dark suits. They seated themselves at a round table by the bay window, unfurled their napkins, and ordered cocktails.

Lloyd saw him and crossed the room. "Waiting for someone?" he said.

"No, sir, I am not."

The words slipped and slurred. His voice was like a disobedient dog.

Lloyd pulled at his chin and pointed at an empty chair. "You mind?"

"Be my guest."

Lloyd's boys were yucking it up with a young waitress. At the edge of the group was the red-faced guy from the first meeting. Bob Perkins's step-and-fetch-it.

"Who's that guy?"

"Which one?"

"With the blue tie. And the bad skin."

Lloyd frowned. "That's Les Newton. Robert's assistant. You've met him."

"Where's his notepad?"

Lloyd sat at the edge of his chair, elbows on his knees. "How much have you had to drink, Emmett?"

"Oh, not that much, Lloyd. No more than I need."

"Why don't you finish what you're eating there and get back to the office. Or home if that would be better."

"And why would home be better?"

Lloyd sniffed. Shoulders pointed. Hair bristling. Mouth like a coin slot. "Does this have anything to do with Fay?"

"What do you think, Lloyd?"

"It's none of my business."

"So why are you asking?"

Lloyd's neck turned red and he checked the nearby tables.

"I'm on the case, Lloyd. Got what you're looking for."

"Keep your voice down."

"Enough to break this town wide open. Give me a couple of days. Signed, sealed, delivered."

As he spoke, Emmett thought of the gun in the car: its cool heft and oily smell and machined-tooled lines.

Lloyd leaned close. "If you have something on the case," he hissed, "go to Roddy." He stood, buttoned his jacket, and returned to his pals, who were laughing and lighting cigars. "And goddamn it, Emmett, pull yourself together."

Emmett sent Mrs. Johnson home early and napped in the office. He woke with drymouth and a headache. It was after five.

After a beer at the Terrace Club he walked down Twentieth Street and into the Negro district. Business was brisk. The clubs were flourishing. The photographs and drawings of the riot dead were still in the shop windows, and the air of menace was as thick as ever. But with the .45 in his pocket and alcohol in his blood, Emmett was right at home.

Charles Bibb had said that the Friendship Brotherhood met on Tuesday nights at this time, but when Emmett reached the offices its windows were dark and the door was locked. He knocked hard for several minutes, peered inside, and circled round the back. A plank fence bordered the back yard, and he stood on a broken chair so he could see over. The yard was cluttered with half-built coffins, rusty nails, and raw lumber. As he was about to climb down, he saw Bibb exit the back door carrying a strongbox.

"Hello there," Bibb said.

"Are you hard of hearing?"

"What's that?"

"Unlock the goddamn gate."

Emmett followed him into the funeral parlor. Bibb tried to squirrel the strongbox under his desk.

"Wait a minute," Emmett said. "Let's have a look inside."

"You ain't interested in this old thing."

"Open it."

Inside was a thick bundle of cash, a book of blank city work dockets, and a spool of badly printed tickets, the type used in the numbers rackets in the district. Emmett took the cash and dumped the paper on the desktop. Bibb was breathing unsteadily, and supporting himself with a hand against the wall. "I reckon I best sit down," he said.

"You do that."

He slumped into a straightback chair. "This ain't what you think."

"So what is it?"

"That ain't my money."

"Good. In that case I guess I can take it for safe-keeping."

Bibb's face glistened. His eyes were watery and watchful, his skin slick with sweat. "You do that, mister, and you may as well just put a gun to my head and pull the trigger."

Bibb's face was slack with despair. The office's wood floor was mottled with tobacco stains. Pile of trash had been roughly swept into the corners, and a Panama Canal Railway Company calendar hung crookedly on the wall, two months out of date.

"If it isn't yours," Emmett said, "whose is it?"

"I's just a bagman."

Emmett waved the wad of cash. "Same as Eddie Sloan? And Virgil Barnes?"

Bibb reached for his drawer.

"Wait a minute," Emmett said.

"Only gettin' my snuff."

Emmett slid open the drawer and handed him the canister. He took a pinch and tucked it under his lip.

"I asked you a question."

"What if I don't answer?"

"Then I take the cash. And you have a date at the Jackson County Courthouse."

Bibb started rocking back and forth in the chair, puckering his lips against the strength of the snuff. He gestured dismissively at the strongbox. "These here tickets, they go to the pool halls and clubs and such. Them that be sellin'. We collects and pays out every Monday. Eddie, yeah, he done the same."

"What about the dockets?"

"One gets filled out for each job. That ways we get paid."

"By who?"

"By the man."

"C'mon, Charles. You can do better than that."

"Be a different individual every time."

"Was it ever Richie Timmons?"

Bibb was deadpan. No doubt.

"How do you like working with the devil?" Emmett asked.

"Better'n bein' dirt po'."

Emmett snapped the rubber band off the wad and peeled off two hundred bucks in twenties, which he stuffed into his pocket. "Why'd he kill Eddie, Charles?"

Bibb's face was all stretched and rubbery, and he looked as if he'd lost his breath.

"Well?"

Bibb shook his head. He was breathing through his mouth.

"Where's Virgil Barnes?" Emmett said.

"You axin' a mess of questions of a old man."

"When you tell me where Virgil is, I'll give you back what's left of your dough."

Bibb wiped his nose with the sleeve of his shirt and Emmett turned to leave.

"Hold on, now."

"Yeah."

"His sister. Could be she knows."

"Keep talking."

"Ida Barnes. Live out Richmond way. Ray County."

Emmett nodded, but Bibb was looking at the money, his tongue resting on his lower lip.

"I'll be back," Emmett said. "You think a little harder about who it is you're working for and what they're doing to the district."

He threw the rest of the cash across the room. The bills fluttered to the floor like dead leaves.

As he left the funeral parlor, Emmett saw an old Ford parked across the street that had not been there when he went in. He looked in the front seat. It was empty. Feeling watched, he walked down Sixteenth Street as far as Indiana. The very poor lived along this stretch, in sagging, splintered shacks with packed-dirt yards and scrap-wood fencing. The few people he passed looked at the ground. He felt his pistol against his ribs, snug in a new holster he had bought that morning at Syke's. He trotted quickly, keen to be back downtown.

By the time he reached Brooklyn Avenue, he knew he was being followed: an occasional flash of a straw hat, a man peering in a shop window, footfalls that stopped when he did. He walked down to Twelfth and crossed the street just ahead of a streetcar. Shielded by its clatter and sway, he ducked into an alley and drew his pistol. A thudding in his ears drowned out all sound, but his vision was sharp, and when the hat appeared, Emmett jumped the guy, dragged him into the alley, and struck him with the butt of the Colt. The man fell to the ground, screaming.

"Don't shoot, pal, I ain't carrying."

"Keep your hands on the ground. Turn over."

It was one of the country boys from the crime scene. Not the guy with the shotgun, but one of the others. Emmett nudged his feet apart and patted him down. He was unarmed. He took the guy's wallet from the back pocket of his overalls. Inside were seven dollar bills, a driver's license, and a Kansas City Police Department ID. The names matched: William H. Mason, with an address in Lees Summit.

"What's your name?" Emmett said.

"Billy Mason."

"Tell me this, Billy: what's a hick from Lees Summit doing working for KCPD?"

"I'm at the academy."

"Who are you working for?"

"Nobody."

Emmett kicked him hard in the ribs, and the man howled and curled up.

"You killed him, didn't you?"

"I didn't kill nobody," he gasped.

Emmett was amazed at how easy it was to stick the muzzle behind the man's ear. "You're a goddamn murderer, Billy."

"I had nothing to do with it. I swear to Jesus."

"Nothing to do with what?"

"The killing."

"What killing?"

The man whimpered. He rammed the muzzle harder. "*What killing?*"

"The musician."

Emmett withdrew the pistol and prodded him with his foot so that he rolled over. Several small pebbles stuck to the man's forehead and his chin was streaked with dirt.

"Why are you following me?"

"I do what I'm told."

"Who told you?"

Mason hesitated, and Emmett stuck the gun in his ear. "A detective," he said quickly. "Red-haired guy in a suit. I don't even know his name."

"Same guy sent you after me down by the river?"

"No. We was just passing that night. We reported the car tag and I got assigned to you."

Emmett was shaking, and he had a sharp pain in his shoulder.

"You were following me."

"No law against that."

"There's a law against murder."

"I told you, I didn't have nothing to do with it."

"So who murdered Eddie Sloan?"

"I don't know."

He stomped on Mason's chest two, three, four times, grunting furiously. He could hear the leather creak of his new holster and the sound of his own breathing. A woman stopped at the alley entrance, and he screamed at her to move along.

Spitting the words, he leaned over and said, "Tell me who killed Eddie Sloan or I'll kill you."

The man was coughing. "I don't know."

"Who did it?"

"You want me to say any goddamn name just to save my ass?"

Mason clutched his chest and spat blood on the ground. His overalls were covered with dirt and his boots were worn and filthy. Not the clothes of the man who'd stepped through river mud in leather shoes.

Emmett holstered his gun and straightened his jacket. He put the man's license and ID into his pocket and dropped the wallet in the dirt. "I have a message for your red-headed friend," he said. "Tell him to tell Richie T to go fuck himself."

36

Arlene was sleeping poorly. Without Wardell, the house was lonesome. The temperature had dropped and the crickets were quieter. The walls creaked. Mice rustled beneath the floorboards.

Reverend Jones's men were long gone. She discouraged visitors. When she got home from the Sunset, she sat at the kitchen table with a glass of water and a pack of cigarettes. She smoked more than ever. Her voice, Piney said, was nice and dark these days, but his forehead crinkled with concern when they talked, and he kept pushing food on her that she didn't want.

Several times a night she wandered into Wardell's room. He had taken his pictures and baseball mementoes and bed linen to Columbia, so the walls were bare, the bed stripped. The curtains were open. She stared at the moonlit mattress as she had once stared at his crib.

First thing each morning she wrote him a letter. She told him what she was going to do that day and reminded him to be clean and alert and respectful of his kin. After breakfast she walked to the post office on Twelfth Street to mail the letter and check her post office box.

Charlotte was a teacher at Douglass Elementary. She brought Wardell to school every day and reported on his progress. Two boys close to his age lived next door. Alvin was not terribly bright, but he was a good, non-drinking man who had a way with kids and a generous spirit. He and Charlotte had not been blessed with children, and they'd always had a soft spot for Wardell.

She kept his letters beneath her mattress. *Me and Uncle Alvin gone fishing. I keeps you in my mine, mama.*

When she reread these words, she felt a shiver as if she'd passed over the grave of a dead child.

On Friday evening, there was a knock at the door. She was dressing for work and threw a housecoat over her slip. A neighbor, most likely, or Alice dropping by with groceries. But it was a white man, and for a moment she thought that the detective had returned.

It was Emmett Whelan.

"Arlene," he said.

She buttoned the housecoat. "Hello."

"May I come in?" he said.

He did not look good. His face was unevenly shaven and his tie stained. He held his hat in his hands, wheeling it by the brim. His eyes searched out the corners of the porch.

A white man at her house was never going to be good, but better for him to be inside than out where all could see, so she brought him to the kitchen. Wardell's letter lay on the table. She scooped it up, showed him to a chair, and excused herself. In her bedroom she changed into her dress, brushed her hair, and checked herself in the mirror.

"Would you like some lemonade?" she asked him.

"You don't have anything stronger?"

"No, I don't."

She poured two glasses. Propped on an elbow, he slumped at the table. One of his jacket lapels was torn. As she moved around the kitchen she was aware of him looking at her. When he swallowed his lemonade, the cords of his neck moved like old rope.

"Where's Wardell?" he said.

"With his kinfolk."

"In Columbia?"

She nodded.

He started to speak but went quiet. He fidgeted. She didn't know if he was holding something back or confused.

"I owe you an apology," he said. "About what happened by the river."

"All right."

"But Wardell... he was never in danger."

"What about now?"

"Well, he's not here, is he?"

"So I was right to send him away?"

He took a handkerchief from his pocket and wiped his face. "No harm being careful." Again his eyes lost their focus and his jaw grew slack.

"Mr. Whelan – "

"You can call me Emmett."

But as she started to speak, he rested his forehead on his palms so that she was looking at the top of his head. He had a bald spot the size of a silver dollar.

When he hadn't moved for a while, she said, "Are you all right?"

His hands trembled. He turned from her and coughed and spat into his handkerchief. "I'm worn out. It gets too much sometimes."

"Don't I know it."

"The case. My wife."

"It must be a great strain on a family," she said, "working on something like this."

"I need your help," he said abruptly.

"How?"

His eyes grew wide, almost manic. "The police killed Eddie Sloan."

"Don't say any more," she warned. The windows were open.

"I'm going to nail them for it."

"Why are you telling me this?"

"I need your help. I need to know why he did it."

"They need a reason?"

"A motive."

"Wardell helped you and he had to leave town. If I didn't have to work, I'd be with him."

"Don't go." He spoke quickly, desperately. He had a look on his face that she had only seen on colored folks.

He reached across the table and touched her arm. She recoiled.

"Listen to me for a minute and don't say anything," he said. "You let your son help me. He brought us to the crucial evidence."

"I don't want to know this."

"You have to trust me. I can find Virgil Barnes. I need you to help me. If he tells me what he and Sloan were doing for the police, then I'll have a case."

"Eddie had nothing to do with that man."

"I think you may be wrong about that."

"And I have no desire ever to see Virgil Barnes again," she said.

From his inside jacket pocket he withdrew some crumpled papers. She glimpsed a gun and holster beneath the jacket. He laid the papers on the table and smoothed them out. He paused, reached again into his pocket, and showed her a small metal canister. "Do you know what this is?"

"Film?"

"That's right." He lost his train of thought and slipped the canister back in his pocket. By now she was keen for him to be gone.

"These are documents from the Friendship Brotherhood offices. Barnes and Sloan were bagmen for Richie Timmons. These papers prove it."

"You'll have to leave," she said.

"What's wrong?"

"I have to go to work. I'm already late."

"I need to find Barnes. And I need you to come with me. He'll talk to me if you're there."

"I have to go."

"I'll walk with you."

"No."

"Can you help me on this? Please?"

His eyes, she saw now, were asking for all sorts of help.

"I told you," she said. "You have to go."

37

Emmett had been sitting in the reception area of Perkins & Graves for half an hour. The ceiling fans clicked steadily and the typewriters rattled. Lloyd's receptionist tapped her pencil on the desktop between phone calls. She had finger-waved hair and a small mouth with too much lipstick.

"He knows I'm here, right?"

"I've told him three times, Mr. Whelan."

Emmett was stone-cold sober, but Lloyd didn't know that. The old man was making him stew.

On Emmett's lap was a manila envelope containing a notarized log, descriptions, and photographs of two .38 cartridge cases. In his pocket was a glassine bag with the cases: the shell from the crime scene and another from the gun club. Henry Conway had delivered, and Leo Gilligan had confirmed: a perfect match.

That morning, Gilligan had run out of the Sharp Building like a kid on Christmas morning. "Like I said."

"You're sure?"

"Of course I'm sure, it's like identical fingerprints."

Still wearing rubber gloves, he handed Emmett the glassine bag, along with his benchnotes. "I won't testify. I'm telling you that up front. But send this to any lab worth its salt and they'll confirm the match."

Emmett paid him the rest of the money. As he counted out the bills, he felt the nudge of the film canister in his jacket pocket. It was like an uncracked fortune cookie. Again he'd intended giving it to Gilligan to develop. Again he stalled. One mystery unveiled at a time.

He relished showing Lloyd he could do the business. But the news didn't give him the fizz of triumph he'd expected. The question remained: why? Mickey was right: without motive, evidence was only half the story. Proof was not enough. Emmett wanted a narrative. His gut told him something was missing. Too many gaps in the plot, too many unanswered questions.

After an hour, a secretary led him to Lloyd's office. To his surprise the whole gang was there: Robert Perkins, like a Buddha in a leather chair, Roddy and Les Newton. The men stood around Robert like figures in a painting. No one said hello. In the false silence, Emmett knew that they'd been talking about him. It got his dander up.

"Emmett," Lloyd finally said. "You have news?"

Newton took out his pad and pencil.

"You the stenographer?" Emmett asked.

"I beg your pardon?"

"Every time we meet, it's out with your little notepad. I feel like I'm in court." He said to Lloyd, "Does he really need to be here?"

Newton's acned cheeks grew even redder. Robert lifted a hand from the arm of the chair. "Forget about that. What's the news?"

Emmett emptied the glassine bag on Lloyd's desktop. The shells jangled like coins. "We have a match."

He pointed at the first, marked by Leo with a spot of blue dye. "This is the case found at the scene of Eddie Sloan's murder. The other one, with the red spot... it's from Richard Timmons's bay at the Paseo Gun Club. Right after he'd been there. The two were fired from the same gun. No question about it." He set the manila envelope beside the shells and tapped it with a fingernail. "Cartridge cases have been logged, photographed, and examined."

"How'd you get the shell from the club?" Lloyd asked.

"Kid that works there."

"How did you arrange that?"

"What difference does it make how I arranged it?"

Lloyd reared back ever so slightly, crinkling his eyes. Newton scribbled while Roddy reached across and picked up the envelope and the shells. "Who did the analysis?"

"A bona fide lab. But the source has to remain anonymous."

"What good is the match," Lloyd said hotly, "if the lab can't be identified? And by the way, it makes a hell of a difference how you acquired the second shell. Or have you forgotten the rules of evidence?"

"Hey," Roddy said, "let's cool down here. We can get another lab to verify the match. That's the easy part. The crucial question is, will the kid testify?"

"I can ask him," Emmett said.

"You can *ask* him?" Lloyd said. "You can make goddamn sure he does so, or you can forget the whole thing. This is a federal case we're constructing, not some back-room exercise."

Lloyd was stiff as hatrack. His face was dark and tight. On his upper lip was a small, purple blister. His hair had fallen across his brow.

"Can I get you a glass of water, Mr. Perkins?" Newton said.

Lloyd waved away the offer and stared at Emmett, who rode out the scrutiny. Lloyd's face reminded him of Fay.

"Do you understand?" Lloyd said.

"Of course I understand."

"Then do it," he said. "Bring him in and get a statement. Roddy, you call the Feds tomorrow and set it up."

"Not so fast," Emmett said.

Up to this point Robert had seemed to be taking nothing in. He'd sat passively in the soft chair. But now his small, hard eyes focused on Emmett.

"We can go to the second lab," Emmett said. "We can get the kid to testify. But we'd be foolish to move. What if Timmons says his gun was stolen? What if he has an alibi? What we need is a motive. You asked me to find out why the Pendergast organization is killing Negroes. Well, I'm close to an answer. Once we know that, the evidence turns harder. And the case comes cleaner."

Newton had stopped writing. The men bent their heads towards Robert, who cleared his throat. "That was a nice little speech, Whelan. But we have a bird in the hand. We move on the shell."

"Why?"

"We move on the shell."

Lloyd's anger had turned to watchfulness. He looked at his brother.

Emmett sensed a shift in power and purpose, but he was in too far to pull back. "Move now, we risk losing the case. Or settle for a lot less than what we could get. I'm talking about a conspiracy that includes KCPD, the mob, and who knows who else. It's big."

Roddy raised a hand. "That's enough, Emmett."

Robert struggled up from the deep chair. His whole head turned crimson with the effort. He straightened his tie. "We have a plan here, Whelan. Keep digging on the wider case, sure, and keep us informed. But Roddy's going to take this evidence to the FBI and move this to the next stage. We can't wait any longer."

"But I don't see how waiting until – "

"Lord Jesus, Lloyd, how much more of this bullshit do I have to listen to? There's nine million bucks on the line here!"

His outburst was like a train roaring by. Alarmed, Lloyd glanced at Emmett. Newton slipped his notepad into his shirt pocket and Roddy coughed.

Lloyd stepped quickly around his brother and clapped Emmett on the shoulder. "Let's not get impatient, Robert. Sounds like we have a plan. Roddy, you do what you have to. Emmett, you're right. Stay on the case. We're making progress here, I can feel it."

Lloyd was moving herky-jerky, like a marionette. Robert had gone to one of the deep windows. Legs apart and shoulders hunched, he gazed onto the street below. Roddy and Newton whispered as Lloyd guided Emmett to the door and asked his secretary to call him a cab.

"I can walk," Emmett said.

"Good. Fine," Lloyd said. "Give me a call later."

Half a block away Roddy caught up with him. "Hold on."

Emmett kept moving. He didn't want to stop. He didn't want to think about what Robert had said.

Roddy grabbed him by the arm and swung him around so that they faced each other. "Lloyd kind of hustled you out of there."

"Is that what he did?"

"We're all on edge, Emmett. We've gone critical here, I think you can see that. And your contribution is essential. It won't be forgotten."

Roddy flashed his most charming smile. He had cut himself shaving, and the red nick was like the blister on Lloyd's lip.

"Contribution?" Emmett said. "What is this, a fundraiser? Nine million for big Bob to pad his empire?"

"Pendergast is a scourge. Last of the crooked machine bosses. You're helping to bring him down. It's a moment in history."

They were poised on the street, between the high limestone buildings of Grand Boulevard. The tangled noise of the city flowed around them.

Emmett waited for a streetcar to pass and leaned close. "History my ass, Roddy. Nine mill. You think I don't know what that fat prick was talking about?"

Roddy slowly lit a cigarette and dropped the spent match on the sidewalk. "I'd be very careful about using language like that to describe Robert Perkins. You're not in West Bottoms now."

"No shit?"

"It's dangerous to jump to conclusions."

"What conclusion *should* I come to?"

"It's a complex case. The Pendergast family has been blocking business in this town since the turn of the century. The prosperity of the whole state is at risk because of the corruption."

"Save your breath, Roddy. I'm in the family, remember? Lloyd's been on this case for nearly five years. They're after the insurance, the federal fire insurance premiums in escrow."

Roddy pulled on his cigarette, hollow-cheeked and attentive. "So what if they are?"

"And I thought you guys were worried about Negroes being killed." Emmett looked at the sky. "What a chump. The State of Missouri will arbitrate on the insurance claim and Pendergast controls the state. Lloyd and big Bob want Timmons so they can squeeze Pendergast and get a favorable judgement. It's all about money. How could I be so stupid?"

He needed a drink. He needed to get off the street and into a quiet bar.

"You haven't been stupid," Roddy said. "And don't go stupid on me now. What did you expect? Like I said first time we met – they see an opportunity. So they're fudging their motives. The endgame's the same. And you... you'll benefit too. Don't forget that. Careerwise. Financially."

In court, when a case was going well and Emmett had evidence and argument perfectly aligned, he often knew what his opponents would say before they spoke. And if they left something out, it was as obvious as a missing front tooth.

"What about you, Roddy? What's in it for you?"

Roddy hitched at his jacket. "You mess with these guys, Emmett, and they'll chew you up and spit you out. Family or no family." He took a final drag and flicked his cigarette butt into the gutter. "I've said my piece. Just don't do anything you'll regret. Go home, spend time with your wife, get a good sleep. Things will look better in the morning. You'll see."

He raised his shoulders and walked up the street. *Spend time with your wife.* Was that a cut? Had Lloyd been airing the family's dirty linen? He watched Roddy return to the law offices. He did not look back. More business to attend to. All of them sniffing the money like bloodhounds. Big Bob probably still at his window perch on the fourth floor, staring down at Emmett right now.

He didn't bother to check. He turned on his heel and headed downtown, in search of the nearest saloon.

38

Emmett Whelan was as color blind as a white man could be, Arlene had to admit that. But there was something careless about him. Something blurred. As if he'd lost sight of himself.

She had seen it in the men in her life. An unraveling. A slow desperation. Alcohol usually had something to do with it. These men lost track of their feelings, even when they seemed able to function day to day. They started wanting the wrong things. The wrong women, mostly. Maybe Emmett was losing his wife, or maybe she was losing him, but his marriage came into it. That much she could sense.

Men in his shape lost their judgement. They couldn't be trusted on matters of the heart, even if they believed everything they said. Which he did. She'd seen that look in his eyes. But what he was looking for was beyond bad judgement. It was dangerous. How could he not see that? A black gal getting involved with a white man only meant one thing. And she wasn't that stupid.

But she decided to help him. She had to think about Eddie. About justice. She had given Virgil Barnes up for dead. If Emmett was right and he was still out there, wouldn't she be a fool not to meet him? Probably the last man to see Eddie alive. Except his killers.

So, even with her reservations, she found herself sitting beside Emmett in his big car, driving along Route 10 towards Richmond, in Ray County. Another clear fall day, full of yellow and blue, the kind that made her think of Wardell in the country, hunting snipe with Alvin or playing hide and seek in the brush with the neighbor kids. She had placed her hat between them on the wide seat, as if marking a boundary. Emmett drove nervously, moving his hand between gear stick and steering wheel. But he was sober. She made sure of that before getting into the car.

They left Kansas City and passed through the good farming country and soon reached the hardscrabble cabins of western Ray County. Poor whites lived here. The men worked the coal mines whenever work was going, and the women and children tilled the fields, raising corn on an acre or two. It was no place for a Negro woman. Arlene kept the window up and slouched low in her seat.

As they approached Richmond, she told Emmett pull over.

"Why?"

"Go on. Beside that bunch of cottonwoods."

He pulled up. She checked to make sure no one was around.

"Drive in to town and park where you won't attract attention," she said. "Then walk back this way along the railroad tracks. You'll see me."

"Why the cloak and dagger?"

"All due respect, I am *not* driving into town with you."

"Let's go straight to Ida Barnes."

"She sees a white man in a Packard, no *way* she answers the door. You *do* want to talk to the woman?"

He did as she suggested, and they met near a ramshackle railroad hut on the edge of the Negro district. Ida lived in the worst part of the neighborhood. The dirt road leading to her shack smelled of raw sewage. Piles of trash sat in the front yards. Emmett waited behind a cypress tree while Arlene knocked on the raw-plank door. She heard a rustling inside and knocked harder. "Ida, open up."

A dark-skinned woman in an organdy dress unlatched the door and squinted at Arlene. Coils of hair sprang from her head in all directions. "Yes'm," she said.

"I want to speak to Virgil."

"Who you?"

"A friend of his."

"Virgil ain't got no friends."

"Let me in, Ida. Let me in and you won't have any trouble."

The plank-door opened on to a small room with a brushed dirt floor and rough-wood furniture. The glassless windows were screened with muslin. An oil-lamp sat in the corner on an old barrel. There was a strong smell of corn liquor.

As soon as Arlene was inside, Emmett appeared, holding his hat. "Where's Virgil?" he said.

His face was red and agitated. Ida couldn't speak. Arlene wondered if she had done the right thing. Another Negro woman being cowed by a white man.

Emmett looked at Arlene in exasperation. "Ida," she said gently, "the man just wants to talk to him. We'll be gone before you know it."

Ida pointed at a blanket-draped doorway. Behind it Virgil was sleeping on a straw-tick mattress, surrounded by empty jugs and tin cans and the buzz of flies. The stink was overwhelming.

Emmett shook him awake. Virgil blinked at them with drooping, bloodshot eyes.

"What you gone done now?" Ida said from the doorway.

"You shut up," Virgil said hoarsely.

With a little moan, Ida left the room. Virgil sat up, lifted a jug, and took a swig.

"You know who I am?" Arlene said sharply. She held her chin high against the smell.

"Yes, ma'am, I do."

Tears pricked her eyes. "It never cross your mind to contact me? Tell me what you know?"

Virgil wiped his nose with the back of his hand. Bits of fluff clung to his hair. His face was pale and he breathed through his mouth. "I don't know nothin'."

"You know about Eddie."

"Eddie's done gone."

"That's right. And Mr. Whelan's doing what he can to make sure no more colored go that way."

Virgil took in Emmett with his watery eyes. "You police?"

"No."

"I ain't got no money. Landlord gone kick me and Ida out come Friday I don't give him money."

"I'll take care of the landlord. And I'll take care of you if you help us out."

When Virgil didn't answer, Emmett said, "The Friendship Brotherhood. Charles Bibb told me how it works."

"Charles Bibb owe me thirty dollar."

"I talked to Rube Gilmore, Virgil. He told me about you doing numbers running."

"He tol' you that?"

"Yes he did."

Virgil moved forward so that he sat on the edge of the mattress. He waved flies away from his face. "I had me a good job at the packin' plant. Four years on the floor and I ain't missed but one day. Mr. Axton, he tol' me my services was no longer needed. Jus' like that."

"When was this?"

"May. June maybe."

"Why do you think that happened?"

"Don't reckon I know. Bibb, he be tellin' me I ain't got nothin' to worry about. Tellin' me the Brotherhood look after me."

"In what way?"

"Like you say. Numbers work and such in the distric'."

"How long did you do that?"

"Month or so."

"Where'd you bring the money?"

"What money?"

"The money you picked up."

Virgil leaned forward and spat on the floor. Arlene took a step back. "Bibb," he said. "We done everything through Bibb."

"You ever deal with the police?"

"No."

"Why are you lying to me, Virgil?"

"I ain't lyin'."

"Does the name Richard Timmons mean anything to you?"

"No sir."

Virgil was staring at the floor, his shoulders pulled in. Emmett hovered over him.

"There was a man in a hat," Emmett said, "with bad skin and thin hair. He came to meetings."

"Could be."

"How often would he come?"

Virgil stuck out his lower lip and said nothing.

"Nothing we discuss will go beyond this room. I promise."

"He come every once in a while," Virgil said.

"Why?"

"Special deliveries."

The rhythm of their back-and-forth seemed to have made Virgil more alert. He wasn't as drunk as he was letting on.

Emmett stood above him with his mouth tight and his hands clenched.

"Something happened," Emmett said. "What was it?"

Virgil scratched the back of his head. "Don't rightly remember."

Emmett grabbed him roughly by the chin and forced his face up. "You want to end up like Eddie Sloan?"

Arlene put a hand on Emmett's arm and said to Virgil, "He's trying to help you."

Emmett let go of his chin. Arlene could hear his breathing. With his foot, Virgil pushed away the jug. "I never done it but once. Run a parcel to a place in the North End."

"From where?"

"Police station. Not headquarters but the precinc' on Campbell."

"What was in the parcel?"

Virgil's eyes lost their haze of innocence. "What you think?"

Arlene's eyes had grown used to the room's darkness. It was pure squalor: tin cans, piles of rags, cigarette butts wedged between the floorboards. A broken mirror above a rust-streaked wash basin. The mattress sheetless and soiled. Everything soaked in that sour, closed-in smell.

"What happened to Eddie?" Emmett said.

Several times Virgil made as if to speak, then shook his head. Emmett had balled both hands into fists.

"Don't hit him," Arlene said. "Please don't."

"Tell me, Virgil."

He took a long swig from the jug and spoke without looking at either of them. "Before Eddie was killed, Rube Gilmore done a run."

"Did a run for who?"

"Man you mention."

"Richie Timmons."

Virgil flinched. "Like I said, no names was used. Anyhow, somethin' went wrong. Two days later, Rube come down the Brotherhood all red and hollerin'. Mr. Bibb, he come to us and say he need a volunteer. I wouldn't do it, so Eddie said he'd go."

Arlene groaned.

"What went wrong?"

"I don't know," Virgil said. "But Eddie never come back from that run and then we *all* scared."

Arlene walked over to the window. She felt faint. Through the torn muslin she saw two kids throwing rocks at a pop bottle propped on a fence.

"Rube start drinkin' and cussin' and carryin' on. Sayin' he's gonna tell the truth 'bout the police. Then he done disappeared. I ain't waitin' round to be next on the list, so I left the boarding house and come here."

After a long silence Emmett said, "I think we can go now."

Still gazing out the window, Arlene said, "He told me that he was going to see you."

Virgil toyed with the top of the jug.

She faced him. "Did you see him that night?" she said.

"No, ma'am, I did not. If he had a job, he'd tell you he was meetin' me. We worked it out such."

She let her hands fall to her side. Emmett gave Virgil twenty dollars and they left the shack.

In the car they sat for a long time, staring out the window. In her mind's eye was Eddie, as he left her on that last night. Tall, green-eyed, hip. Lying to her because he had to. Carrying her curse into the night. Still loving her.

"Are you all right?" Emmett asked.

She didn't answer.

"He was just trying to earn a living."

"He was mixed up with the police," she said. "Who'd've thought?"

"I don't think it was that simple."

She shook her head. "It doesn't matter now."

Black birds flapped above the shorn wheat fields.

"What are you going to do?" she asked Emmett.

"I'm working that out."

"Drive me home."

But Emmett was distracted. "Timmons had Bibb put a team of runners together for special jobs," he said. "Paying off criminals, I would guess. Sensitive payoffs. Dangerous."

"Don't say anything more."

"It's a motive," he said. "Can't you see? One of the payoffs went wrong – a disagreement over the amount, probably – and Eddie got caught in the middle. He learned something he shouldn't have, and Timmons killed him."

"Please be quiet."

He looked at her and she saw that he was still miles away. "Get the kid to testify, and I can go to the FBI," he said.

"Stop it!" she shouted.

"You asked me what I'm going to do. I'm going to help the Feds get Timmons. Before he hurts anyone else."

"Please," she said. "Just bring me home."

39

At the Paseo Gun Club, a new man was behind the desk. "Maguire around?"

The guy shook his head.

"I need to talk to Henry Conway," Emmett said.

The guy looked him up and down. Emmett was aware of his five-o'clock shadow and soiled collar. "And who are you?" the man said.

He flipped open his billfold and flashed his ID. The guy took his time examining it. "He's busy right now."

"You've got a choice. Either I take the kid downtown or I take you."

The guy tensed his shoulders and stared but didn't answer. He disappeared into the bays and returned with Henry.

Outside the club, Emmett pointed at his car. When they were seated inside he said, "I appreciate your help."

Henry nodded, fidgeting in the seat.

"I've got another favor to ask."

"Yeah?"

"You've heard of the FBI?"

"Sure. Who hasn't?"

"I want you to come with me and tell them what you told me."

He frowned. "I don't know about that."

"You don't have much choice here, Henry."

"I better talk to my uncle."

Emmett grabbed the kid's shoulder. "I told you before, you can't talk to anybody. You're coming in with me."

Henry squirmed beneath his grip. "This ain't the way they said it would work."

"The way who said?"

"Nobody said nothing about the FBI."

"We're just taking it to the next step. Those shells you gave me are now part of a criminal case. We need your testimony to verify the find. I'll make it worth your while."

"How much?"

"We'll work that out later."

Emmett started the car and edged away from the curb. As he pulled into traffic, Henry opened the door and jumped out. He hit the street hard, rolling, and a car behind had to swerve to avoid him, horn blaring. The passenger door of the Packard was flapping like a broken wing. Emmett hit the brakes and pulled over, and the door hit a telephone pole and slammed shut. He jumped out and bolted after Henry. He huffed and puffed and his lungs burned, but the kid was limping and he closed the gap. Henry ducked into an alley, and he caught up with him as he was climbing a fence. When he tried to pull him down, the kid kicked him in the face.

In a rage, Emmett pulled him to the ground, took his Colt from its holster and hit him on the side of his head with the butt of the gun.

The kid howled. "Goddamn you, Mister!"

"Tell me right now, you little son of a bitch – tell me you didn't lie to me about that shell."

"I didn't lie about nothing."

"Why'd you run? What are you scared of?"

Emmett's face throbbed from the kick. He held Henry by the collar and stuck the barrel of the pistol to his cheek.

"I'll do what you want," the kid said. "I'll do everything they told me to."

"Everything who told you?"

"You and the other guy."

"What other guy?"

"Please don't shoot me, mister. Please."

He pushed the kid away and holstered his gun. He was shaking – from the chase, sure, but also from shock. He had pulled a gun on a kid. Hit him with it.

"I'm not going to shoot you," Emmett said breathlessly. "Don't worry."

Henry had his hands at his face, like a boxer. His lip was swollen.

"Now," Emmett said, "you going to tell me what's going on?"

"The other guy didn't say nothing about the FBI. He told me you were from county."

"I'm going to ask you again, Henry. Listen to me. What other guy?"

Henry touched his sore lip and swallowed. "He told me if I said anything, he'd kill me."

"Nobody's going to kill you. What other man?"

"The man I gave the shell to."

"You gave the shell to me."

"And someone else."

The world lurched on its axis. Like when Mickey told him about the roll of film in the locker.

"You mean you gave some other guy one of the same shells you gave me?"

"Yeah."

"When? Before you gave them to me?"

"Yeah."

"Think. *When?*"

"In the summer. Before school started."

"Middle of August."

"I guess."

He helped the kid up. His trousers were torn and bloodied at the knees. Emmett touched his own face and found blood. "Look what you did to me."

"I didn't mean it. Jesus, Mister, I thought you were going to shoot me."

Emmett was tired. If only he didn't have to find out anything more.

"This man you gave the first shell to: describe him."

"Wore a suit, like you. Blue tie."

"Blue tie. With stripes going across?"

"Yeah."

"What color hair."

"Kinda brown. His skin was all red on his face. All pimply and sore looking."

Emmett's own skin crawled.

"Swear you won't say anything, Mister. He said he'd kill me."

"OK, kid. OK. Don't worry. Go back inside and get cleaned up."

"We're not going to the Feds?"

"Not today."

40

Mrs. Mac opened the door. She wasn't smiling.

"Is he in?" Emmett said.

"Where else would he be?"

He stepped into the house. The hallway was overheated. Smells of sweat and antiseptic and something baking.

"How's the patient?"

She didn't answer. Brushing flour from her apron front, she walked into the kitchen. He followed.

"Are you not going to ask after your Ma?" she said.

"She's here?"

"Not at the minute. But she's still staying with us, if that's what you're asking."

Emmett straightened his tie. More than once, when he was a kid, Mrs. Mac had smacked him on the butt with a wooden spoon when he needed it.

"Does she need any cash?"

She flapped her hands. "Sweet Jesus, you're worse than your man," she said, nodding towards Mickey's bedroom. "Look at the state of you. I'm glad she's *not* here. Offering money and looking like you slept in the gutter."

"It's been a rough week.

"Has it? Well, your Ma wouldn't know that, would she?"

"It's this case we're on, Mrs. Mac."

But she had her back to him.

"Go on," she said, rattling dishes in the sink. "Go in to him. The pair of you deserve each other."

Mickey lay on his bed, his broken leg resting on a pile of pillows and a copy of the *Star* spread across his lap. His face was lumpy and pale. A gray bandage covered his left eye.

"Someone looks like shit," Mickey said. "What have *you* been doing?"

"Working."

"Getting closer?"

"Too close."

Mrs. Mac banged pots and slammed drawers.

"On her high horse again," Mickey said. "You say something?"

"The Ma."

"Don't talk to me. They tell you they want you around and then all they do is complain. Like I'm good for anything except lying here. Can't even get her to bring me a drink."

"How are you?"

"How am I? How's the *case*?"

"They carry you in here on a stretcher?"

Mickey nodded at a pair of crutches leaning against the wall. "I can just about get around. Emmo, what's the matter? Talk to me."

Emmett took the gun from his holster and laid it on the bed.

"Shit," Mickey said, shoving it under the blanket. "Ma sees that, she'll murder me."

"When you told me what was in the locker, you didn't mention a piece."

"Didn't stop you from taking it, I notice."

"Big mistake."

Mickey folded the newspaper and dropped it on the floor. He was unshaven and smelled as if he hadn't bathed in weeks, but the sheets were fresh and his good eye was clear and sober. "How so?"

"I don't like how it makes me feel."

"God made man, Sam Colt made him equal."

"Equally evil."

"Goddamn it, Emmo, are you going to talk like a priest or let me know what the hell is going on?"

He closed the bedroom door. "It's all over," he said.

"You found out."

"I found out."

"Timmons?"

Emmett shook his head. "Bigger than that."

"You're shitting me."

"The cartridge case," Emmett said. "It was a plant."

"What?"

"We were set up."

"By who?"

Since pistol-whipping little Henry Conway, Emmett had been driving up and down the river road, watching the water flow and piecing together the narrative. It was easy enough to figure once he knew that Les Newton had been a step ahead of him.

He told Mickey the story. All the Perkins bullshit about the Pendergast machine had been a smokescreen. The brothers were dancing with the devil. And why not? With the judiciary, the state superintendent of insurance, and the governor in his pocket, Tom Pendergast held the key to the nine million. How much would it take to get him to free it up? Five percent? Even if Pendergast's kickback was half a mill, it would be worth it. The insurance companies would get their windfall, and the brothers would structure the deal and build in fees that would make them and their cronies even richer than they already were.

Timmons was Pendergast's front man, the money mover and the arranger. When the amount of the bribe was agreed, Timmons dipped into his stable of bagmen and told Bibb to send Rube Gilmore to collect. All went smoothly. So far so good.

But something went wrong. Irish Tom Pendergast was no gentleman. The way Emmett figured it, he got greedy. Knowing the size of the prize and seeing how easily the money-bag was filled, he held out for more. The Perkins boys stayed tight-lipped and played along, and when Timmons sent Eddie Sloan to collect the extra juice, the boys killed him, probably using hired muscle from Chicago.

The murder was a message. But Lloyd and his boys were Kansas City businessmen. They knew how to turn trouble into opportunity. Why not pin it on the machine? They got Roddy Hudson on the team, planted the shell, and roped in an ambitious and easily fooled young prosecutor with no ties to the city. With the Feds baying for Pendergast's blood, it must have seemed like a perfect plan.

Mickey's face was a whiter shade of pale. "Jesus. Emmo."

"My own family, Mick. My wife was screwing God knows who while her old man was screwing me. And just about everyone else in the state of Missouri."

"Go to the Feds."

"Yeah? And tell them what?"

"What you've told me. It makes sense now. Motive and method. Round up Virgil and Conway and get them to testify."

"I don't think it's that easy."

"You think it's better to wait until someone else is killed? Who the fuck you think would be next on their list?"

"I've had enough, Mick."

He handed Emmett the gun. "At least protect yourself."

"I don't want it." He stood up, took the canister of film from his jacket pocket, and threw it on the bed. "And I don't want this either."

"Where are you going?"

"For a walk."

"You mean you're running."

"Whatever you want to call it."

Mickey lifted the canister. "You don't want to know?"

"I know too much already."

"This isn't you, Emmo."

"Me? What is me?"

"Do the right thing."

"That's what's fucked me over. Every time."

He opened the bedroom door.

"Do the right thing!" Mickey shouted as he left.

He let himself out without saying good-bye to Mrs. Mac.

He drove home. Middle of the afternoon, middle of the week. Fay's car was in the driveway. He found her in their bedroom, hunched over her dresser, rooting through what remained of her clothes. An open suitcase lay on the bed.

"What are you doing here?" she said.

"I could ask the same of you."

They faced each other across the bed like gunslingers. Her hair was done up like Joan Crawford's and she wore a new ruffled blouse. But her cheeks were streaked with tears.

"You look awful," she said. "Daddy told me you're drinking again."

"My chosen vice."

She threw a few pieces of clothing into the suitcase.

"I'm only here to get a couple of things. Then I'm going straight home."

"Home?"

"Daddy's."

"How's he doing, anyhow?"

"Why do you ask?"

"Oh, I don't know. He seems a little wound up lately."

She lifted a handkerchief from the dressertop and blew her nose. Her hands were shaking. "What did you do to him, Emmett? Why does he hate you so?"

She didn't know. Of course not. But who did? Lloyd had set the whole thing up with perfect deniability.

"Why does anyone hate me?" he said.

"He's going to sell the house. This house. It's in his name."

"Good riddance. To the house, to you, and to your fucking old man."

She was breathing heavily and her lipstick was smeared. He was reminded of the night she had disappeared during the country club party and emerged from the basement at the last moment, flushed and disheveled and triumphant. Though now she just looked abandoned.

Another mystery unraveled into narrative.

"He's left you," he said, "hasn't he?"

"What are you talking about?"

Her narrowed eyes and tight chin told him he'd hit on the truth.

"The guy you've been fucking. He's deserted you."

"No wonder I hate you. You've become so vulgar."

"But I'm right."

She closed the top of the suitcase. "Daddy had you pegged all along. Careful about how you drink and speak, but Irish to the core."

He watched her car float down the street. The brakelights winked as she turned the corner and disappeared behind a grove of trees.

He went downstairs and took a bottle of whiskey from the lower cupboard and emptied it in the kitchen sink. He didn't want that where he could reach it. Not tonight.

In the morning, he showered and shaved and dressed in clean clothes. He ate a good breakfast. Checked his brief-case for all he needed. Drove to the Piggly Wiggly and gassed up the car. Then headed for the federal offices on Summit Street. He would trust Mickey. Virtue was its own reward.

He asked to speak to the agent in charge. The young woman at the reception desk wrote his name on a yellow pad. "What is the purpose of your visit, Mr. Whelan?"

"It's a private matter."

She tapped the pad with her pen. "I have to write something here."

"I'm from the Jackson County prosecutor's office. I'm here on a jurisdictional issue."

The agent appeared immediately and led him to a dusty office. He was a tall man in a blue suit with jug ears and oiled hair. He did not introduce himself.

He seated Emmett and left the room. It sounded as if he locked the door, but Emmett couldn't bring himself to check. After a long time he returned with another agent in an iden-tical suit. The new man's jacket swung open as he entered, and Emmett saw the gun in its shoulder holster and a pair of handcuffs dangling from his belt. This man stood behind him while the agent in charge moved behind the desk and set a brown folder on its empty surface.

When neither of the agents spoke, Emmett said, "I'm here about the murder of Eddie Sloan."

"We know that."

"You know the case?"

The agent in charge opened the folder and fanned several pages across the desktop. Above his ear was a slash of skin where hair didn't grow. He studied the pages. Emmett turned in his seat. The man behind him was staring at his partner, hands folded in front of him.

"I've been working on it," Emmett said, "since Sloan's death, six, seven weeks ago."

"So this is a county case?"

"Not exactly."

"You are..." – he glanced at the paperwork – "assistant prosecutor. Jackson County."

As the agent spoke, Emmett noticed that the room had no windows and nothing hanging on the walls. The desk was bolted to the floor and he was seated in the only chair.

"Strictly speaking," Emmett said, "it is not county. I *had* been working with Roddy Hudson, who heads the state criminal division out of Jefferson City."

"He sent you down here?"

"No."

"Not exactly, huh?"

He tried to stand up, but the agent behind him pushed him down by the shoulders. "Hey," Emmett said.

"Take it easy, sport."

"What's going on here?"

"You tell me."

"That file, who gave it to you?" The agent closed the folder without answering. "What my investigation has led to," Emmett continued hoarsely, "is that Roddy... Roddy Hudson is the man you're looking for."

"Hudson? Looking for Hudson?"

"He had an involvement. Along with Lloyd Perkins."

"Your father-in-law?"

"And Lloyd's brother Robert. And a guy named Les Newton. I've put together the whole case." He lifted his briefcase. *I've got the evidence,* he wanted to say. *The men who killed Sloan. Feud with the Pendergast machine, see? I can lay it all out for you guys.*

But he stayed silent. The words in his head were like something out of a movie.

The man facing him pinched his lower lip with thumb and forefinger. "So you're not here to turn yourself in?"

Emmett steadied himself with a hand on the desk. "What?"

The agent looked at his partner, who swiftly and neatly pinned Emmett's arms behind his back and cuffed his wrists.

"You're under arrest."

"For what?"

"For the murder of Edward Sloan."

"But I'm the *investigator.*" The agent who had cuffed him lifted him roughly to his feet. "I can tell you the whole story," Emmett said.

"Good. We're all ears. And you can tell Roddy Hudson, too, because he's working with us on the case."

The agent picked up the folder and Emmett's briefcase while his partner pulled Emmett out of the room and brought him to his cell.

41

L ate on Wednesday afternoon, Arlene was at her weekly
cleaning job at Mr. Jefferson's law office beside the Plaza.
Two women sat with their backs to her in the waiting room,
speaking in low tones, though loud enough for her to hear. She
wasn't listening but she wasn't blocking it out either – in this
part of town she was used to being treated as if she wasn't there.

The women wore fox fur stoles and netted hats and silk
stockings. Plaza money. They were younger than Arlene but
had the tones and gestures of older women. Or movie stars.
Above them, the ceiling fan clicked as it rotated.

"She doesn't even bother to pretend anymore. Doesn't try
to hide it."

"Would you, darling?"

"Well, I wouldn't be in that position in the first place, now
would I?"

"Position?"

The women laughed. One of them was smoking, and ash
from her cigarette floated to the marble floor that Arlene had
just cleaned.

"I can't imagine what Ed would do if he found himself in
that situation."

"Ed would run him out of town. So would Bob."

"At *least* run him out."

"Any man with a *whit* of self-respect. But Whelan? Didn't know how to handle her from the start. Hadn't a clue."

The woman tisked. The name she'd mentioned hung in the air like a child's balloon.

"What ever did she see in him?" the other said.

The woman shrugged. Mr. Jefferson came out from his office and the women stood up and there was laughter and loud voices and talk of having a drink since it was after five in the evening.

On the way home it began to rain. A dense rain that dripped from the tips of the oak leaves and blurred the trolley car windows while mild thunder rumbled in the dark skies overhead. Arlene thought of Wardell, out in Columbia. Charlotte, in her last letter, had mentioned misbehavior. Poor schoolwork. Sulking. Arlene would have to go out there. But what was really needed was for Wardell to come home. Not to testify, as Emmett Whelan wanted, but to take up where he belonged, with his mama, sleeping in his bedroom with its pennants and baseball photographs.

Whelan. If he messed up this case like he was messing up his life, then who knew when Wardell could return. A good man, maybe, but bad news for her.

There was a loud bang and the trolley came to a sudden halt on Troost Avenue. Sparks showered down from the overhead wires and the smell of burnt rubber filled the car. Arlene gathered her cleaning bags and quickly filed out with the other passengers onto Eighteenth Street. The rain had stayed heavy and she sheltered under the trees. The driver peered at the wires and walked away. After ten minutes, she decided to brave the weather and walk the mile or so home. The ugly burnt smell was still in her nostrils.

As she crossed Paseo, a funeral band marched out from behind a line of brick buildings on Olive Street. Coming from a funeral at United Baptist, it must have been, leading the mourners to Pinewood Cemetery. She could not recall anyone in the district who had died in the last week. Waiting respectfully for the band to pass, she recognized a number of the musicians. Lee Garrison lifted the bell of his trombone in greeting. They played "Just a Closer Walk with Thee" at dirge tempo, and she sang along under her breath.

A horse-drawn funeral coach followed, and behind it a train of mourners. The horses wore black plumes. The open coach had a small white casket inside, a child's casket, with flowers along the side that spelled JULES. As the train passed, Jules's mother, younger than Arlene and propped up by two older women, threw her head back and shrieked so loudly the whole world seemed to stop its motion.

The scene went blurry for Arlene. Sound vanished. As if waking from a dream, she slowly became aware of the band and its music.

Long after the funeral had passed, Arlene stood motionless on the side of the road, her tears mingling with raindrops.

42

The day after his arrest, a Thursday, Emmett was allowed to read the complaint against him in the presence of the agent in charge. It accused him of engaging in a conspiracy to murder Edward Sloan and was signed by a federal magistrate. Attached was an affidavit, sworn to by Roddy Hudson, declaring that Emmett and Les Newton had tampered with physical evidence germane to the case.

His cell guard told him that Newton and the Perkins brothers had been arrested on the same day and jailed in another part of the building. News of the arrests had not reached the press. The shit would hit the fan on Monday, when the US Attorney in St. Louis was to file formal charges and establish dates for preliminary hearings.

Emmett asked to see Roddy before the hearings. The agent told him it was out of the question.

On Friday morning, the agent told him he would be detained pending his hearing, when it would be determined if he was eligible for bail. But he had the right to consult counsel. He didn't have a regular attorney, so he sent a note to Stanley Pearson, his fellow assistant county prosecutor. Stan came to his cell in the early afternoon. His was the first friendly face Emmett had seen in twenty-four hours, and his story flowed forth in a jumbled rush.

Pearson was floored. "When was all this going on?"

"Over the last two months."

"Fleming didn't say anything to me about it."

"Fleming didn't know."

"He didn't know? Your *boss*?"

Stan's face was like a telegram with bad news.

"Stan, listen, I need help here."

"Right. OK… You said you had the evidence assembled and analyzed, and then gave it to Hudson."

"Yes. Except he took it, really."

"And what was the connection between you and Newton?"

"No connection. Newton planted the shell, not me."

"I don't follow you."

"The Perkins brothers had Newton plant the cartridge case at the crime scene figuring I would discover it. The plan was for me to put a false case together – unwittingly – which would implicate Timmons in a murder the Perkins brothers actually ordered."

"Lloyd and Robert Perkins killed Sloan."

"Had him killed, yes – but I didn't have anything to do with it. *Hudson* did."

"But Hudson is driving this investigation."

"He saw the lay of the land and pulled a switch. And set me up as a patsy."

Stan looked like a kid who forgot his homework.

"Goddamn it, Stan, it's obvious. All this time he's been associating with them, meeting them, planning – how hard can that be to document?"

"But he brought the evidence to the Feds. And even if he took it from you, who's to say he wasn't undercover from the start?"

Stan had grown up on a farm outside St. Joseph. He was smart, he was shrewd, and he called it like he saw it. Great at finding holes in cases and no good at hiding what he felt.

Panic spread in Emmett's chest. If he couldn't convince his attorney, who wanted to help him, how was he going to convince a grand jury? "You don't believe me," he said.

"I'm not here to believe or disbelieve, I'm here to represent." They stared at each other for a few moments. "Listen," Stan said, growing fidgety, "the best thing I can do for you right now is get the paperwork in order for Monday." He looked at his watch. "I've got an hour before the court offices close. I'll see you tomorrow. Write the whole story out and we'll get it into deposition."

Stan stood up and called for the guard. Above the door to Emmett's cell someone had scrawled the phrase *your fucked*.

"There are witnesses, Stan."

"Witnesses to what?"

It was good question. A prosecutor's question. The witnesses would corroborate everything Roddy Hudson and the FBI accused him of. The evidence that proved his innocence could as easily prove his guilt. And the only people who could vouch for his innocence were guilty themselves – his father-in-law, Robert Perkins, and Les Newton.

And Mickey.

"One other thing you can do for me," Emmett said. "I need to let a couple of people know what's happening."

He scribbled two addresses while the guard unlocked the door. Pocketing the slip of paper, Stan avoided his gaze and hustled down the dank corridor. Desperate to be the hell out of there.

Arlene came to see him after breakfast on Saturday. They met across an oak table in the visiting room, deserted except for an armed guard at the door. Emmett had had a sleepless night. He was numb with stress.

Her face was pale and concerned. "What's going on, Emmett?"

He could not remember her using his name before. The way she said it was musical and soothing. Everything he planned to say stuck in his throat, and he broke down, crying into his hands.

"They set me up," he said.

"What do you mean?"

"They're saying I helped kill Eddie Sloan."

She shrank back in her chair. "I told you not to involve me. This is what happens."

To Negroes. He knew that was what she meant.

"You have to help me," he said.

"Why? What could I do?"

"I don't know."

The guard watched them. "What about the witnesses?" she said.

"Who, Virgil? The kid at the gun club? Whatever they say would make me look guilty."

"And what about Wardell?"

"What about him?"

"Is he still in danger?"

"Arlene, they're saying I did it. Do you understand that?"

She smiled wanly. "They won't do anything to you."

"Why?"

"It's all a mistake. You'll tell them what happened and they'll clear it all up. You'll see."

It sounded as if she was trying to convince herself.

"I need you, Arlene."

She glanced at the guard. "Talk to your lawyer," she said. "Get your police friends working on it."

"The police? *You're* saying this?"

He started to tell her the story. He was brimming with the need to confide. Guilt and innocence, mystery and proof. Corruption and its own rules. His city, his family, his marriage. He would tell her all. She was a Negro. She knew the score. There was no point trying to fight the weight of history.

But she waved away his words.

"Arlene, you have to listen to me."

She stood up.

"Arlene. You're the only one who's helped. Who understands."

"I have to go."

"Stay. Please."

"Your friend," she said, "the ex-cop. Talk to him."

"Come to the hearing," Emmett said. "Can you? If I can only see you there."

But she was talking to the guard, telling him she had to leave.

Two hours later, the guard brought Emmett back to the visiting room. Mickey sat where Arlene had, his cast angling out from beneath the table. Freshly shaven, he wore a striped shirt and straw hat. His crutches leaned against the table and a cigarette smoked in the ashtray.

"You all right there, son?" the guard said to Mickey.

"I am, Joe."

"I'll leave you to it."

Emmett sat as the guard took his position by the door. "You know him?"

"Joe Casey. Worked with my dad at the cement factory during the boom. You need anything, just give him a nod."

"What I need, I'm not going to get from him."

"What's going on?"

"I followed your advice – I went to the Feds."

"So I see."

Again, Emmett told the tale. Mickey sat through it coolly, leaning back in his chair while he smoked and fingered the buttons of his clean shirt. His injured eye, now unbandaged, fixed Emmett with a watery gleam.

When he was finished, Emmett said, "We have to find a way of getting to the Perkinses."

"Why?"

"Lloyd's my only chance. I know he doesn't like me, but I can't believe he'd let his own son-in-law take the fall. He's not a monster."

"He's not? How about Roddy Hudson – is he a monster?"

"That son of a bitch. Goddamn it, Mick, what am I going to do?"

Mickey stubbed his cigarette in the ashtray. "I'll tell you this for nothing, Emmo: the only thing Lloyd and Robert Perkins are thinking about right now is how to save their own asses from the chair. If they think for a second that sending you down the river could do that, they won't hesitate."

"You always were a cynic."

"A realist."

"What about Newton? He knows the truth."

Mickey shook his head. "He'll be loyal. And if he isn't, they'll buy him off."

Emmett stood and paced around the table. "Roddy Hudson's ratted them out, and instead of working with me to nail him they'd let me go down? I can't believe that."

"Roddy's played this inch perfect. Tell me one thing he's done that can't be positioned as part of an investigation."

Emmett examined the ragged walls of the windowless room. Less than two months ago he had stood at his tenth-floor office window, looking down on the city like a king and reveling in doing a pal a favor.

What a dupe.

"All that talk we had about the old neighborhood," Emmett said, still looking at the peeling paint. "No wonder I got your goat."

"Let's keep focused here, Emmo."

"You were right. I carried a romantic view. All ambition and no common sense."

"Don't beat yourself up. I've been in this with you all the way, and I didn't see it coming. You were set up."

"If we could figure out when Hudson first became involved." He stopped and looked at the floor. "No. Bring a note to Lloyd for me. I've no other choice."

Mickey shook his head.

"Then what the hell am I supposed to do?" Emmett said.

"Hudson's your man. We go after him."

"Ah, you have it all worked out. Just how do you think we do that?"

Mickey stuck a fresh cigarette between his lips and patted his pockets, looking for a light. He struggled to his feet and propped himself on his crutches.

"Where are you going?"

"To get a light off Joe." He took an envelope from beneath his belt and slid it onto the tabletop. "Have a look at that."

He lurched across to the room, keeping his body between the guard and the table.

Hands covering the envelope, Emmett watched Mickey lean into a lit match and banter with the guard. He slowly slid his finger beneath the sealed flap and peeled it open. Photographs.

Today of all days, why had Mickey done this to him?

His breathing thickened. Mickey glanced his way, kept up the chatter. He pulled the envelope on to his lap, removed the pictures, flicked through them. Lovers entwined across a lacy bedspread, their limbs dusky in the muted light. But there was no mistaking the faces.

He put the pictures back in the envelope and waited until Mickey had returned to his seat. "The negatives?"

"Safe and sound."

"I want to talk to him."

"I think that can be arranged."

He passed the envelope beneath the table. "Can you make sure he gets copies tonight."

"I'll make damn sure of it."

Mickey gathered his crutches again.

"Mick. Thank you."

"Just doing my job, pal."

43

"What do you want?"

"What do you think?"

"Are you going to make me play guessing games?"

"I'll do whatever I wish. And you'll do whatever I tell you to."

"And if I don't?"

"The pictures go to the *Star*, the *Post-Dispatch*, and the *Chicago Tribune*."

"They wouldn't be interested."

"I think they would."

"It could be anybody in those pictures."

"It could be, but it isn't. It's you. You and my wife."

"Keep your voice down."

"That's what she used to say to me whenever I accused her of what the pictures prove is true."

"You mean whenever the two of you were at each other's throats?"

"Talk like that and all deals are off. I go to jail and your career goes into the garbage can."

"You still haven't told me what you want."

"All charges dropped, public recognition for what I discovered, and a police pension for Mickey McDermott."

"That's impossible."

"Which part?"

"How can I get the Feds to drop charges for something I swore in an affidavit that you did?"

"That's your problem."

"It's not a problem, it's an impossibility."

"What was it like?"

"What was what like?"

"Screwing my wife and then an hour later having a drink with me."

"I don't believe that specific scenario ever arose."

"That's just one scenario the papers will be detailing."

"I am willing to work with you on this."

"Is that right?"

"There are ways of getting you off the hook."

"Give me an example."

"You could testify against the men in question in exchange for immunity from prosecution."

"The men in question?"

"Lloyd and his brother."

"I don't think that would work."

"Why not?"

"Tell me where I'm wrong here: you want me to pretend that I conspired to kill Eddie Sloan, pretend that Lloyd told me what to do, and then perjure myself so that you can solidify a false case against him."

"There's nothing false about it. You know what he did."

"With your help."

"You know well that nothing I did can be construed as a conspiracy to do anything other than solve two murders. There is no evidence."

"Unlike your affair with Fay."

"That was unfortunate."

"Fuck you. Fuck you and the train you came in on."

"Are we going to find a solution here or call each other names?"

"*You* are going to find a solution. By Monday at noon."

"You've told me what I have to do. What do I get in return?"

"The pictures don't go to the newspapers."

"And I get the negatives."

"No."

"How do I know you won't use them again?"

"You don't."

"How can I trust you?"

"You can't. But you have no other choice."

"I can choose not to be blackmailed."

"Let's get back to the real world here. You can choose to let me suffer for something I didn't do. And bring disgrace upon yourself."

"I'll need all day Monday. At least."

"The photos are ready to go. If you're not here by five o'clock I pull the trigger."

"I will be here."

"I bet you will."

As he was leaving, Roddy looked over his shoulder. Emmett pointed his forefinger at him, cocking his thumb like the hammer of a gun.

44

R oddy Hudson met the press on Wednesday afternoon in the mezzanine hall of Jackson County Courthouse. Word had leaked out that something was up, something big. The room hummed with the chatter of newspaper reporters and off-duty cops, politicos and gossipmongers. A hedge of radio mikes bordered the lectern. Old Glory and the state flag of Missouri drooped on either side of the dais, swaying in the breeze of ceiling fans. An Indian summer had fallen on the city, and the hall was stifling.

From the back of the room, Emmett watched Roddy approach the lectern, buttoning his suit jacket and smoothing his tie. He was flanked by federal agents and assistants from state. His greased hair shone in the pale light and his eyes were crimped with self-importance. The murmur in the hall grew louder. Laura Hudson stood off to the side, gazing up at her husband and clasping her hands. She wore long white gloves and a gardenia at her breast.

Roddy scanned the hall, looking, Emmett felt certain, for him. He avoided his eye. The babble subsided as Roddy cleared his throat.

"Good afternoon," he said into the microphones. "It is unusual, I know, to summon the press at a time when the golf courses beckon." Light laughter. "But the state prosecutor's office has been working closely with federal authorities for some time on a case of huge importance to the city and the nation. And we have had a major breakthrough."

Oh, he was puffed up, all right. The guy could lay it on thick. And as the rhetoric swelled, Emmett fanned himself with his hat and looked through high windows at a hazy sky. It was hard to listen. He had only come to make sure Roddy honored their bargain. And as his mind wandered, he thought of Fay, holed up with her mother in an unidentified location while the Feds combed the Perkins house for evidence.

"...and indictments have been handed down this week for a number of men – including Lloyd Perkins, Robert Perkins, and other prominent members of the business community, as well as key operatives in the Jackson Democratic Club – charging them with conspiracy to murder, perversion of the course of justice, and insurance fraud so massive it beggars belief."

The newsmen scribbled in their notebooks. The flashbulbs popped. Yes, Fay in hiding while Laura paraded with her white gloves in the limelight, watching her husband with eyes like a vixen's. How much did she know? There was one mystery Emmett would never unravel.

"...could not have been done without the outstanding contribution of Assistant Jackson County Prosecutor Emmett Whelan. With the help of former Kansas City police officer Michael McDermott, Mr. Whelan conducted his investigation in strictest secrecy – in fact, his discretion was so thorough that he drew down suspicion on himself until such time as his critical role was clearly realized. So vigorous, so single-minded was Mr. Whelan's pursuit of..."

Emmett slipped out of the room.

As he jogged down the courthouse steps, he heard a whistle. A hand waved from a Monarch cab parked on the corner. It was Mickey. Emmett joined him in the back seat.

"Say hello to Horace," Mickey said.

The cabbie turned his head and smiled. The front passenger seat had been removed so that Mickey could extend his cast in comfort. He handed Emmett a bottle wrapped in a paper bag.

"No thanks," Emmett said.

Mickey took a swig himself and slapped him on the shoulder. "You did it, you son of a bitch."

"*We* did it."

"Hudson still spouting bullshit in there?"

"Sticking to the script."

"Yeah, yeah." Mickey handed the cabbie a dollar. "Horace, old buddy, run across the street and get me a pack of Luckies."

When Horace was gone, Mickey said, "I got the word from downtown. I'm back on the force."

"No more than you deserve."

He slapped the cast. "I'm even getting benefit until I'm back on my feet."

"I told you, didn't I?"

"So you did."

The courthouse doors flew open and reporters galloped out to file before the afternoon deadline.

"Just so you know," Mickey said in a low voice, "the negatives? Safety deposit box in First National." He handed Emmett a card. "Those pictures were a fucking gold mine."

Emmett looked away.

"Sorry, Emmo. You know what I mean."

"I don't disagree. I'm happy for you."

"And me for you."

"What are you doing today?"

"I'm going have Horace drive me all over KC while I get shitfaced."

"Not a bad idea."

"Want to join me?"

"Not today, pal."

Emmett drove his Packard slowly out to Oakwood, watching fallen leaves swirl in the wake of passing cars. The autumn sun spackled the windshield. He passed Penn Valley, Westport, and the country club. He crossed Brush Creek, cemented solid by the city a few years ago in a sweetheart deal with Pendergast's concrete company. Mickey's dad had worked on that project. The trees of Loose Park were turning red and yellow and a kite hung lazily above the tennis courts. The whole city seemed to be basking in late good weather and fine health. He wished he could lie in the sun and fall asleep for a month.

Outside the house a FOR SALE sign was stuck in the grass. A moving truck sat in the driveway. Two men were negotiating Fay's vanity through the front door.

Ophelia was in the kitchen, wrapping dishes in tissue paper and placing them in a cardboard box. "Hello, Mr. Whelan."

"Hello, Ophelia. Where's this all going?"

"You axin' the wrong person. Ophelia jus' doin' what she tol'."

He sighed. "I know. How's Fay?"

"Her mother sick."

"Mrs. Perkins?"

"Yes sir."

"And Fay?"

She didn't answer.

Emmett wandered the rooms of the house, packing up his clothes and personal items and bringing them out to the car. He swept out the garage and got his golf clubs from the basement. His neighbor, Mr. Hollis, who'd been watering his lawn, went into his house without a word. A strange hush had fallen across the neighborhood, and a vague scraping sound rose from somewhere behind the trees.

Ophelia stood at the front door, hands on her hips. "What Ophelia spose do now, Mr. Whelan?" she said loudly. Kinky wisps of hair had escaped from her bun and quivered in the air.

He guided her back into the house. "You're still here, Ophelia. You're still working."

"I get this here packin' done and I'm gone."

"Give me your telephone number."

"I ain't got a phone."

"Your address then."

She blinked her big yellowed eyes and returned to the kitchen.

After the moving men were gone, he found her sitting on the stairs, crying. He made her a cup of coffee and helped her finish the packing. She locked up and climbed into the Packard. He gave her a ride to the streetcar, and as she got out of the car he handed her fifty dollars.

He looped back to the house and sat in his car until dusk, watching the empty rooms grade into darkness and thinking of the night when he had sat there with the gun in his lap, waiting for Fay. A bad smell hung in the air. The scraping sound had grown louder, and a pair of squirrels ran back and forth across the road.

At eight o'clock, he started the engine and put the car into gear. Mr. Hollis peered at him through parted curtains.

45

Wardell heard a loud honk. He looked out the bedroom window. Mr. Watkins's car sat in the sunshine. The front door slammed and Charlotte ran down the porch steps. A woman got out of the car and hugged Charlotte. It was his mama.

"Alvin! Wardell! Look who's here."

Mr. Watkins got out the driver's side. He wore a straw hat and a red tie. He came around the car and shook hands with Alvin.

"Wardell!" Charlotte shouted. "Where are you, son?"

He left the bedroom and went out onto the front porch, and his mama ran up the steps and grabbed him tight. She smelled like flowers.

"It took us three hours," his mama said.

They drank iced tea in the sitting room. "Straight out Route 40."

"That some chariot you got there, Cal," Alvin said.

"Oldsmobile."

"They lettin' black folks buy Oldsmobiles now?"

"Man I buy from, he only care about the color of my *money*."

They men laughed. Wardell sat in a wooden chair by the door. His cowhide case, packed since early morning, was already in the trunk of the car. His mama's wildflowers were in a clay vase on the coffee table.

Mr. Watkins sat on the edge of his seat. His elbows were on his knees, and his new hat sat on the floor beside his shiny shoes.

The adults went quiet. Mr. Watkins wiped his face with a checkered handkerchief. Charlotte brushed bits of fluff from her dress. Through the screen came the cackle of chickens from the Cooper house.

"So it's safe now," Alvin said to Cal. "That's what you reckon."

"All over."

"Wardell," his mama said, "put your suitcase in the car."

"I did."

"Go check your room," Charlotte said, "Make sure you haven't left anything behind."

The sheets were stripped from his bed, and the bare mattress looked thin and lonely. The grown-ups murmured in the next room. He looked beneath the bedframe and found a nickel in the dust.

When he returned, Mr. Watkins had gone outside. His mama stood by the door. She saw Wardell coming and stretched out her arms. "I can't thank you enough," she said to Alvin and Charlotte. "But we have to go home now."

He and his mama got in the car. Alvin and Charlotte stood on the porch and waved good-bye.

They drove along the new highway with all the windows down. His mama dangled her bare arm from the window. Her hair danced in the wind. She looked over her shoulder at Wardell.

"You're going to miss Alvin, I suppose," she said.

"Him and me, we played catch every night."

"Did you want to stay there?"

"No. I want to go home."

Mr. Watkins's eyes looked at him in the rear view mirror. "Wardell. The Monarchs are playing again next week. How would you like to go?"

"Is Satch coming back?"

"No. But Jess Willard will be there. And Cool Papa Bell."

"Yes sir."

A flock of starlings rose from the field beside them. A cloud covered the sun.

"He wanted to come out himself," Mr. Watkins said to his mama. "Said he appreciated everything the boy did to help on the case. Said he wanted to see you."

"Not a very good idea, Cal. Not today, not tomorrow."

"That's what I told him."

Wardell leaned forward in the back seat and touched his mama's shoulder. She smiled and patted his hand and said, "We'll be home soon."

"Yes, mama."

She sang:

Go down, Moses
Way down in Egypt's land
Tell old Pharaoh
To let my people go

Wardell closed his eyes and listened to her voice. It was like honey. He knew that Jesus should be in his mind, but he wasn't. Satch was. He was pitching: high kick, little jink when he reared back, arm whipping so fast it was a blur. Pop of the catcher's mitt and a called strike.

He tipped his hat and made for the third-base line. Walked across the diamond like he was walking on water. Caught Wardell's eye and winked as he ducked into the dugout.

His mama said, "You all right, sugar?"

"Yes, mama. I'm all right."

ACKNOWLEDGEMENTS

My thanks to Breffni O'Malley, who read an early version of this novel and gave me invaluable advice; and to Svetlana Pironko, for her clear-eyed guidance and support as we have brought this book to life.

ABOUT THE AUTHOR

Kevin Stevens is the author of two novels published by Simon & Schuster UK, *Song for Katya* and *The Rizzoli Contract*, and *This Ain't No Video Game, Kid!*, a novel for young adults published by Little Island.

His superhero fantasy for children, *The Powers*, was a Dublin UNESCO City of Literature Citywide Reading Project for children.

The Cops Are Robbers, his true crime account of New England's largest bank burglary, was made into an NBC Movie of the Week starring Ed Asner and George Kennedy.

Kevin lives in Dublin and Boston and writes about jazz and American politics for *The Irish Times* and other publications.

To learn more about Kevin Stevens, visit *reachtheshiningriver.com* and *www.betimesbooks.com*

www.ingramcontent.com/pod-product-compliance
Lightning Source LLC
Chambersburg PA
CBHW030649260626
47157CB00007B/2556